The Crooked Albatross
and Sweet Fanny Adams

Hey Kastle!
I hope you like it.

[signature]

The Crooked Albatross
and Sweet Fanny Adams

LEIGH CROSS

TWOHARBORS
WWW.TWOHARBORSPRESS.COM

Two Harbors Press
322 First Avenue N, 5th floor
Minneapolis, MN 55401
612.455.2293
www.TwoHarborsPress.com

ISBN-13: 978-1-63413-346-3
LCCN: 2015900798

Distributed by Itasca Books

Edited by Katie McCabe, author of *Justice Older than the Law*
Cover Design by Fabrizio Cross
Albatross Photographs by Roger Cain

Printed in the United States of America

Acknowledgments

If Nils Christensen, member of Canada's Aviation Hall of Fame, had not maintained my airplane, my yellowed bones, feeble brain, and shriveled entrails would have long since decorated an oldgrowth hemlock somewhere North of Campbell River and South of Prince Rupert.

If Katie McCabe, author of *Justice Older than the Law*, had not given me the benefit of many hours of advice, editorial assistance and help, this book would be decorating a dung-heap.

If Roger Cain had not generously allowed me to use his excellent photographs of an Albatross, Fabrizio Cross would not have been able to construct a great cover around it. The island in the background is actually Cocos Island.

If Velma Cross, my dear wife, had not patiently tolerated my absence from household chores while, daily, I retired to my crypt, this book could not have been written. Velma's cheerful encouragement brightens my days and makes writing possible.

Prologue

"Who are we hanging today, Ratcliffe?" Sir John Seede leafed through the stack of warrants on his desk.

"Rare treat we have today. Pirates, Sir John. Our cells are graced by none other than Captain Thompson and his crew of twelve." Ratcliffe reefed a tin from his leather vest, opened it, and crammed a wad of snuff under his upper lip.

"Snuff! Filthy habit, that, Ratcliffe. Remember my position. Not appropriate behavior for you as my personal secretary. Snuff leads to a bad end. Madness. Holes in your face. All that sort of thing, don't y'know."

"Right, Governor." A drop of drool ran from the corner of Ratcliffe's mouth, meandered over his chin, and dripped onto his vest. "Dreadful sorry about that." Ratcliffe did not look the least bit sorry. He clasped his hands on his vest, twiddled his thumbs, gazed at the ceiling, and hissed, quietly, through his front teeth.

Sir John fiddled with the objects on his desk: a jar of quill pens, an inkwell and sand-shaker. On his left, tucked under his case of dueling pistols, was the manuscript, which Sir John hoped would be his ticket to a niche in history: *Personal Encounters with Noted Pirates: The Memoirs of Sir John Seede, OM, MBE, FRGS,*

Governor of Jamaica. "Hmm. Yes. Pirates, eh? Stroke of luck, that. Perhaps even a new chapter for the book."

"No doubt, sir. And how is dear Lady Charlotte today? Better, I trust?"

"Ah. Yes. Better, but still too thin. Damn these tropical fevers anyway. Hasn't been the same since we came here. Between ourselves, I'm afraid I married a girl a bit too young—I mean too young for the tropics, that is,— but let's get back to Captain Thompson. I'd thought that Captain Thompson's hunting grounds were in the Pacific. What's he doing in the Caribbean? And what prizes can be seized by a pirate crew of twelve? A shite-punt on the Thames would be about their speed, eh? Or perhaps a *fufu* junk on the Yangtze?"

"There were seventy of the ruffians then."

"What became of the other fifty-six?"

"Fifty-eight, sir."

"Whatever. Whatever, dammit. What became of them?"

"I'm getting to that, sir."

"Well get to it, man!"

"For a while, our sly captain had a run of good luck in the Pacific. He had taken his schooner, *Pride of Gloucester*, into Lima for stores and water. Lima was still Spanish then. While he lay under the guns of the fortress, Thompson played the part of a bluff English merchant skipper, shrewd perhaps, but honest as the day is long—he plays that role very well—when who should pull alongside in a longboat but His Excellency the Viceroy. He was looking for someone to carry the treasures of Lima out of reach of the rebels—"

"Oh my suffering great aunt! The rebels, eh? That would

be our current allies, the Argentines under San Martin, eh?"

"And don't forget our own Admiral Cochrane's fleet approaching by sea. Anyway, Thompson managed to convince the Viceroy of his reliability. You can say what you like, sir, but an Englishman, particularly an English Gentleman can spin a better bald-faced lie than any Frog, Lascar, Diego, Swamp-Singer—"

"I say, Ratcliffe! Hold on, now! That's quite enough! That's cheek!" Sir John stiffened his back and tucked in his chin. "An English gentleman always keeps his word!"

"Of course, Sir John, of course!" Ratcliffe hawked a compact and snuff-colored goober into Sir John's dustbin. Sir John shuddered. "But Thompson didn't keep his word. The Viceroy and his men brought the treasure out to *Pride of Gloucester* and stowed it below. The Viceroy posted guards and went ashore. As soon as it got dark, Thompson's bullyboys slit the guards' throats and popped them into sacks weighted with lumps of ballast. They plumped the sacks overboard. Thompson slipped *Pride of Gloucester's* cable and drifted away on the tide. As soon as they were out of sight, they cracked on sail. By dawn they were over the horizon. They sailed to a speck of an island, Isla del Cocos it's called, about three hundred fifty miles west by south from the Gulf of Panama. It's uninhabited, visited by the occasional whaler. You may remember, sir? Captain Colnet took the frigate, *Rattler,* into Cocos some thirty years ago. You've read his account?"

"I suppose. Don't recall at the moment."

"Well, Colnet reported the island has faults: hotter than hell, rains every day, the clothes rot on your back, anchorages are difficult—foul ground, shallow. However, in every other way, Cocos seems close to heaven. The creeks run with plenty of good, sweet water. The reefs teem with tasty fish. The hills leap with wild goats and pigs for the taking and mountains of fresh coconuts grow on the palms by the shore. Delicious!

"When Thompson arrived, he worked his men without stopping until they'd landed the wealth of Lima and buried it. Then he let them break out a great hogshead of rum from the hold and tow it ashore. Our Captain Thompson quietly rowed back to *Pride of Gloucester* and spent the night on board and alone. Picture that beach: looming jungle hills, a drizzle of rain, and a great cluster of heavily armed cutthroats, guzzling rum and capering around fires on which they singed some unlucky hogs and a goat or two. Picture the quarrels toward midnight when they were all mad-drunk. Captain Thompson dozed snug and safe in his cabin. Occasionally he'd roll over in his bunk, put his spyglass out the porthole, and watch the shrieking, cursing mob shoot, stab, and slash each other to ribbons. Every point-blank pistol shot in a soft belly, every cutlass slash spurting bright blood into the firelight, it was one less share for the crew and one more for Captain Thompson, you see?"

"Yes, I see. Elegant phrase, that. Damned good. Graphic. May I quote you? 'Every point-blank pistol shot into a soft belly, every cutlass slash spurting bright blood into the firelight' and all that?" Sir John scribbled notes.

"But of course, sir." Ratcliffe nodded graciously. He helped himself to another pinch of snuff and dusted the crumbs off his leather vest. "By morning, there were thirty men left alive sitting miserably on the beach, shivering in the drizzle, serum and blood leaking from their gashes and shot-holes, their heads throbbing with rum. It was an easy matter for Captain Thompson to row to the beach and restore order. Our captain never approached his men without a brace of loaded pistols in his belt and a naked cutlass in his hand."

"Clever chap, that."

"Too clever by half. Thompson's luck had changed. No sooner had he got the remnants of his sorry crew on board than he spied the royals of a ship on the horizon. After Thompson left, our Admiral Cochrane had arrived and corked the port of Lima tighter than vintage port. He found out about Thompson's escapade and ordered one of his captains to crack on every rag his frigate, *Porpoise*, could carry and bring Thompson back.

"Thompson had outsmarted himself. He'd not enough men left to fight. He had to slip his last cable and run. However, *Pride of Gloucester* was a Yankee-built schooner with a clean bottom and a good pair of heels and, in spite of being shorthanded, and a miserable, sick, sorry few hands they were, Thompson kept clear for four days. But *Porpoise* was gaining on Thompson; she was a much larger vessel and, even though her bottom was foul, she had more speed off the wind. *Porpoise* was trying occasional shots from her bow chasers when, off Punta Mala, the wind changed to a northerly gale. *Pride of Gloucester* could be rigged fore-and-aft and could beat to windward like a razor, whereas *Porpoise* was a full ship, slow and clumsy when she was on the wind, and, as I said, her bottom was foul. She had to claw her way up the Gulf of Panama and watch Thompson get farther and farther away. Thompson had the City of Panama in sight when his luck failed again. The wind died to a flat calm. There he sat with his sails slatting, watching *Porpoise* close on him. Fluky wind, you see. *Porpoise* still had a light breeze on her quarter. A mile off shore, *Porpoise* caught up with *Pride of Gloucester* and pounded her to flaming rags and splinters. Thompson and twelve men managed to lower a boat and sneak away under the smoke, but the rest of the crew was blown to hell with *Pride of Gloucester*.

"Thompson and his lot disappeared into the City of Panama and crossed the Isthmus to the Caribbean shore, committing only casual acts of loot and rape. There they stole a fishing smack and sailed to Jamaica. A few nights ago, they were well into drink in a cheap stew when Starret, sailing master of *Wasp*, recognized Thompson and informed the guard. They caught the pirates with their breeks down rutting with some of our local whores. The magistrate found them guilty of piracy and sentenced them to hang. The hangman awaits your signature on the warrants, but I thought you might wish to have a look at them before they swing for it, perhaps interview them for your memoirs? They're downstairs, Sir John, in chains, under guard and awaiting your inspection."

"Jolly good!" said Sir John. "Let's have a look at them, Ratcliffe. Bring them up, one—no, two at a time, and we'll see what kind of songs they can sing. I shall take notes."

Ratcliffe wiped the snuff-drool from his chin. "Very good, sir."

The first pair the guards brought in consisted of a somber giant and a wee little ratlike man.

"Name!" Ratcliffe demanded of the giant.

"*Cangrejo, señor. Pero estoy un hombre honrado y inocente—*"

"Shut up. Answer my questions only," Ratcliffe said. "Guards! Look sharp. I'll have no insolence here."

"What does the rascal say?"

"He says he's an honest and innocent man."

"Oh yes. No doubt about it. No doubt at all. Gad, but he's an ugly monster. And big!" Sir John said, scratching busily with his pen. "I say, are there enough chains on him? And that face! The French disease on top of smallpox scars, I'll wager. And how does he eat with those rotting teeth? Faugh! Get him to stand farther away, Ratcliffe. His breath would stun a hyena."

"A bit farther back, guards," said Ratcliffe.

The soldiers standing behind the big pirate jerked at his chains. Cangrejo backed up two paces.

The small prisoner squeaked: "Don't 'af to speak Dago to that scum, sorr. He 'spicca da ingels' when tha makes him."

Sir John sniffed: "Thenks awfully."

"And who might you be?" Ratcliffe asked.

"Crabbe, sorr, Israel Crabbe at tha service, Your Worship. And, if I may be so bold, I'd like to thank you most heartily, for saving me from this band of ruffians. We're going to kill me, sorr! Me! Imagine! And after I'd labored so perilous hard to save their souls, Your Worships. As you can see plain as day, Your Worships, I'm no pirate, I'm a minister of the gospel."

"What's that? What's that?" said Sir John. "Damn his eyes! What's that rascal saying? He's a what?"

"He's a 'minister of the gospel,' sir," Ratcliffe said.

"Oh, quite! Oh, rather! Oh my great aunt Matilda's arse!" Sir John raised one eyebrow. "I should have realized it immediately. Typical 'minister of the gospel,' if I do say so myself: shirt filthy and stained with blood and purple vomit, a chancre consuming a large portion of his nose—also the French disease, I'll wager—and missing, let me see—" Sir John craned his neck to examine Crabbe. "—three fingers on his left hand, two on the right." Sir John scratched away at his notes.

"And that's not half, Sir John. Look at that scar on what little skin is left of his nose," Ratcliffe said. "Slit for a cutpurse or my name's not Ratcliffe."

"Ah, delighted to make acquaintances with Your Worships!" said Crabbe. "Mr. Ratcliffe, is it? And Sir John? Delighted. I can explain these disconfigurationments easy, sorrs. Honorable scars o' me calling, no more, no less. Not for me the easy congfligations of honest farmers and tradesmen, no sorrs! Me call led me a perilous path amongst the real sinners of the world—"

"A minister of the gospel, eh?" Ratcliffe dragged down the under lid of his left eye. "In that case, allow me to introduce myself. I'm the late Queen Mother."

"Yes, and I'm the Dowager Duchess of Prawn," said Sir John.

"It's God's own, bright, honest truth, sorrs," Crabbe squeaked through his ratlike nose, what was left of it. He fluttered his little hands. Ratcliffe glanced around the prisoner to detect the possible presence of a bald, skinny tail. "I would show Your Worships me ordination papers had these swine not confisticated them from me and burned them."

"Hmm. Yes. Of course. Pity, that," Sir John said.

"Fairly took the words from my mouth, sir," said Ratcliffe.

"As God is my judge, sorrs!" Crabbe rolled his eyes piously to heaven.

"Oh shut up, do!" Sir John snapped. "I've heard quite enough from you." Sir John stabbed his pen in the air at Cangrejo. "You there, do you understand me?"

Cangrejo nodded. "*Si, señor.*"

"Very good. Now look here, don't waste my time with protestations of innocence. I know, beyond the slightest shadow of a doubt, that you are guilty of piracy many times over, and I hang pirates. But I could perhaps be persuaded to commute the death sentence of the pirate who gave the most precise details concerning the treasure."

Crabbe squeaked, "Well, then, that's simple. I'm your man, sorr! I saved a trifle for myself, sorr, for to construct a small chapel in me village. While these other ruffians were fighting and drinking, I took the scepter of the Bishop of Lima with a diamond as big as a child's fist on top. I buried it fifty paces back from the beach. When you pardon me, being an innocent man of the cloth and all like that, I'll lead you direct to it I will."

"Don' leesten to zat *ijo'e puta*, señor," said Cangrejo. "He only ze cook. I, *mismo*, was presently at all the buryings and I will tell you everyzing. Pieces of eight, señor, reevers of them—"

"Well!" said Crabbe. "Of all the bleddy—"

"Guards!" said Sir John. "Remove the small cutpurse for the moment. We'll listen to the big Diego first."

***

"Well, sir, that's the lot. Except for Thompson himself."

Sir John blew the sand from his latest page of notes. "Fascinating. Utterly fascinating. Marvelous material for my memoirs. They all agree on the location of the main loot: 'In Chatham Bay, on the northeast of the island, find a big spreading tree with four notches carved in the butt. Walk three hundred fifty yards south by west, a quarter west, then walk due east to align yourself with the stream as it flows through a U-shaped notch,' and so on and so forth. But each of them has his own personal tale to tell. I rather liked the Reverend Israel Crabbe's narrative of how he absconded with the golden scepter of the Bishop of Lima adorned with a diamond as big as a child's fist. Of course, only he knows the location, what?"

"Yes, sir. Very nice, sir. And Cangrejo's yarn: 'Señor! Zee life-size, solid gold statue of zee Blessed Virgeen Maria wit' zee eyes of esmeraldas—'"

"Yes. Absolutely marvelous. How much do you think such a statue would weigh, Ratcliffe?"

"No less than two and a half tons, Sir John."

"Yes. Quite. I thought so. And our elegant Señor Cangrejo tucked two and a half tons of gold casually under his coat and tiptoed off into the bushes with it."

"So he would have us believe. And, of course, he must be saved in order to lead us to this treasure. Only he knows the location."

"Well, let's have the pièce de résistance, the noted Captain Thompson himself."

"Very good, sir." Ratcliffe shouted: "Corporal! Bring in Thompson."

The man the guards pushed into the room had spent several days in a filthy cell; however, he'd cleaned up a bit and had somehow managed to take a shave. He bowed politely to Sir

John and smiled like a mischievous schoolboy called before the headmaster: "I seem to have made a fair pickle of it this time, eh, Sir John?" he said.

"Indeed."

"Sir John, I have a matter of some delicacy to discuss with you, man to man, between gentlemen, so to speak." Thompson glanced at Ratcliffe and the guards. "Could we do so in privacy?"

Ratcliffe said, "Careful, Sir John!"

Sir John looked up from his notes and shook his head. "I think not. What could we possibly have to discuss in private?"

"Why, the true and accurate location of the Loot of Lima."

"We have had ample instructions from your crew," said Ratcliffe.

"Yes," Sir John said. "I don't really know what else you could add to: 'In Chatham Bay, on the northeast of the island, find the big spreading tree with four notches carved in the butt. Walk three hundred fifty yards south by west, a quarter west, then—'"

Thompson laughed. "Surely, you don't think I'd allow those scum a chart or a true compass? That rabble wouldn't know a map from a monkey's arse. Lord-a-mercy, Sir John, a man must watch out for his interests."

"Hmm, yes, I see your point," Sir John said. "But Ratcliffe stays." Sir John moved the pile of manuscript to the other side of his desk, opened the mahogany case and took out one of the dueling pistols, cocked it, and laid it on the desk before him. He spoke to the guards. "I believe we have the situation in hand, Corporal. You may wait in the other room."

The guards left, closing the door behind them.

"Well then, I know when I'm beaten," Thompson continued. "I propose a straightforward business exchange: my life for the Loot of Lima. I'll even lead you to it."

"No, you won't," Sir John said. "You'll give us the correct instructions. We'll lead ourselves to it and we'll consider sparing your life, perhaps even setting you free."

"You drive a hard bargain, Sir John." Thompson rubbed his head briskly. His short, fair hair stuck up like the quills of a hedgehog, a boyish gesture which Sir John found engaging. "But beggars can't be choosers. Give me your word of honor between English gentleman that you'll set me free."

"All right. Fair enough. You have my word." Sir John threw a quick glance over Thompson's shoulder to Ratcliffe, who stood behind. Ratcliffe responded with a grotesque elongation of his face.

In his chains, Thompson shuffled to the door and shot the bolt. "Gentlemen, let's understand each other. I'm speaking of such wealth that no one's trustworthy. No one. We must have complete secrecy. Let me use a piece of your paper and a pen, Sir John, and I shall draw you the true directions to a king's ransom."

Sir John slid a fresh piece of paper, a pen, and the inkwell to the front of his desk. Thompson took the pen awkwardly in his manacled hands and drew a broad inverted cup shape at the bottom of the paper.

"Forget what that rabble told you about Chatham Bay on the northeast of the island. Go to the bay on the northwest of the island. Called Wafer Bay, incidentally, after Lionel Wafer, the surgeon of the British sloop of war *Bachelor's Delight*. Her skipper, Davis, put into Cocos with half his crew rotten with scurvy— but dear me, how I do ramble!" Thompson laughed and rubbed his short hair again with the same schoolboy gesture.

Sir John smiled. He couldn't help but like this charming rascal.

"On the westerly side of Wafer Bay, there's a creek which appears to flow inland at high tide." Thompson scratched a sharply pointed V that pointed still farther inland. "That's because there's a rock ledge, don't you see, right here at the top of the beach, keeps the tide out until high slack." Thompson drew a wavy line across the top of the V. "Now, Sir John, you follow the bed of that creek upstream and the stream forks. Follow the fork that passes a big tree with four large notches carved in the butt for about three-hundred-fifty yards and you will find a place where the creek courses over a U-shaped notch in the hillside. The treasure is buried fifty yards from that notch on a bearing of—now, Sir John, I must use your rule to draw the bearing."

Sir John leaned over the sketch. Ratcliffe craned forward to peer over Thompson's shoulder. Thompson reached for the rule but snatched the cocked pistol, aimed it deftly under his arm, and drilled a neat hole through Ratcliffe's heart. Thompson whipped the other pistol from the mahogany case, jumped behind Sir John's back, and flipped a loop of his chains over Sir John's head. In the same charming schoolboy tone: "Isn't this too, too cozy. We're twins, Sir John. You're my passport. Tell the guards we leave together and we board a ship together. You will live, Sir John, as long as you're useful. So, be useful."

"It would appear you have the upper hand," Sir John said. "I shall inform the guards." Coupled with Thompson, Sir John stepped over the corpse of Ratcliffe, twitching in a pool of gore, and unbolted the door. The guards tumbled in and stopped at seeing Thompson holding a cocked pistol in Sir John's back. Sir John said: "Guards, seize this man."

"No you don't!" shouted Thompson. "One false move and Sir John dies."

"I think not. That pistol is loaded with a blank."

Thompson snickered. "By God, sir, you are a cool one! No English gentleman would give an opponent a dueling pistol loaded with a blank."

"Guards, you *will* follow my instructions immediately."

The charming schoolboy disappeared. "Piss-begotten son of a dog-fucked whore! You die with me." He pressed the muzzle of the pistol against Sir John's spine.

The pistol fired as a guard smashed his musket butt onto Thompson's skull with the thump of a ripe cantaloupe falling from a chiffonier. Thompson dropped like a poleaxed steer. The guards helped Sir John disengage himself from the loop of chain and get to his feet.

"Damn and double-damn!" Sir John shrugged out of his jacket and beat out the sparks around a smoldering, ragged hole.

The Captain of the Guard said, "Sir John! Are you all right?"

"Oh, I'm quite all right. But my jacket! I do believe this blackguard has ruined it. Is he dead, by the way?"

The Captain examined Thompson, who lay on the floor,

blood drooling from nose, ears, and mouth. "I don't believe so, sir. Not quite yet. He seems to be breathing."

"Well, then, let's take no more chances, shall we?" Sir John sat down and busily scratched signatures on the pile of death warrants. "Drag him out and hang him. Immediately, before he recovers and tries some other caper. He's certainly too clever by half, but he doesn't know much about English gentlemen."

"Very good, sir."

"And send a detail in here to clean up after poor Ratcliffe. Dreadful pity and all that, but he did go on so." Sir John wiped a gout of Ratcliffe's blood from his shoe onto Ratcliffe's vest. "I say, Captain, I shall have to replace him. I must have a secretary. Check for any likely lads among the merchant's clarkes who can write a good hand. And who damned well do not use snuff."

"Very good, sir. And the other pirates?"

"Hang them all. Hang every last rotten one of them."

***

On Cocos Island, an unusually strong nor'easter abated in the evening, but not before the surf had ripped the last supporting earth from under one side of a large tree, the boudoir for two hundred greedy boobies. As the tree leaned and finally fell into the surf, the boobies screamed, tweaked each other savagely with their beaks, and held each other to blame for the situation. Most of the adult birds took wing before they were immersed in the waves.

Booby chicks were also in the tree. Booby chicks are pink and so stupid as to make their parents' feeble intellects glitter like René Descartes. Before they were immersed, the more vocal chicks said "Gork?" and clutched the branches tightly with their rubbery feet. Many of the chicks held onto the branches until they were drowned or crushed in the surf. Small, industrious sharks hustled about in the shallows and munched greedily. Those chicks that escaped the sharks floated soggily to shore and waddled up the beach, plaintively questioning: "Gork?" Others fought peevishly amongst themselves, "Skree!"

Their parents ignored the decimation of the flock of young. They had a more important thing to do: an avian court-martial on the subject "Who tipped over our tree?" The prosecutors mercilessly questioned the suspects, pecking them savagely to extract confessions of guilt. The suspects did not cooperate. The line of distinction between prosecutor and suspect blurred and the court-martial degenerated into a screaming, flopping carpet of feathers under a cloud of leaping lice.

Daylight was fading fast. The flock adjourned the court-martial, refreshed themselves with a few morsels of marine garbage, including scraps of their young leftover from the sharks' dinner, and flew away in search of a new boudoir. Not far inland, they infested a suitable tree and settled down to sleep. The surviving chicks waddled inland to the new tree, gorking plaintively, and joined their parents.

During the night, the flock passed the products of their evening meal. Booby shit is the foulest, most adhesive shit in the world's catalog of excrement. By morning, this stinking, gluey, snot-like material had obliterated four large notches carved in the butt of the big spreading tree.

During the night, more torrential rain fell and precipitated a landslide which plugged the creek and buried a U-shaped notch under tons of mud, rocks, and shattered tree trunks.

***

When his father died, Sir John Seede came into the estate and retired from colonial service. He returned to England, where he occupied himself with polishing his manuscript, *Personal Encounters with Noted Pirates of the Spanish Main: The Memoirs of Sir John Seede, OM, MBE, FRGS.* He also gave liberal attention to the table and the bottle. In the salubrious English air, Lady Charlotte recovered completely from her tropical fevers and put on enough weight to become 'a fine figure of a woman.' She was twenty years Sir John's junior. Sir John, too, put on weight—a great deal of weight—and became quite red in the face, what the English call a 'ruddy complexion.'

One Sunday in early autumn, the couple drove home from church in their stylish low barouche drawn by their matched pair of black Hanoverians. Passing a meandering brook, Sir John gave a great shout. "Yaah! Stop! For God's sake, stop the carriage!" The coachman reined in the horses. Before the footman could dismount to assist, Sir John tumbled out of the barouche and rushed headlong through the spreading oaks to plunge his head into the creek.

Lady Charlotte, the coachman, and the footman looked on in amazement. Lady Charlotte tapped the footman with her fan. "Charlie, dear, whatever can the dear man be doing?"

"Haven't the foggiest, madam," said Charlie, a tall, strapping fellow and a great favorite of Lady Charlotte. "Perhaps he feels the heat?"

"Gracious, Charlie, it's not that warm. He's had his poor, dear head underwater a frightfully long time, don't you think?"

"Yessum, indeed, that he has."

"Well then, you two. Driver! Charlie! Lively now. Fish him out. Directly."

The two servants did as instructed and helped Sir John back into the barouche. His eyes were unfocused and his few remaining strands of gray hair plastered wetly to his face. "Wazi na fobba," he said. "Hurtsh, hurtsh!"

"Whatever is the matter with your voice, John? Oh well, never mind. Driver? Driver! Whip up your pair and take us home tout de suite. Then go and get dear Dr. Cadavré. Accept no excuses, mind. Bring him directly. Probably unnecessary, don't you think, Charlie? But we mustn't take any chances with dear, dear Sir John." She leaned forward to pat Sir John's knee. "We'll take you home, dear, and fix you a dear hot cup of tea. I'll warrant you'll be as good as new when dear Dr. Cadavré arrives to bleed you and put some dear, outrageous, French or Latin name to your dear little escapade."

"Hurtsh! Hurtsh!" Sir John mumbled.

Near Seede Hall, the coachman had to rein in while a span of oxen and a big-wheeled farm cart trundled across the road and into a farmyard. The farmer's seven tousle-headed children sat in a row on the top rail of the farm fence. They stared unblinkingly at the barouche, picked their noses, and wiped their fingers on their filthy jerkins.

"Yaaaah!" screamed Sir John and leaped from the barouche. He stumbled crabwise, hopping more than walking, into the farmyard and plunged his head into a stone watering trough.

The farmer's children abandoned themselves to helpless laughter and clutched each other for support. One of them even fell off the fence to lie flopping and gasping on the ground like a fresh-caught smelt.

Even Lady Charlotte giggled. "Really, Charlie, this is too amusing! The dear man has become quite eccentric!"

However, when they hauled Sir John's head from the horse trough, they discovered the dear man had become quite dead. The children continued to point, guffaw and tumble until their mother bundled them away into the thatched farmhouse.

After the funeral, Lady Charlotte gave Charlie the sack. As a further act of contrition, she cracked on her finest suit of forty-pound weeds: broad-brimmed hat, billowing veils, unreefed courses, tops'ls, royals, t'gallants, skysails, and even a few stuns'ls to port . With the manuscript under her arm and the wind on her quarter, she boomed downwind on a broad reach to the office of a publisher, where she arranged to have Sir John's *Personal Encounters with Noted Pirates of the Spanish Main: The Memoirs of Sir John Seede, OM, MBE, FRGS* published in octavo on fine French paper, handsomely bound in calf, the spine lettered in gilt. In spite of her layers of veils, she made a devastating impression on the publisher, a recent widower, a snappy dresser, and a handsome devil at that. Lady Charlotte managed to indicate through the high pathos of the moment that she herself was not unimpressed.

At first, very few read Sir John's book of memoirs. Lady Charlotte glanced at it to confirm the quality of type and paper and sent copies to all the relatives, Sir John's college, and the library of the British Museum. Over the years, a few of Sir John's descendants leafed idly through it. But a hundred years later, an enterprising plagiarist happened on the copy in the British Museum. He extracted the story of Thompson, included it with several other pirate yarns from other sources. He expanded and embroidered the accounts and published them in a tawdry pulp volume that went through three editions of a hundred thousand copies each.

The illustration on the front cover shows a villainously ugly, grinning pirate, complete with eye patch and head bandana and a knife clamped in his teeth, in the act of ripping the décolletage from a screaming and almost unbelievably endowed blonde who has draped herself over a bursting treasure chest. In the background looms a mountain of treasure: gems as big as butter clams, a river of glittering pieces of eight, a scepter containing a diamond as big as a child's fist, and a life-size, solid gold statue of the Virgin with emerald eyes. On the summit lolls a gigantic octopus that seems to have contracted inappropriate sexual tastes. His red eyes glitter and he reaches a questing tentacle for the partially exposed, very ample mammary of the blonde. The pirate doesn't appear to mind sharing his prize with this perverted mollusk.

On the back cover, a commercial artist had created a quasi-photograph of the drunken fracas in Chatham Bay with a quote from the text: "Every point-blank pistol shot in a soft belly, every cutlass slash that spurted bright blood into the firelight was one less share for the crew and one more for Captain Thompson." Even poor Ratcliffe would have his small place in history.

The book was a howling success, and, in the years since, it has caused one hell of a lot of men, who should have known one hell of a lot better, one a hell of a lot of trouble.

Chapter One

Men fall in love with machines. For some, it's motorcycles. For others, it's cars or antique threshing machines. For Longstreet, it was airplanes.

Longstreet was a timber cruiser, a man who earns his living by trudging through forests and counting trees. Not only does he count the trees, he notes their species, estimates their volume, and judges their quality and health. Cruising is as much an art as it is a science, and Longstreet was a real artist, much in demand for his accurate reports. Longstreet was also an owly bugger and fiercely independent.

Longstreet had decided that flying would be an advantage for his work—strictly as a business investment, you understand. He got his private pilot's license. His instructor was an airplane salesman, a polite young man: "Flying is easy. You drive 'em up and drive 'em down." But once Longstreet got the feel of stick, rudder, and throttle, he fell in love with flying. He even began to learn something. He discovered that the pretty airplanes the polite young man sold were not the thing for bush flying. He bought a Super Cub. He learned the basics of bush flying from an impolite old son of a bitch who taught him:

Power approaches: "*Don't* cut that throttle yet. Nose higher!"

Forward slips: "For Christ sake! Lower that leading wing! Keep it *down*."

Short-field landings: "Power, goddammit, *power*."

Longstreet learned about foul weather and ice from several experiences that left him exhausted, bathed in a cold sweat, but fortunately alive.

He even taught himself a few aerobatics.

To a flyer, Coastal British Columbia is a heady cocktail of mountains and water. The weather changes from a relaxed stroll in a summer meadow to a blindfolded stagger under a freezing deluge through a cave populated with murderers with baseball bats. The weather can do this in minutes and without warning. Longstreet decided he needed an instrument rating. He learned instrument flying from a coldblooded instructor who made his impolite bush-flying instructor look like Mother Teresa after a few stiff drinks. "No, sir, you failed that miserably. Go around. Report to the tower—*now, right now!* Go back to the beacon and try again—*don't lift that hood! Eyes on the clocks*."

Longstreet strained his finances outfitting his Cub with a powerful engine, a constant-speed prop, and enough avionics for instrument flying. Then he put her on floats. For a float-plane, coastal British Columbia is one big landing field.

Longstreet's Cub was his magic carpet. A potential client would tell him: "It'll be a snap. All nice timber on easy slopes. Gimme a good price on this one. I got a lot more work for you."

After an inspection trip in the Cub, Longstreet could say: "Most of your trees are growing out of cracks in a granite cliff. No contract price. Cost plus, and I need two thousand bucks up front."

Coastal logging begins in the early spring. Through the summer the chainsaws howl, the yarders thunder, whistle signals shriek, logs splash into the water, and the air sizzles with logger language, probably the world's raunchiest dialect. But in the late fall, the days shrink down to a scant seven hours of fog and freezing rain. Felled and bucked timber is piled like slippery jackstraws over lakes of bottomless mud.

Then logging throws in the sponge for the winter. Loggers with homes and families crave their warm hearths, hockey on television, and a jug of rye in the kitchen. Loggers without families are eager to get out of the cold air and into a nice warm bar for their hockey and rye-and-ginger. Longstreet didn't follow hockey and didn't drink rye, but he was ready for a change. He had finished the fieldwork for this job. It was time to go to town, clean up his notes, submit his report, and get paid. This contract had been with a major timber company, and he was staying at their company camp—easy living for him. He usually slept in a tent and cooked his own meals over a campfire.

The rigging crews had built their lunches, climbed into the crummies and gone up into the hills. The dry-land sort crew rumbled in their front loaders building bundles of logs. The boom men scooted in their boom boats making up sections of bundles. The cooks made bread. The bull cooks swamped out the bunkhouses. The Push and Longstreet lingered over a last mug of coffee. The Push in a logging camp does not have an easy job. He is the interface between the Suits in the office downtown and the loggers in the bush who hate them. When the loggers succeed in breaking a huge, greasy machine, "Hee-hee, Boss, it broke," it's the Push, not the Suits, who must get

3

it fixed. When the washing machine gets plugged with chewing gum and gravel, it's the Push, not the Suits, who must fix it. When the cook goes shrieking apeshit in the night and has to be shipped out in a big, white laundry bag, the Push must cook until the Suits send in a replacement. It's the Push, not the Suits, who must stand, nose to nose, with giant, drunken psychopaths and say, "You're fired."

The Push slugged down the last of his coffee and plastered an insincere smile on his face. "So, you've finished your contract, but listen, I've got some good news. I got a radiophone call from the office. They've been offered a timber lease, a section of really nice poles. Poles are scarce right now and they're getting top dollar on the market. All you'd have to do is—"

"No. I don't 'have to do' anything. I'm going where it's warm and dry."

"Yeah, but you got to understand, they want to make a quick offer and they really need a cruise on those poles, and since you're up here already and—"

"I do understand. I don't care what they 'really need.' It's time for me to get warm and dry."

"Yeah, but I don't think it would take much time and the money would be great. You've got them over a barrel."

"They can shove that barrel up their ass. If they want me, they'll have to wait till next spring. Right now I've got enough money. I'm going where the sun shines all day, the food is great, the beer is cold, and they speak Spanish."

"The office won't like—"

"Look, man, quit trying." Longstreet made a horizontal sweeping motion with his hand. "The name of the game is 'no

4

more cruising until spring.' That's final. Get the office on the blower and tell them."

The Push heaved a sigh and left for the radiophone in the kitchen. He would have to give the Suits the bad news. They would whine and try to pass the buck onto the Push. The Push would have to be sweet and conciliatory while he ducked out from under the buck. The Suits would complain about the extra expense of flying in another timber cruiser. The Push would sympathize—carefully. That buck still floated around in the air looking for someone's back. Eventually the Push would mention the expense of long radiophone calls. That usually made the Suits shut up.

Longstreet got his pack out of the bunkhouse, toted it down to the float, and tossed it into the back of his Super Cub. He checked the oil in the engine.

A raven flew out of the underbrush and perched on the rudder. He looked Longstreet over carefully with one eye. He flirted his head to ogle with the other. *"Grack-grr! Chuckle-chuckle-squeak?"* This phrase in Raven language translates to: "Hey there, kid. Whatcha doin'?"

Only a fool is rude to a raven. Longstreet might have been owly, but he was not a fool. He said, "Well, sir, I'm going to fly my sorry, battered birdie to Victoria for maintenance. Then I'm going to see if I can hustle a trip to where the beer is cold and the skies are not cloudy all day."

"Dork-dork-dork-dork, snickle?" ("Ha-ha. Is that a fact?") The raven flirted his tail and reefed a louse from under his wing with his beak.

"Yeah, that's a fact."

"*Graak-graak-graak. Snee! Snee!*" ("You're gonna be sorry!") The raven flew away across Thompson Sound. On his way, he did a couple of snap rolls.

"You sooty bastard! Snap rolls, no less!" Longstreet had never done a snap roll. He didn't know if a Super Cub could do a snap roll. On wheels? Maybe. On floats? Never!

Longstreet inspected the Super Cub's wings and control surfaces for frost. No frost. He bled his fuel tanks into a cup and looked for water. No water. He took a look at his floats. A season's worth of barnacles and weed looked back at him. No help for that. He pushed off from the dock and used his paddle to turn into the wind. He climbed in, closed the power switch, turned on the magnetos, and thumbed the starter. The Lycoming engine, all two hundred horses of it, started immediately. On taxi, he checked controls, magnetos, fuel tanks, and throttle and cycled his constant-speed prop.

"All right, either you can drag those filthy, dirty floats out of the water and fly, or you can't." He lifted his water rudders and eased full throttle to the Lycoming. The engine's trombone-like moan echoed from the surrounding cliffs. "Come on. Up onto the step. Yes! That's it!"

She flew.

He flew over Knight Inlet and clenched his jaw. The turbulence was sickening. He passed the town of Campbell River. He flew down Georgia Strait and over the warmer Gulf Islands. He began to think seriously about the evening: his digs in Vancouver, a hot shower, a close shave, Chinese food, and perhaps the company of Delia the redhead with the smooth white skin.

Such thoughts don't make for concentration on flying.

He dragged his mind away from Delia the redhead with the smooth white skin. He thumbed the mike. "Victoria Tower, this is floatplane Whiskey-Oscar-Papa."

"Whiskey-Oscar-Papa, Victoria Tower."

"I'm ten miles out, west of Salt Spring, to land in Pat Bay."

"Whiskey-Oscar-Papa, we have no traffic. You are cleared direct to land in Pat Bay."

"Whiskey-Oscar-Papa."

Longstreet racked the Super Cub into a howling forward slip. He straightened up ten feet above the water and plumped his floats into Pat Bay. He taxied onto the seaplane ramp.

During the war, Pat Bay had been a base for military Catalinas, Geese, Albatross, and, on rare occasions, even a hulking Martin Mars, squatting on her ponderous beaching gear like a winged blimp hangar. But the war was over and the military had discarded seaplanes and moved on to helicopters. The adjacent airstrip had passed into civilian hands and become Victoria International Airport. The paint peeled from the old hangars. No signal flags fluttered. The only saluting and strutting martinets were the seagulls.

Most of the old amphibians and flying boats had been scrapped or abandoned in careless dumps, like popcorn bags in the gutter of a prairie cinema. Some of the amphibians still mumbled through the sky many thousands of hours beyond their design lifetimes. A lucky few got complete rebuilds into gleaming corporate limousines; the rest of the frowzy old bitches were patched up to serve as water bombers or freight transport if honest, arms or dope smugglers if not. Coastal logging camps were served by floatplanes.

The Nordic Air pickup swung around the corner and backed a floatplane dolly down the ramp and under the Super Cub's floats.

"Hiya, Angus," Longstreet said.

Angus jumped out of the cab and pumped the hydraulics on the dolly to lift the Super Cub. "My boy, even though the bludy-fookin' English language doesn't contain bludy-fookin' words to express the boundless extent of my hatred for bludy-fookin' airplanes, I am fookin' disgusted by the appalling bludy state you have allowed your poor dickey bird to get into."

The two-way radio in the pickup cab squawked: "Nordic Air pickup, where are you?"

Angus snarled: "Bludy fookin' nosy parkers." He sauntered to the cab, thumbed the mike, and snarled with withering scorn: "Victoria Ground, this is the Nordic Air pickup and, for your information, you can't see me because I'm on the bludy seaplane ramp—and where did you think I usually drag the bludy floatplane dolly, to the corner store for a bludy popsicle?"

"Roger, Angus," said the radio. "Glad to see you in your usual sweet mood."

Angus clipped the mike onto its hook.

Longstreet said, "Where's the Viking? Counting his money? Off chasing pussy in Tuktoyaktuk?"

"The Viking—Mr. Einer Torsen to you—is extracting yet more money from Mr. High-and-Mighty Van Dusen. He's taking the Albatross today."

"Jesus, Jesus, Jesus! That Albatross. I remember when you got her. She came in on the water. Her wheels hadn't been used for a year. Einer had to pull her wings off and hire a lowboy to get her over to the hangar. Her engines looked like moldy corncobs in a coal mine. They dripped so much oil the pigeons were skating on the tarmac. And damn! Did she stink! She'd been carrying fish."

"Mr. Longstreet, sir, would you honor me by gracing the right seat of the pickup with your arse? I have to get your bludy airplane back to the bludy hangar so I can bludy well fix it. And will you be around after quitting time? If I have to listen to your bullshit, I'd rather do it over a pint—I might even buy a round."

Longstreet threw himself to his knees. "He loves me!" Longstreet cooed, clasping his hands to his heart and rolling his eyes to the sky in an ecstasy of ersatz rapture. "He loves me! Angus, the bludy-fookin' Oatmeal Sasquatch himself, actually offered to buy me a bludy beer!"

"Shut your bludy yap. Get in the bludy cab."

Gingerly and in the lowest gear, Angus towed the Super Cub up the ramp. He thumbed the mike: "Victoria Ground, this is Nordic Air pickup. I'm towing a Super Cub back to the Nordic Air hangar."

"Ah, Nordic Air pickup, we have incoming traffic, a flock of water bombers. They're low on fuel and have to come straight in. Hold short of the runway."

"Holding short. Nordic Air pickup."

"The Albatross is finished? In only six months?" Longstreet said. "That's almost a world record! Can't wait to see her. I bet she's a beautiful job. What all did you have to do on her?"

"A bludy smart-ass, that's what you are. No bludy airplane's beautiful; nothing but pains in the arse, they are." Angus turned off the pickup's engine to wait.

"What airplanes don't you hate, Sasquatch?"

"Shut up and let me finish. She was stripped, inspected rivet by rivet—sometimes even with a microscope. All of her aluminum spar caps were replaced with titanium—at ruinous expense, I may add. Any skin, frame, rib, hinge, tube that couldn't be made better than new has been replaced. Inside and out, any skin showing corrosion pits has been soaked in chromic acid and painted with the best primers and paints—which don't come cheap either, my boy."

Angus thumbed the mike. "Victoria Ground, this is Nordic Air pickup."

"Continue holding. Water bomber on short final."

"Holding. Nordic Air." Angus put down the mike. The water bomber, a Catalina amphibian, landed like a dying pterodactyl. "As I was saying before I was interrupted by that sick bludy-fookin' machine, we recovered the Albatross's control surfaces and replaced her rusty old control cables, turnbuckles, and sheaves with the best bronze and stainless steel money can buy—a lot of money. We pulled off her sad engines. We hung two spanking-fresh Wright Cyclone engines on brand-new mounts we had to weld up from scratch—"

"Stay where you are, Nordic Air. Another bomber on short final."

"Holding. Nordic Air."

Another aluminum pterodactyl staggered in and plopped onto the runway.

"—and these engines are none of your cut-rate overhauls, mind you, but zero-time units from Standard Aero, and even I've got to admit that an engine from Standard Aero is a thing of beauty. We hung brand-new three-bladed reversible pitch props on them. We installed airline-quality avionics—"

"Nordic Air pickup, you're cleared direct across the runway to the Nordic Air hangar."

"Nordic Air. Cleared to hangar." Angus snarled and dropped the mike into its cradle. "As I was saying before I was interrupted by those piles of aluminium shite, eight good engineers—myself included—two crackerjack sheet-metal men, the best tig-welder on the coast, together with hydraulic engineers, electricians, machinists, avionics men, radar mechanics, painters, and a trainload of other tradesmen, tinkers, and assorted fetch-and-carry, grunt-and-groan orangutans have spent half a year of their lives to make her right again. And I'll admit we've not done a bad job."

The Nordic Air hangar was a relic of World War II, a giant box as featureless as a barn on three sides and on the fourth, a facade of leaf after leaf of massive rolling doors. Under normal circumstances, only three leaves would have been opened to admit the Super Cub, but today the Nordic Air crew toiled like ants to push them all back. Each leaf that clattered and rumbled open showed more of a gleaming Grumman Albatross that stretched from wall to wall of the hangar. Her tail barely cleared the roof trusses. Lettered on one slab side of her fuselage was "International Historical Salvage Limited" in bold letters of gold, outlined in maroon.

"Damn, Sasquatch!" Longstreet looked up at the Albatross. "Now you got the wings back on her, she's huge! But who the hell is 'International Historical Salvage Limited'? What do they do? Buy old books? Dig for the Holy Grail?"

"I'll answer your questions in order because I'm too polite for my own good. Of course she's huge. A Grumman Albatross isn't a mosquito like that bundle of rags and corrosion in which you risk your stupid neck. An Albatross is one of the largest amphibious aircraft ever built. She can apply almost three thousand horsepower on takeoff; she's close to a hundred feet from tip to tip of her wings, and now that we've extracted World-War-Two JATO, SNOTTO, SONAR, two-ton radar, IFF, and other military shite out of her, she'll carry roughly as much as a DC-3—another real workhorse, but about which the less we have to say, the better."

Longstreet said. "Christ, she's gorgeous! What's that doo-hickey under the tail? I've never seen one of those before."

"That, my friend, is a cage we installed for a magnetom-eter. And there's more. There's a powered cable reel inside the fuselage. The avionics guys installed the readout panel behind the cockpit."

"A magnetometer, eh? That's for a geological survey, isn't it?"

"Aye. That's the business of International Historical Sal-vage Limited, the Vancouver public company that sold enough stock to greedy babes-in-the-woods who should know better, to raise enough money to fork over half a million dollars to fix that airplane."

"So these guys are geologists?"

"No. It's worse. Can you imagine? These poor fools have invested real money in a company that's going to look for bur-ied treasure. If they'd asked me, I'd have told them to save their money and buy a canoe and some shovels. Then, when they'd done digging in the tidal sands, they'd have enough left to move into a cozy loony bin in which they could blather in unknown tongues, chew the rugs, and pick flowers off the wallpaper during their declining years."

"Sasquatch, you got no romance in your soul."

"Arrrr—" Angus snarled and slapped a disgusted backhand at thin air.

A man walked slowly into view examining the gleaming surfaces of the Albatross's hull. "Who's that?" Longstreet said.

"That is none other than Van Dusen, mister bludy-fookin' International Historical Salvage Limited himself."

Einer Torsen, the Viking, followed behind Van Dusen with a clipboard under his arm. He made a quiet remark. The man gave a hearty laugh.

"Christ, listen to that big son of a bitch," Longstreet said. "Big white teeth and great big Ipana smile—goddamn if it ain't Captain America himself."

Angus smirked. "Longstreet, you have unfortunate tendencies to jump to conclusions."

"The bastard's in good shape, isn't he? Probably works out a lot. Got plenty of time on his hands. Doesn't have to make a living."

"Unlike you, of course, my fine industrious friend. Let's see. You've been working fairly steadily for almost nine months now."

"So long as I pay my mechanic's bills, what's it to you? I work hard, cruise a lot of timber, then I goof off, travel, chase women, drink beer. It's my choice."

"Oh for the life of a timber cruiser. If I had to do it all over again, I'd be a timber cruiser. I wouldn't join the RAF as a bludy helper, study hard and get my engineers ticket, grind my arse to a powder keeping the war going, then spend the next thirty years of my life fixing bludy, fookin' airplanes—"

Longstreet pantomimed a gypsy violinist playing "Hearts and Flowers." "Oh, Sasquatch," he howled forlornly, "your sad, sad story has done gone and broke my pore heart asunder."

"Someday, me boyo, you're going to cut one of those smart-ass capers and some big bugger—who's not sweet and forgiving like me—is going to knock your feeble, smart-ass brains out—"

"But until that day, I'll continue to laugh and gambol in the sunshine with—"

Einer shouted across the hangar "And if yü fawney, fawney fellows ver in da müvies, yü'd be rich. But yü ain't and Mr. Longstreet, sir, ef yü'd be efer so kind tü come over here, eye'll introduce yü to Mr. Van Düsen, da owner of da Albatross. Dat vay yü'll leave da Oatmeal Sasquatch alone and he can scrape da garbage off yür airplane and see if he can make it fly again."

Angus opened his rollaway toolbox and began to pull inspection covers and cowlings from the Super Cub. Longstreet walked across the hangar floor to the Albatross. Mechanics were hitching one end of a tow-bar to the Albatross's nose wheel and the other to the front bumper of the pickup. At the left landing gear, Einer explained to Van Dusen a fine point of maintenance having to do with careful inspection, rinsing with fresh water, and applying a special grease to avoid pitting, to avoid corrosion, to avoid chafing a seal, to avoid hydraulic leaks, to avoid—

"Absolutely beautiful job, Einer," Longstreet said.

"Yaw, vell, she's not bad ef eye dü say so myself," Einer

' answered. "Mr. Van Düsen, eye vant yü tü meet anoder old customer, Longstreet."

Van Dusen and Longstreet shook hands. Longstreet said: "Could I look her over inside, maybe eat my heart out a little?"

"Sure. Why not. Is that Super Cub yours? I want to see that."

"Yeah, it is." Longstreet and Van Dusen walked over to Longstreet's Super Cub.

Van Dusen stepped carefully up onto a nonskid patch on a float and looked into the cockpit. "Damn! A constant—speed prop in a Super Cub! How many horses?"

"Two hundred horse Lycoming. Einer put it in when he rebuilt her."

"And from the radios you've got in her you could probably fly her on instruments—but I didn't know you could fly IFR on floats."

"Yeah, well, it's not legal, but when it gets really sticky I climb and file an IFR flight plan over the radio. I cancel the plan when I get in the clear. Damn sight better than blundering around in the rocks. Besides, in the winter I put wheels on her and go down South."

Van Dusen whistled. "Not a bad life you lead. South, huh? You speak Spanish?"

"Enough to get by."

"How about a multiengine ticket?"

"No. I haven't needed it yet, and big, fast airplanes are no use to me. I couldn't afford them anyway."

"Yeah, well—multiengine training—well, that's not hard to fix."

"Mr. Van Düsen," Einer said, "it's getting close to quvitting time. Yü better gaw home while yü still got plenty of light."

Van Dusen said, "That's right! Longstreet, you better do that look-see quick while we tow her out."

Longstreet climbed the ladder and entered the after cabin hatch of the Albatross. He felt a faint jar, then mild rocking as the pickup inched the Albatross out of the hangar. Folding benches were mounted along both sides. Plenty of recessed D rings were provided for lashing cargo. Amidships, two huge ferry tanks almost filled the fuselage, leaving barely enough room to squeeze by. Forward of the ferry tanks and aft of the cockpit was a console, the readout for the magnetometer. In the cockpit they'd retained the massive control yokes and rudder pedals, and the original engine and flap controls still depended from the roof, but almost everything else was new. The instrument panel had been completely rebuilt for modern instruments and a battery of top-of-the-line avionics. Longstreet slid down the hatch and into the nose cabin, equipped with a pair of bunks. An anchor fitted neatly into brackets on the wall. Mooring lines were stowed in a locker. The nose hatch was open. Longstreet stuck his head out. "You got one hell of an airplane here, Mr. Van Dusen."

"I believe she'll do the job."

"I'll bet she'll do whatever job you have in mind." Longstreet closed the hatch, walked back through the cabin, and climbed down the ladder. The mechanics unhooked the towing strut and slid chocks under the wheels. Van Dusen was standing by the ladder, waiting to board.

Longstreet asked: "Where are you taking her?"

Van Dusen said, "She'll be based in Central America. I'll use her to haul freight and backup operations."

"Well, anytime you need a copilot, I know that country. I'm kidding."

Van Dusen didn't look as if he was kidding. "We should talk sometime. Ever hear of the Loot of Lima?"

"That sounds pretty romantic."

Einer said: "Yaw, vell, scrü de Lüte of Lima. Eye need a cold glass of beer. Yü go fly."

Van Dusen climbed into the Albatross and closed the hatch. From an open window in the cockpit, he shouted, "Clear prop!"

"Clear!" chorused the mechanics on the tarmac.

A starter whined; the right prop of the Albatross turned. With a jarring rattle, the engine fired, blowing a cloud of rich blue smoke, steadied down to an even mumble, then accelerated to a vibrating, fortissimo hum as Van Dusen advanced the throttle a hair. The left starter keened, the prop spun, and, with another blue cloud of smoke, the left engine caught. The prop's rotating blades became a translucent disk.

"Goddamn, those engines sound good!" Longstreet shouted into Angus's ear.

Angus nodded.

Van Dusen waved from the cockpit. The mechanics ran to pull the chocks from the wheels. Van Dusen applied a bit more throttle and taxied away from the hangar. The Nordic Air crew strolled out to watch the takeoff, the culmination of six months of hard work.

Van Dusen held short of the runway and did a long and careful run-up. Each engine roared, then snarled down an octave as he cycled the prop to full coarse pitch. He received his clearance from the tower. The Albatross taxied onto the active runway. The engines responded to full throttle with a level trombone bellow. The Albatross accelerated down the runway and lifted off. The wheels snapped up into their wells. At about five hundred feet, the Albatross banked smoothly to head out across Pat Bay. The mechanics breathed again and covered their excitement with remarks:

"I'll be damned, it flies!"

"Glad to see the last of that monster!"

"What the hell, another day, another Albatross."

"Albatross, whatever. I only do it for the money."

Angus nudged Longstreet. "How about that takeoff, eh?"

"All right. All right. He can fly an airplane. Hey Einer, when do you think my Super Cub will be ready?"

"Vell, Longstreet, it really depends on wot we find but ve're going to need at least a veek or two. Suppose yü give me a call in a day or tü and I'll know better. Are yü flying commercial or catching da bus to Vancüver?

"I'll fly commercial, catch the five o'clock to Vancouver. I might even have a date tonight."

Einer sighed. "Ven yü come back, maybe ve go have a cold glass of beer, eh?"

"Sure, Viking, why not."

Back in Vancouver, Longstreet parked his rusty VW Beetle in his own spot behind the coffee roaster's store and climbed the outside stairs to his apartment.

He tossed three weeks' worth of dirty clothes into the washer and put his notecase onto his drafting table. The client could wait. He had more important things. Like a call to Delia the redhead.

"Hiya, Snookums! I'm starving. Chinese? Like soon? Like Hong-Fat's?"

"Where the hell have you been?" Delia sounded snarky, as if she hadn't sold anything for a while.

"Real estate business not too good?"

"Real estate business has been lousy. I had a couple of big-time operators—the kind of guys you would call 'suits.' The kind of guys I would call slimy-fingered four-flushers. They were looking for office space—they said. They just absolutely had to see everything in my book. They just absolutely had to bad-mouth everything in my book. And there I was. Me. All suited up. All made up. Great big smile on my pretty face. Long red pigtail hanging cutely over my shoulder. Laughing appreciatively at all their smart-ass remarks and smutty jokes. At the end of the day, they'd buy the drinks, lots of them. They wanted to get me potted. Hell! Potted? Me? I drank them under the bar while squirming coyly out from under their damp octopus-fingers. And for a weeks' work, all that irresistible charm and a tankful of gas? I get Sweet Fanny Adams—"

"Sweet Fanny Adams? Who's that?"

"It's a euphemism, bonehead. It stands for sweet fuck-all. They said, 'We'll think it over and call you next week. We have to talk to Toronto, the head office, don't you know.' Then, a great big nothing. So, naturally, I tried to call Toronto, the head office. It doesn't exist. It was my slimy, rotten competition snooping my listings. And what about you? Have you been having a good time? Playing in the sunshine with your little airplane?"

"Usual stuff. Twenty percent cruise on a section of mixed timber—mostly hemlock and balsam with a couple of groves of dandy old-growth cedar. Trees beat the hell out of real estate. Either they're there or they ain't there. But enough of this chitchat. I'm hungry as hell. I've got to shit, shower, and shave, but I'm quick. I'll be at Hong-Fat's in an hour. Join me? I'll pay."

"'Shit, shower and shave'! Oh, Longstreet, you're so suave, so debonair you'd be irresistible if you weren't such a grubby wood rat. I have to finish my martini and freshen up. I'll be there as soon as I can. And I hope you understand women of my caliber are not usually so readily available to bush apes on a moment's notice."

"I'm too, too overwhelmed by your noblesse oblige. But I'm even hungrier."

"Smart-ass."

Chapter Two

Hong-Fat's is not easy to find. In fact, if you don't already know where it is, you'll never find it.

Longstreet walked up the alley between Pender and Keefer Street, slipping between the brimming garbage cans and footing the occasional overfed cat out of the way. He took a sharp left turn down an even narrower alley—foot traffic only—until he came to a flickering neon sign saying, '_ong Fa_.' The *H* and the *t* had long since been obliterated by bad little boys with sharp rocks. Anyway, the sign had nothing to do with current ownership. The name 'Hong-Fat' was one of a hundred identical signs made by a neon company long since defunct. *Lo-fan* (non-Chinese) customers had no choice but to call the place 'Hong-Fat's.' Chinese customers identified the place with a Cantonese phrase meaning 'Fat Grandpa's house.'

Longstreet climbed the creaking wooden staircase to the second floor, pushed open the door, and walked into brightly lit, gustatory heaven. He was lucky. There was an empty table. From the kitchen came the roar of burners under woks, rattling utensils, clattering plates, and a continuous monologue from Fat Grandpa, punctuated with shouts of laughter from his assistants—all his children, grandchildren, or products of more complicated social relationships.

Joe, the waiter, his hands full of dishes, pointed Longstreet to an empty table with a quick motion of his chin. When he was seated, Joe brought him a small platter of cold jellyfish strips and sliced pork hocks.

With his chopsticks, Longstreet dipped a slice of pork hock in vinegar laced with strips of fresh gingerroot and popped it in his mouth. He followed with some fiery strips of cold jellyfish.

Joe asked: "Where you wife?"

"I think maybe I've told you about a thousand times she's not my wife, only a good friend."

"Oh yes. Only good flend. Only good flend." Joe snickered, picked a nostril, and wiped his finger on Longstreet's table-cloth. He was one of Fat Grandpa's grandnephews and was allowed a few excesses.

In the kitchen, Fat Grandpa rattled off another joke. He, too, was allowed excesses. He owned the joint, was older than Methuselah, and could cook like the Chinese God of Food.

"I think she come now," Joe said. Delia's heels were clicking up the rickety wooden staircase.

"I think you're right." Longstreet stood to welcome Delia.

She certainly knew how to make an entrance: stretch blue jeans, a green silk blouse, and that gorgeous copper-colored pigtail over her shoulder. In spite of his casual exterior Longstreet's heart pounded. The other patrons even went so far as to stop eating to stare. Even Joe snorted and bumped his shins on a chair. One patron was so impressed he allowed a morsel of eggplant to escape his chopsticks and fall on the floor.

Delia gave Longstreet a quick peck on the cheek, avoiding his more ardent clutch. Joe seated Delia. "Joe, I hope you remember, I want no, repeat absolutely no MSG used in my food. And when are you going to get a liquor license? I like a drink with my dinner."

"OK. I tell Grandpa." Joe went to the kitchen door and shouted a long phrase which was greeted with thunderous guffaws and an equally long Cantonese retort which brought the house down again.

"Joe, I don't suppose you would tell me what Fat Grandpa actually said. If the food wasn't so good, I wouldn't set foot in this crummy joint."

"He say 'No MSG.'" Joe tried to stifle a guffaw, but his nose overflowed. "Snerk! Snerk!" He had to retire to the corner of the room and blow it noisily on a fresh table napkin.

"Joe," Delia barked, "it would be ever so sweet of you to get your comedic sense under control. I too would like some jellyfish and cold pork hock." She extended her chopsticks and picked morsels from Longstreet's plate until her own jellyfish arrived, along with a plate of deep-fried squid and a small platter of sliced, barbecued duck.

They ate in silence for a while.

"So, tell me about these big-timers who took up your week."

But Delia wasn't listening. Like a stunned haddock in spawning season she stared wide-eyed over Longstreet's shoulder.

"Hi there. This place is great. What wonderful smells!"

Longstreet's chair screeched on the tile floor as he turned.

It was Van Dusen, wearing a Hawaiian shirt outside a pair of neatly pressed khaki pants. His shoes were shined. He was wearing his great big Ipana smile.

"Where did you come from?"

"From necessity."

"How did you find me?"

"Einer told me."

"Yeah, I did take him here to dinner once. He asked them if they knew how to boil a codfish head. It's pretty hard to surprise the chef in this joint. They brought him a boiled codfish head."

"Well, that's a Norsky for you. Did he like it?"

"Matter of fact, Einer said it was the best boiled codfish head he ever tasted. Big head, too. Damn near as big as mine."

"Can I join you—and your pretty lady?"

"Sure. Why not. How about a boiled codfish head?"

Van Dusen pulled out a chair and sat down. "I believe I'll pass on that one. What's good here?"

Longstreet chewed his underlip reflectively. "I don't know. How do you like your food? Hot? Mild? Sweet? Bitter?"

"As a matter of fact, I like hot, and I wouldn't mind a shot of bitter either."

"Joe!" Longstreet shouted. Joe had retired to the kitchen to join the chatter. He came out and strolled toward the table, again picking his nose. "How about you leave my tablecloth alone and see if Fat Grandpa will make us one of those peppery *fou-qua* dishes and maybe two orders of those dumplings with delicious juice in them? And we definitely need some sturgeon fillets in that peppery-greasy sauce—oh yeah, how about that preserved fish and eggplant hot pot?"

Joe nodded and headed towards the kitchen.

Van Dusen said, "Would you be so kind as to introduce me to your lady?"

"I'm Delia," she said and assumed her most winning, wide-eyed smile.

Longstreet thought, Look out, you big-time-operator pilot with the great big Ipana smile and the gorgeous Albatross, you've stepped in it. She'll get her axe and chainsaw out and fall you and buck you into a boom-stick like she does all the big-time operators.

"You're such a stunner. You must be in show business, perhaps films?"

Longstreet waited for Delia to burn him right down to his ankles.

But she didn't. She twinkled and cooed, "No. Actually, I'm in real estate."

Van Dusen whistled. "Pity the customer with somebody like you on the selling end. They don't have a chance. Longstreet? How about you? You ever do any selling?"

"No. I couldn't sell poontang on a troop train."

Delia cooed again, "He's right. His choice of language guarantees that."

Van Dusen said, "Great little airplane, your Super Cub. I've put in more hours than I can remember in one of these."

"It does the job," Longstreet said.

"I'll bet. These little buggers will fly with anything you can close the doors on. Those floats of yours must spend a lot of time in salt water to pick up growth like that."

"Yeah," Longstreet said. "I work all up and down the coast. Don't get into fresh water much."

"All you have to do is build a seaplane ramp at your home base."

"I don't have a home base. When I'm in town I've got digs over a coffee roaster. The Super Cub is my home base."

"Yes, but your plane has 'Longstreet Log Services' painted on the side; you must have an office of some kind. How about your billing, your phone, your mail, your laundry? Surely you don't sleep in a Super Cub?"

"My answering service takes my phone calls. Steady clients call me on high-frequency radio or talk to my bookkeeper. I pick up my mail once every few weeks—such as it is. My parents are dead and my sister married an asshole and never did write letters anyway. Besides, she's pissed off at me for kissing goodbye to 'the home of the slave and the land of the flea.' I got no back seat in the Super Cub—did you notice? That's where I keep my tent, sleeping bag, grub box, and some other useful crap. When I'm not sleeping in one of a client's bush camps, I live wherever I pitch my tent."

"Great stuff. If you can live like that, what I have in mind would be duck soup for you."

"What do you have in mind?"

"I need a guy who can do a lot of things: copilot the Albatross, handle a boat, navigate, maybe speak Spanish, ride heard on a bunch of Englishmen, to name a few."

"If I felt like it, I could probably do most of that stuff except the copilot. I don't have a multiengine rating and I've never flown anything bigger than a beaver. What are you going to do, anyway?"

Van Dusen sighed. "Well here goes. Did you ever hear of the Loot of Lima?"

Delia said, "That sounds so utterly romantic I might have to throw up."

"I know." Van Dusen sighed again. "The trouble is it's probably true." He reached into his briefcase and pulled out a book. The tattered cover depicted a grinning pirate, a chest of treasure, and a screaming, over-endowed blonde being groped by a giant octopus.

"Oh-*hoh*, my-*hi*, gaw-*hawd*!" Delia groaned. "Surely a great big grown-up boy like you doesn't, for one single solitary minute, believe—" She rolled her eyes at the ceiling.

Van Dusen grinned. "Yeah, I know. But, believe it or not, this book covers the basic story. Give it a read. But only a damned fool would rely on this account alone. After I'd done a fair amount of research, I found some guys who've done the whole research job from A to Z. They've been worming around in the British Museum and other dusty, obscure basements, and they've found a lot of stuff that's neither in this book nor in the historical references this book is drawn from: Sir John Seede's memoirs of his time as governor of Jamaica. They're Brits. They don't have any money, so they've become stockholders in my company."

"Treasure maps? Stuff like that?" Longstreet said. Joe brought several steaming platters and a bucket of rice out of the kitchen. "Treasure maps are okay, but this here is more important: real food!"

"Yes!" Delia said. "And Joe, leave your damned nose and our tablecloth out of it."

"Plus which," Van Dusen said, "we've got financial muscle, an amphibious airplane, and what with modern instruments, magnetometers, metal detectors, things like that—"

Longstreet wouldn't have it. "No. Not when food like this is in front of us. We eat. Then maybe we talk."

Between mouthfuls Delia and Van Dusen chatted about movies, books, and music. Longstreet ate in silence. When the platters were empty, Van Dusen tossed a couple of twenty-dollar bills on the table and gave Longstreet a business card: International Historical Salvage Limited. "Great dinner. That should take care of my share. Look, if you're not too busy, why not drop around to my office tomorrow morning and we'll talk?"

"I might do that."

"I hope you do. I think we could work together, and with the right breaks you might get filthy rich." On his way out, Van Dusen patted Delia's shoulder.

Delia looked as if she liked it.

Longstreet didn't.

Delia threw another twenty on the table. "Don't sulk, Longstreet. I'm a free agent. You don't own me. I have an early day tomorrow."

"Hey! I invited you to dinner, and I was thinking we might—"

"—well, we won't. Not tonight."

Chapter Three

In the morning, Longstreet felt better. He had his first cup of coffee and got busy organizing the field notes and charts of his latest cruise. He typed a summary report on his portable Underwood. He put these materials in a nine-by-twelve mailing envelope, addressed it, and stamped it. He would mail it later.

"That does it," he said aloud. "Now for some breakfast." When he was alone, Longstreet always talked to himself.

He fried himself a New York steak, rare, buttered up a couple of slices of toast and spread on a liberal ration of ginger marmalade. After he finished eating he washed his dishes and boiled out the cast-iron skillet. He made himself another mug of strong coffee and sat back down at his table.

He felt even better. "It's time for me to go someplace warm and dry, where they speak Spanish, where they know how to cook beans and brew decent beer." He fished Van Dusen's card out of his pocket. "What the hell. What've I got to lose?"

He opened the tattered copy of the book Van Dusen had given him and read the chapter on the Loot of Lima. "Every point-blank pistol shot in a soft belly, every cutlass slash that spurted bright blood into the firelight, it was one less share for the crew and one more for Captain Thompson." (The spirit of

Ratcliffe took a ghostly pinch of snuff.) "Damn! That's graphic enough. What a story!"

Van Dusen's office was not easy to find. Longstreet drove to the Vancouver airport's south terminal and spent some time groping around among buildings until he found a hangar that displayed the sign "International Historical Salvage Limited." The office was a small lean-to crouched beside the hangar. Longstreet peeked through the dirty window into the office. Van Dusen was there at a desk, talking on the phone. Longstreet rapped on the window. Van Dusen looked up and gestured for Longstreet to come in. He was off the phone by the time Longstreet entered. "That was my broker," he said. "We've sold more stock. I think we're ready to go."

"Sold more stock? How's that?"

"That's what I've been doing for the last few months. Rebuilding an Albatross and treasure- hunting are very expensive. I've been charming the socks off of every woman's club, Lodge meeting, and Legion Hall in the whole province of British Columbia—Alberta, too—peddling this story."

"You must be good at it. Rebuilding an Albatross doesn't come cheap. What kind of a deal are you offering these stockholders?"

"It's simple enough. After we deduct expenses, the company splits everything right down the middle with the stockholders."

"The company?"

"That's me. I take a quarter and the rest of the crew splits the balance."

"The rest of the crew? How big is the 'rest of the crew?'"

"Not that big. There's the three Brits that did the research, MacTavish, and you—if you join."

"MacTavish?"

"He and I go way back."

"You've got MacTavish. What do you need me for?"

"In the field, you're the Push. I can't be in the field all the time. Somebody's got to run the job while I'm up here raising money. MacTavish is a good fellow. As I said, we go way back, but he has his weaknesses. When he sees a pair of tits he forgets everything, and he has a few other limitations. He can't do celestial navigation, and to tell the truth, he can be a bigmouthed smart-ass. He can piss people off and he doesn't know when to shut up. That leaves you, if you want to join."

"Celestial navigation? Timber cruisers are supposed to know where they are. I learned a bit about it, but I've never actually practiced it."

"It's pretty simple. I'm pretty sure you wouldn't have any trouble with it."

"Yeah, maybe. I've read about treasure hunting expeditions. From what I hear, these efforts usually end with the sea rushing into an enormous and expensive hole at the bottom of which are many interesting rocks but not treasure. Then the treasure hunters have a big fight and murder each other or spend the rest of their lives suing each other—from their cozy nooks in the poorhouse."

"Yes, I must admit that's a possible scenario for us. But I don't think so. When push comes to shove, I'll be running the show and I'll call the shots. We've got solid information. We're well-financed and I think we can build a workable crew."

"So tell me about these three Brits, now. Supposing they're goofy as shit-house rats. Have you met them in person?"

"I haven't met them myself. They're not here yet. They'll fly in when we're ready to go, but their research is solid as a rock. The leader, Spatchcocker, sounded sane when I talked to him on the phone, and he can write a decent letter."

"Spatchcocker? What kind of a name is that?"

"Well, uh, he claims to be a descendant of a 'Duke of Spatchcocker,' one of William the Conqueror's lieutenants. That sounds a bit fishy to me. More likely he's a descendant of someone who split chickens for the duke's dinner."

"Did you say he's not goofy?"

"Well, he says he did time in the RAF during the war."

"Along with some other goofy people."

"Dammit, Longstreet, anything's possible. You're a flyer and you've worked in the bush. Sometimes things work and sometimes they don't. It's the breaks. If you're going to do anything in this world you have to take a risk once in a while."

"Okay, okay! I guess that's true. So fill me in on the plan."

"We need a boat. I've got one lined up. She's a small tuna clipper that was converted into a yacht. She's got ample quarters for all our people. She might be able to carry a backhoe. We'll have to move a lot of dirt. No point digging by hand—"

"—and I'm supposed to sail this bucket all the way down to Central America?"

"No, we don't have to. *Sweet Fanny Adams* is—"

"*SWEET FANNY ADAMS!* Little snuff-colored Jesus! Who the hell would name a boat the *Sweet Fanny Adams!*"

"The fisherman who built her. I got the story from the

boat broker. At first, the fisherman named her *Hermione*, after his wife. Her first few trips were terrible. No fish. Then his wife flew the coop. She ran off to Moose Jaw with a Hungarian piano tuner. The fisherman renamed the boat *Sweet Fanny Adams*. That turned the trick. He caught plenty of fish until he retired—to Thailand, as a matter of fact, with the cutest—but that's another story. He sold his boat to a rich drunk who rebuilt her as a yacht. The rich drunk wanted to circumnavigate the globe, but he knew nothing about seamanship. So he hired my old friend MacTavish as a yacht captain. MacTavish sailed her down to Panama and the rich drunk died on the way. His widow couldn't wait to get rid of the boat. I bought her for a song—"

"—I've heard that song before. I'll sing it for you. 'Beautiful yacht for sale cheap.' They don't tell you she has a burning desire to be a submarine and has been settling down into the water, which is now lapping over the bed in the master stateroom. The engine has been under salt water for a month and is not salvageable. The planking—"

"Easy does it, Longstreet. MacTavish is still on board—crazy coot, but he's ex-navy and knows his way around a boat. He says she's okay."

Longstreet mused. "Well, this whole thing sounds like it might make a good winter vacation. It's warm in that part of the world, and this treasure sounds like fun too, whether we find anything or not."

Van Dusen grinned. "Hey! That sounds like you might be coming around."

"Yeah, I might. Fill me in on the financial arrangements."

"Everybody's on shares. Nobody gets paid. The company takes care of room and board and travel arrangements."

"That doesn't sound too bad. Supposing I signed on, what would be my first job?"

"Fly down to Panama. Look over *Sweet Fanny Adams* and tell me if she'll do the job. I want her to go to Cocos Island, house and feed the crew, and carry the supplies and maybe some kind of a digging machine."

"What about the electronics? You mentioned something about a magnetometer and perhaps some other treasure hunting stuff?"

"That's on the Albatross. As soon as you get to the island, you'll be using our channel to call me on the high-frequency radio, and I'll be joining you."

"Where do these Brits come into the picture?"

"As soon as you tell me the boat can do the job, they're going to fly to Panama, join you there, and sail out to Cocos Island with you and MacTavish."

"So there I am. I'm supposed to go to sea with MacTavish, who I don't know, and three Brits who might be goofy as—"

"—shit-house rats. Yeah, yeah, yeah. You said that before. Look, we're talking about a caper. You know capers. Sometimes they are a lot of fun. Sometimes they turn sour. The stakes in this particular caper are enormous: the Loot of Lima. You struck me as a guy who was willing to take a chance, not some old fart who wanted to spend the winter in a deck chair sipping drinky-poos with little umbrellas in them. I'm not trying to tell you there's no risk. There's plenty of risk. Are you on board or not? I'd like to know now."

Longstreet sucked his underlip.

Van Dusen grinned and said, "There's the Albatross, too. I'm betting you'd like some time in her."

Longstreet nodded. "That does it. I guess I'm on board."

"Good stuff! You'll fly down to Panama, commercial, as soon as I can get a ticket—business class! The stockholders can afford that."

"I'd like to take Delia along if she'll go. I could pay her airfare."

"I think the stockholders could afford that too, but maybe we won't mention it to them. Delia's a smart lady and a real knockout."

"You got a deal."

Chapter Four

Longstreet met Delia for coffee. He didn't have far to go, since his apartment was on the second floor above a coffee roaster and the best place to drink coffee in Vancouver. Moustache Petes went there to talk politics in Italian or Greek, wave their hands, and bitch about how "I'm tellin' ya, kids today. They ain't like kids was when I was a kid."

On the other side of the room sat the freaks in their beads, ponytails, and embroidered overalls. "Man, like wow! Man like it was that I tell you I never saw anything like that. Unbelievable. Fantastic, like."

Longstreet went there. Delia joined him. "So, is your nose out of joint that I didn't succumb to your blandishments last night?"

"Yeah, it is, a bit. Delia—uh—I get horny out in the bush."

"Longstreet—uh—I get horny selling real estate. But sometimes I feel like it and sometimes I don't. Last night, I didn't."

"Okay. Enough said. But I got something else on my mind."

"Such as it is. Your mind, that is. Tell me about that 'else.'"

"It looks like I might be working with that guy, Van Dusen. I'm going to give it a try. For openers, he wants me to go to the City of Panama and see if an old boat is seaworthy. How would you like to go with me?"

"Oh, goody! Florida! Long sandy beaches leaping with fleas! Leering, smirking, randy old bastards in wheelchairs! Lousy food! Mosquitoes! Endless, filthy, cut-rate shopping malls! Sultry, sticky heat! Longstreet, you have such groovy ideas. But I think I could skip Florida. No thanks. I'll stay here in Canada."

"Hey, wait. You got the wrong Panama. I'm talking about Panama, the capital of the nation, Panama. Down in Central America."

"That's different! I've never been south of the United States. I'd love to go, but I have some conditions: Separate hotel rooms. We fly business class."

"Okay. Anything else?"

"When do we leave?"

"How about tomorrow?"

"It's a deal."

Flying was easy in the nineteen eighties. You bought a ticket and got on the airplane. Longstreet and Delia were too sleepy to do anything but drink lousy coffee in the Vancouver terminal before their early morning flight. They changed in Los Angeles, where they chatted over club sandwiches. Delia had a double martini, Longstreet had a beer. They changed in Mexico City, where Delia snarled over a margarita and a bowl of *sopa de tortilla*. They changed in San Jose, Costa Rica, where they were both too tired to even snarl before catching a DC-3 for Albrook Field in the Panama Canal Zone.

Their hotel? Standard Central American digs: stark bathrooms, Jesus bugs in the toilet tanks, patched sheets, holes in the screens through which the occasional mosquito hummed but they were too tired to notice. They slept like logs.

They had breakfast at the sidewalk bar next to the hotel. Fried eggs on hot tortillas, fried rice and black beans called *gallo pinto*, crisp bacon, and espresso coffee.

They took a taxi to the Balboa Yacht Club.

Traffic through the Panama Canal begins in the morning. The pilot boats shuttle the pilots to the vessels and they slide up the channel to Miraflores Locks, one at a time like a circus parade of elephants.

Longstreet and Delia stood on the dock of the Balboa Yacht Club and watched the parade. They waited for the water taxi to carry them out to *Sweet Fanny Adams*. From the dock, the old tuna clipper didn't look all that bad. She rocked gently at her mooring on the waves caused by the passing shipping. She wasn't banged up. She floated on an even keel. She had been a bait boat, not a seiner, but her bait tank had been completely removed and her low afterdeck made into kind of a sundeck with an awning and deck chairs. Her fishing stations had been retained, low platforms outboard around the stern and a foot above the waterline. When she was a tuna boat, the fisherman had stood on these stations, each man with a pole and sometimes as many as three poles to one hook. A deep-sea tuna can be a big fish.

It didn't seem as if the late owner had screwed her up too badly: no swimming pools, no cigarette boats in special davits, no helicopter pads, none of the superfluous garbage the rich insist on adding when they convert an honest workboat to a yacht. Besides, *Sweet Fanny Adams* was too small for such additions. At seventy feet, she was small even for a tuna clipper.

Under the awning on the afterdeck, a man sat in a deck

chair reading a newspaper. He appeared to be dressed only in a sailor hat and jockey shorts.

The water taxi arrived. Longstreet and Delia climbed aboard. When they were abeam, Longstreet shouted: "Hey! *Sweet Fanny Adams!* Can we come aboard?"

The man heaved himself out of the deck chair and pulled up a boiler suit from around his ankles. "Denied! No tourists! Do not enter! Keep away! Fuck off! Light a rag!" He walked to the rail and scowled at Longstreet.

Delia pushed her sunglasses up on her head and scowled back at him.

A lecherous smirk spread itself across the man's sweaty, whiskered face. "Well hello, Sugar-Lump! I'd love to welcome your dear little body aboard, but the boss ordered me: 'Nobody boards her but company folks.'"

"Well, I'm 'company folks.' My name is Longstreet. I think Van Dusen told you about me."

"Humph. In that case, come aboard. Yeah. Bring Angel-Tits with you, by all means."

Delia muttered: "That old bastard is going to be trouble."

Longstreet scrambled up to the deck. The whiskered man was leaning over the rail staring down into Delia's cleavage.

"So you're Longstreet, are you? Well, I'm MacTavish. And you're here to look over the boat, eh?" His eyes stayed on Delia and he might have offered his hand to Longstreet if it hadn't been so busy scratching his crotch.

Delia stepped onto one of the fishing platforms and started to hoist herself over the rail. Of course MacTavish stopped scratching and just had to help her aboard with much laying on of hands—all over her. One hand even slipped into the halter of her sunsuit—accidentally of course. "Awfully sorry about that, Princess Dumpling-Knockers. Accidents will happen you know."

Delia smiled. "Yes, accidents certainly will happen, Whisker-Snout, but if I were you, I'd avoid another accident like that."

"Goodness! You are a peppery little morsel! I like 'em like that!"

Sweet Fanny Adams rolled in the wash of a passing fifty-thousand-ton bulk carrier, loaded with a cargo of Canada number-one red wheat for Europe. Delia stumbled, but in the process of regaining her balance, her parasol handle accidentally gave MacTavish a swift clout on the crotch.

MacTavish doubled over and grabbed the rail.

Longstreet whistled in admiration. "Damn, Delia! That was fast! But if you two wouldn't mind postponing the chit-chat, I'd like to inspect the boat." Longstreet helped MacTavish to straighten up and catch his breath.

MacTavish wheezed and gasped. "Jesus Christ! What'd you do that for?"

Delia smiled sweetly. "Awfully sorry about that. Accidents will happen you know. I must have lost my balance. I don't have my sea legs yet."

Longstreet said, "I should have warned you, MacTavish. Don't monkey with Delia. She bites. Van Dusen said you had sea-time on this vessel?"

MacTavish's voice came out in strangled wheezes. "Yeah. The stiff—I mean the late owner—hired me as a yacht captain for when he was too drunk to handle her himself—which was always. I flew down from Canada and joined her in San Diego."

Longstreet said, "Do you think we could carry a small backhoe without making her top-heavy?"

MacTavish sucked his underlip and shook his head. "I think a full-size backhoe might be too heavy on deck, but maybe we could carry one in the cargo hold. What about one of those dinky Japanese hydraulic excavators you see around these days? They look like toys but they can do pretty good work."

Longstreet's pencil scribbled in his notebook. "How do you know Van Dusen?"

"In the Navy. I was his dog robber before he got cashiered—unofficial dog robber that is. Lieutenant commanders don't rate a real dog robber."

"Huh! That's news to me. Navy. Lieutenant commander, eh? Which navy? And cashiered? Cashiered why?"

"The US Navy, of course. Why he got cashiered? I think it was something about beating up some Korean hooker—maybe she died? I don't know. But Van Dusen took the whole mess right in his stride. As soon as he was out of the Navy he fell in love with a rich Canadian broad, married her and emigrated to Canada. He talked me into taking early retirement and I went to work for him and his new wife on their estate on Vancouver Island. I was kind of a general handyman, pretty much like a civilian dog robber."

"Estate? Vancouver Island? He didn't say anything about that, either."

"He didn't say anything about it because he doesn't have it anymore. Swanky joint, it was. She called it a ranch. She loved horses and had a bunch of them. Miles of board fences all painted white. Man oh man, did those fences know how to rot! I worked my ass off. The broad kept the estate when they split the sheet. It was hers in the first place. But Van Dusen landed on his feet again. He came out of the divorce with a nice chunk of dough. The ex-wife didn't need a dog robber, and for damned sure she didn't want Van Dusen's dog robber even if he did fix fences. I got the sack as soon as she noticed me. She said, real nasty-like, 'Hey, you! Are you still here?' So then Van Dusen helped me get this job as a yacht captain."

Longstreet whistled. "Wife. Estate. Horses. That's interesting as all hell. That's more about Van Dusen than I knew before. Suppose we take a look at the engine room?"

MacTavish led the way, from the after-sundeck, up a companionway ladder to the main deck, past the main fish-hatch and to the after side of the main cabin. MacTavish opened a door to a companionway. "Down we go," MacTavish said.

They climbed down a ladder. Accidentally, of course, MacTavish's right hand slid up Delia's leg almost all the way to her crotch as she followed. Delia slipped but she caught herself and her other foot accidentally crushed MacTavish's left hand on a rung of the ladder. "Ouch!" MacTavish yelled.

They reached the engine room deck. Forward of the main engine, the generator set filled the air with a hot oil smell and made conversation difficult.

The main engine looked new. It was a clean Detroit 12V-71, a modern, supercharged engine. "Hey! That's something! A Screaming Jimmy and a Buzzin' Dozen at that!" Longstreet said. He checked the crankcase oil level. "The Seventy-Ones are all great engines and this one must be pretty new, other-wise there'd be dirty oil all over everything. Noisy bastards but horsepower by the year, four hundred fifty horses. Fire her up. Let's hear her." The engines stuttered for a minute, then settled down to the typical, Seventy-One screaming clatter. Longstreet yelled: "Sounds okay. Let's let her run while we look at the rest of the boat. Then we can see if she's making oil or running too hot."

MacTavish yelled back, "Seems you know a little bit about engines, Sonny."

"Yeah, Popsey. I've seen a few of them. And since it looks like we're going to be shipmates, you can cut the 'Sonny' crap and call me Longstreet. And maybe I'll call you MacTavish in-stead of Shit-Face or Fuzzy-Nuts or maybe the Great Groper."

"Okay. Fair enough. Longstreet it is."

Longstreet lifted up one of the deck gratings and looked down into the bilges. They stunk, and a scant teacup full of oily water swirled in a corner. "Not bad. Looks as if she hasn't been leaking."

"She's pretty tight. We only had to pump her once on the trip down, and that was after a cloudburst. I think the water leaked through the deck."

They climbed up out of the noise and smell of the en-gine room and out the door onto the main deck. The engine's scream faded to a bearable mumble. In the middle of the deck was the main hatch, much larger than necessary for handling fish. It had probably been enlarged during the refit. To star-board was a motorized seine skiff, to port, a smaller skiff with a dinghy lashed inside.

"Hey," Longstreet said, "we got enough boats. That's going to be handy." He read their names: "*Gin, Vodka, Tequila.* I bet the late owner named them."

"You got it. He did," MacTavish answered. "And he got me to paint on the new names, but if you notice, I painted them on masking tape. I hate to monkey around with a boat's name. It's bad luck. If you peel off the masking tape you'll find the original names underneath."

Longstreet peeled the tape off the seine-skiff. "*Waltzing Matilda.* Now there's a decent name for a skiff."

"Peel off the others."

"*Cunning Punt,* another good name, but I wouldn't like to have to shout it out around the ladies, particularly if I'd been drinking." Longstreet peeled the name off the dinghy: "*Chicken S.* I agree with that. I wouldn't want to take her through the surf. That old tuna skipper, now, he had a real talent for names."

"Didn't he. Goofy old bastard."

Longstreet said, "Goofy, maybe, but according to Van Dusen, a stunningly beautiful Thai seductress holds him up to the light every morning to see if there's any blood left in him."

MacTavish sighed. "Lord-a-mercy! What a terrible fate! Do you think if I was rotten enough I could draw the same sentence? How about you? But I guess you're pretty well fixed, eh?"

Longstreet shook his head. "I don't know. Things are a bit rocky these days."

"Sorry to hear that. A broad like that redhead—I could eat a yard of her—"

"Hey! I don't want to hear this. Lay off!"

"—just to get to kiss her—"

"Goddammit, Mac. You don't know when to shut up, do you."

"—ass." MacTavish stared at his feet and studied the cracks in the deck. "And no, I guess I don't know when to shut up. I have to say that when I was a deck-ape that cost me plenty."

"Alright, Mac, let's make a deal. How about you learn? I got to ride herd on a bunch of nutcases while we go and dig holes in a goddamned tropical paradise. We're going to be shipmates and I'm going to need a lot of help. For Christ's sweet sake, could you maybe, please learn when to shut up?"

"All right. I'll give it try."

Aft of the deckhouse, the mast and cargo boom had been retained, even beefed up. Her cargo winch had a lifting drum with a clutch and a brake. Either side of the drum two gypsy-heads projected for swinging the boom, altogether a shipshape arrangement. Longstreet couldn't figure out why such heavy lifting gear had been retained until they climbed down into what had been the fish hold. It was empty and had been converted for cargo. Securely lashed down was a small, open automobile, a Moke, a lightweight jeep, very popular in south sea countries. The boom and winch were intended to offload the Moke for onshore excursions. The main hatch had been enlarged to make this possible.

"That Moke has a current California license," Longstreet said. "What do you think? We could offload it and use it for running our errands."

"Why not," MacTavish agreed.

Delia joined them when they climbed back out of the hold, up to the main deck, and forward into the deckhouse. It had been

left the way it had been as a tuna clipper. Aft was the main saloon where the tuna fishermen had waited until the lookout spotted fish. This was where they had their meals, lounged, smoked,
played cards, and shot the breeze. Built into the saloon were eight
pilot berths, four to port, four more to starboard. In the middle
stood the dining table and benches, all firmly anchored to the
cabin sole. Forward, the galley occupied the starboard side. This
galley had been modified. It was more like a kitchen in an expensive penthouse than a galley; however, it was serviceable enough.
To port was the main head with two showers.

They climbed down a companionway ladder that led from
the main cabin to the lower deck that had held the ship's stores.
MacTavish said, "The owner converted it into his dream love
nest. Poor bastard. Too drunk to get it up."

They opened a door. "Yuck!" Delia said and gagged. The
stench was ghastly. A huge, round, king-size bed with black silk
sheets and a mirror above filled most of the cabin. Evidently
the late owner's corpse had spent a few tropical days before the
undertakers scooped him out. Delia covered her mouth and
nose with her scarf. "Good God! MacTavish, open those portholes right now. If you have any Air Wick on board, open a few
dozen bottles and leave them in here."

"Aw, Sugar-Lump—"

"MacTavish, get this straight. My name is Delia. Now, I'm
getting out of here before I throw up." She left the cabin.

MacTavish sniggered and winked at Longstreet. "Broads!
Can't live with 'em. Can't live without 'em."

"Whatever. But I don't think you have that choice. She's
right about the smell. Do you have a hot plate or camp stove or

something? We'd better get started burning a few handfuls of coffee. And we'll give all that bedding the deep six. Maybe the whole bed. I can't think of anything more useless at sea than a Playboy fart-sack."

They went back on deck. Delia had retreated to a deck chair under the awning on the afterdeck and was reading Mac-Tavish's newspaper. Longstreet and MacTavish climbed up the companionway ladder to the top deck and into the pilothouse. To the starboard of the steering station, a radar screen stood on a pedestal. Maybe it worked, maybe it didn't. Longstreet didn't care much. To port of the steering station was a rack of engine instruments, a shortwave radio, and an autopilot. "Does that autopilot work?"

"Yup," MacTavish told him. "Works like a hot damn."

"That's great," Longstreet said. "I hate steering for hours watching a compass."

"You can say that again," MacTavish said. "Without that autopilot I wouldn't have made it down here. The owner was dead drunk most of the time until he went ahead and was just dead. He was useless as tits on a boar, alive or dead. I had the con twenty-four hours a day."

Aft of the steering station were a couple of lockers and a chart table. A Hamilton hack watch swung on its gimbals in its wooden box. Longstreet opened the drawer and thumbed through the charts. "Good enough. The sextant?"

"I think there's something in the locker there," MacTavish said. "I've got no use for all that fancy stuff. Dead-reckoning, a good pair of binoculars and the radio direction finder are good enough for me."

"Well, let me take a look. We're going to sea, not blundering down the coast. We need celestial navigation."

"Jesus, Longstreet, you know that stuff? Where'd you learn it? You must have some sea time under your belt."

"Yeah, I have a little sea time, but mostly I picked it up for my forestry work. It's useful if a timber cruiser can figure out where the hell he is. He's got to know just a few surveying essentials. I've never actually practiced celestial navigation, but I think I could fake it until I learn how." Longstreet opened the locker and found a surplus Navy sextant, a set of HO-214 tables, a current nautical almanac, a good batch of plotting charts, parallel rulers, pencils, a protractor, and a couple of compasses. "Will you look at that! I think that's all we need."

In the back of the pilothouse were two tiny cabins, one for the skipper, one for the first mate. MacTavish had used the mate's cabin. It was shipshape, except for a couple of extreme girlie magazines.

They went back down to the engine room. Longstreet pulled the idle cutoff on the Detroit diesel. The engine stopped and was comfortably warm, not overheated. The oil level was the same as before. "I think she's okay," Longstreet shouted over the hum of the generator.

"She didn't give a speck of trouble all the way down the coast. I think she got a new engine as part of her rebuild. You worry too much."

"Not too much. It's my ass that's going to be in her when we go to sea. Okay, I think I've seen enough for now. Delia and I are going back to the hotel to give Van Dusen a call." They climbed the ladder to the deck. Delia sat in MacTavish's chair under the awning aft and reading his newspaper.

MacTavish winked at Longstreet. "Why don't you leave Sugar-Muffins here? I could fix her a cup of coffee and we could chat or maybe—"

"Jesus, Mac! If I left Delia here, when I came back I'd find you overboard with a hook through your ass at the end of a fishing line as bait for sharks."

Delia shook her head. "I wouldn't do that. It's complicated, and besides, I'm used to sharks; I'm a real estate salesman. I would keep it simple and kick him in the balls." Delia smiled sweetly at MacTavish.

Longstreet put his fingers in his mouth and whistled shrilly for the water taxi. When it arrived, MacTavish moved to help Delia down the ladder, then thought better of it and returned to his deck chair.

Longstreet said, "See you later, Mac."

MacTavish sat down in his deck chair and picked up his newspaper.

When they got back to the hotel Longstreet, phoned Van Dusen—not that easy in the 1970s. Central American telephone services were on the rough side. After quarreling with a half-dozen switchboards he got through. "Hi, Van."

"I just got in from speaking," Van Dusen said. "We're still raising money. Have you seen the boat yet?"

"Aye-aye, sir-Commander-sir. She's okay, sir. I think she'll do the job, sir."

"Can the military jargon, Longstreet. I don't hold any rank

now. I gather you've been getting some of my history from MacTavish. He always did have a big mouth."

"And sticky fingers. Delia damn near killed him. He doesn't know how lucky he is to still be alive."

"Quite the girl, that one. Oh, by the way . . ."

"'Oh, by the way . . .' Dammit, I hate that. The worst things in the world are usually announced with 'oh by the way . . .'"

"No, no, it's not that bad. It's that the Brits should be arriving tomorrow. Could you meet them at the airport? They'll be coming in to Albrook Air Force Station in the Canal Zone."

"I guess so. How do I spot them? What are their names, anyway?"

Longstreet heard Van Dusen rustling some papers. Then he said, "Brian Spatchcocker, Kevin Ratcliffe, and Joe Houlihan. I think Spatchcocker does most of the talking. It shouldn't be all that hard to recognize them. They're coming from Jamaica where they've been doing some research."

"Okay. What do I do with them?"

"Maybe you could bunk them down on the boat? I don't know. Play it by ear. I'll be down soon. I've got a freight run in the Albatross."

"Freight run, eh? What's that?"

"Don't worry about it."

"Aye-aye, Commander-sir. I'll sit here like the good little discharged Korean private-first-class ground-pounder I am and not worry about it."

"Come off it, Longstreet. It's got nothing to do with the business at hand. The Albatross has to earn its keep. I take a job on the side every so often."

"Okay. So I'll go meet these Limeys. Delia has had enough of Panama."

"See if she wants a ride back with me in the Albatross. I'll be down there in two or three days. Meanwhile, she might be useful in helping to calm the Brits down."

"Okay, I'll ask her. Longstreet over and out."

"Van Dusen over and out."

Chapter Five

Albrook Air Force Station does double duty, at one end military: noisy fighters, hulking, olive-drab transports, jeeps, saluting and chicken shit. At the other end, an ordinary civilian airfield: DC-3's, boarding ladders, Coke machines, and candy wrappers stuck in chain-link fences. Longstreet and Delia stood behind one such fence and watched a DC-3 discharge passengers.

Delia couldn't tolerate heavy sun, particularly after the toasting she'd received on *Sweet Fanny Adams*. Except for her pigtail, there was almost no Delia visible outside of a long-sleeved cotton dress, a floppy, southern belle–style hat, and very large, dark glasses.

The Brits were easy to identify. The first was a bloke in bulletproof tweeds with a matching tweed cap clamped on his double-jointed, peanut-shaped head. In the middle of this head sprouted a sparse mustache. His shirt was starched, slightly frayed and closed at the neck with what resembled an old-school or regimental tie. He walked briskly over to the fence and offered his hand to Longstreet. "Ian Spatchcocker here. And you might be Longstreet?"

"Right the first time."

"And who is that pretty, pretty lady with you? This will be a jolly old trip with such a tempting seductress along don-cha-know-sniff-sniff. Kerchuckle-snerk-sniff."

Delia snapped, "And how would you know? There's not much of this 'tempting seductress' visible. Jolly old sunburn, don-cha-know. Anyway, seductress or not, I wouldn't go on this 'jolly old trip' for all the jewels in Elizabeth's crown. Sniff-sniff. Kerchuckle-snerk-sniff-sniff right back at you."

"Oh my goodness! A saucy wench, indeed! Sniff-sniff. Kerchuckle-snerk." Spatchcocker winked over his quivering mustache.

Delia shook her head at Longstreet. "Oh-*hoh*, my-*hi*, gaw-*hawd*. And you're going to go to sea with this mollusk? I'll bet he fucks squid when nobody is looking."

Spatchcocker began to inflate. "I beg your pardon! Fucks squid, indeed! Ne-vah! In all my life! Have I been subjected to such offense! If I were back with the jolly old RAF, you can bet that—"

A fellow in very loose embroidered cotton clothes oozed over the ground besides Spatchcocker. "Hello there, Longstreet. Isn't this exciting! I'm Kevin Ratcliffe."

Longstreet extended his hand.

"Namaste," Ratcliffe said with a bow and shook hands with himself inside his shirt. "It's as hot here as it was in Jamaica. But not as hot as the edge of the Dead Sea in the Holy Land. Anything can float in the Dead Sea, anything. I will never forget the time when I dropped my watch, a gold one I inherited from my great-uncle, Tobias Ratcliffe, when he died—in squalor, I must add, he drank—and it floated away. I barely caught it in time. Shallow water, you see, in the Dead Sea. I was able to wade right up to it. Little pebbles. Quite sharp. Of course, my shoes and socks became salty. It took five washes in fresh water to desalinate them. It isn't only salt, in the Dead Sea other corrosive chemicals are in solution. Fortunately, I was able to catch my watch before the water penetrated the case. It still worked perfectly, until the time I found myself in a boozing kennel in Port Said and this sultry odalisque plumped herself down in my lap. She oozed on it—my watch, that is, and oozed a bit on my lap, too. I had to send my pants to the cleaners. This odalisque also played the oud besides oozing, and most fetchingly, I must say. Of course, she specialized in secular music, very secular, oh my goodness, my goodness! How very, very secular, I may add, tee-hee, not like the Sufi meditation oud music, deeply introspective and spiritual, it is. I will never forget how profoundly I was moved when I first heard Sufi oud music—"

"Fascinating, utterly fascinating, Kevin," the third man said. "But let's save the Sufi and that oozing odalisque for later, shall we? I'm Joe Houlihan." He extended his hand to Longstreet. "Please to meet you, Longstreet. Up until now, I've been providing the money for travel and research."

Spatchcocker said, "Sniff-sniff. Kerchuckle-snerk. And I hope you brought plenty of that money. We must book our flight directly to San Jose in Costa Rica. Fucks squid, indeed! Ne-vah in my entire, bloody life have I—"

"Let it go, Ian," Houlihan said.

"—been subjected to such bloody insolence."

"Enough. Put a sock in it, Ian. Talk about something else."

Longstreet asked, "You're going to San Jose? Why's that?"

"I should think it would be perfectly obvious. Cocos Island is Costa Rican sovereign territory. We absolutely must have permission to visit."

"But nobody lives on Cocos Island. The Costa Rican government doesn't have the faintest idea what goes on there. Why look for trouble?"

"We simply will not violate Costa Rican sovereignty. Everything must be done aboveboard and absolutely tickety-boo."

Longstreet shrugged. "Tickety-boo, eh? Have you any idea what kind of swamp you're strolling into? Central American greed? Central American politics? Central American jealousy? All that wonderful 'tickety-boo' stuff?"

"We have absolutely no intention of emulating your high-handed, Amiddican ways—"

"Not 'Amiddican,' we're Canadians. At least most of us are."

"Canadian? Then you should have inherited some smidgen of the proper, British way of doing business. We don't intend to ride roughshod over Costa Rica. Tickety-boo it must be."

"Tickety-boo, your ass," Longstreet snorted. "But go for it. I ain't nothing but your humble chauffeur—and an equal shareholder, by the way."

"Equal shareholder! My goodness! But aren't you just a hired hand, a boat driver? Mr. Van Dusen said—"

"Too bad. I'm a shareholder. We boat drivers don't come cheap these days."

"Hmm. Snerk-snerk. Is that a fact? I certainly don't think so! I'll have to have a few words with Mr. Van Dusen about that."

"Have as many words as you choose, but I am, in fact, an equal shareholder. It might be easier to get used to it."

"Perhaps. Perhaps not. Come along, Joe. We must book our flight to San Jose."

Overhead, the subdued rattle of two Pratt & Whitney Twin Wasp engines on low power setting announced that an approaching DC-3 was on a downwind leg. The public address system blatted: "Squalk-squalk—Lacsa Airlines flight three-gobble-garble-leaving immediately for San Jose-garble-garble-garble-squawk-click."

Spatchcocker said, "By George! This is a stroke of luck! Sniff-sniff! We shall take only our overnight bags to San Jose. We shan't need more than a day to get permission. We shall leave our heavier duffel with you, Longstreet. Stow it in our cabins, please. All tickety-boo."

"Aye-aye your Grace, sir, and tickety-boo-hoo. Your 'heavy duffel' might make it on board, assuming we don't lose it, a distinct possibility. But if you think you can handle Costa Rican politics in one day, you've got to be one of the world's most tickety-boo optimists. 'Only a tickety-boo month' would be more like it. How's your tickety-boo Spanish?"

"We RAF chaps know how to handle these things. These fellows understand English very well if one speaks loudly and plainly, don't y'know."

Houlihan said, "Spatchcocker has got a bit to learn, but bear with us. I can speak serviceable Spanish. Before you take the duffel bags, let me pull out my shaving gear, a few shirts, and maybe a clean pair of pants."

Spatchcocker tipped his head back and twitched his long upper lip with its skimpy moustache. "Really, Joe, I can't imagine we'll be in Costa Rica more than a day at the most. Sniff-sniff-sniff."

"Whatever, Ian. I'll bring along some spare duds, just in case." Houlihan pulled some clothes and his shaving gear from his duffel bag.

Longstreet went outside, found a taxi, and woke the driver. The driver followed Longstreet back into the terminal.

Ratcliffe fumbled with the handle on his enormous bag as if fondling the trunk of a somnolent baby elephant. He paused and gazed into the air. "I will never forget that early morning when I had to catch a ferry across the Bosporus. You can't imagine the glory of the sunrise on the Bosporus. The domes of the Grand Mosque gleaming! The mysteries of Hagia Sophia! The strident cries of the street vendors: 'Chai! Chai! Hushibubula!' The exotic and spicy aromas of dusty carpets rapidly unrolling on the sidewalk. 'No, no, sir. For you to viewing, no buying! I love practicing the English. You are being English? I am loving England! My cousin is living in London.' The ferries weren't running yet. I had to vault over the carpets and parlay with the oarsman of a small dhow, a villainous chap in a skullcap. This oarsman, as are all oarsmen on the Bosporus, was a Muslim, of course. Muslim men almost always cover their heads. It is said in the Koran—"

"—fascinating, utterly fascinating, Kevin, but suppose we skip the Bosporus, Koran, skullcap, and all for the time being? Why don't you drag your bag out to the taxi?" Houlihan shouldered his bag and carried it out.

Ratcliffe opened and shut his mouth several times. Spatchcocker sniffed and twitched his mustache. Given enough time they might have helped with the luggage, but apparently they didn't have enough time before the DC-3 left for San Jose.

After the plane took off, Longstreet, Delia and the taxi driver stuffed the enormous duffel bags into the taxi. They took up the entire trunk and back seat. Longstreet had to ride in the front seat with Delia in his lap. When they arrived at the yacht club, they rolled the bags down the ramp to the dock and into the water taxi.

MacTavish had seen them coming. He'd unlimbered the winch and had a cargo net waiting. He lowered the cargo net. The water taxi driver studied the sky and whistled while Longstreet and Delia bundled the bags onto the net. MacTavish hoisted the bags on board. They dragged them down the companionway and into the storeroom. What was even more remarkable, MacTavish managed to keep his hands off Delia.

Chapter Six

That evening, Longstreet and Delia had their dinner in a sidewalk café overlooking the Gulf of Panama and the sunset. After margaritas, Longstreet switched to beer, Delia to another margarita. Longstreet's steak was stringy and tough but the flavor was excellent. Delia topped off her dinner of breaded and pan-fried corvina with slices of fresh papaya and a shot of Panamanian Añejo rum. Longstreet chose flan caramel and had another beer. He got his courage up. "So, look, not to get snarky about it, but it's been a long dry spell with you and me."

Delia stared down at the table. "I thought maybe it might be obvious, but I guess not. So we'll talk about it. I should have brought it up sooner. First, I need a refill."

Delia rapped on her rum glass with her spoon. The waiter brought her another shot of Añejo.

"When we first met at the University, you were a forestry student, an intense, young expatriate, a Korean War veteran burning with hatred for the Vietnam War and the US government. Such a glamorous rebel! And you had a beard! How totally, totally unacceptable to my parents! How could cute little me, a naïve, bright-eyed MBA student from Prince George and running on a full tank of hormones, not fall madly in love with you? We stuck to each other like flypaper and screwed like crazed weasels in May. It was great. I'm not saying it wasn't great. But now I'm pushing forty. So are you. You've shaved off your beard. I've shaved off my beard too, in a manner of speaking."

"Things have changed?"

"Yes they have. Look, you make your living in the bush. You eat bush food. You sleep in a grotty bush sleeping bag. You dress in grotty bush clothes; you speak bush language. You're a bush ape and you always will be. That's the size of it. But me? I'm not a bush ape. I'm a downtown girl and I like it. If I hook up with anybody, he'll be a downtown guy."

"So. Downtown? A big-time operator? A mover and shaker? A captain of industry, maybe? Monarch of all he surveys with a great big Ipana smile?" Multicolored ropes of anger, frustration, jealousy, and hurt started to writhe and twine in Longstreet's abdomen.

"You and your damned 'great big Ipana smile.' I've heard that too many times. It's old stuff."

"Old stuff, huh? So I'm getting to be old stuff?"

"Hey! Don't do that. Don't push it. I don't want to dump on you. Let's stay good friends."

"So now we are 'good friends?' But supposing I don't want to be just 'good friends'?"

Delia put her hand over Longstreet's. "I'm truly sorry. But it takes two to tango, and I don't want to tango anymore."

"That's the way it's going to be?"

"Yes. I'm afraid that's the way it's going to be."

Longstreet's eyes smarted. The multicolored ropes writhed

themselves into a tight Turk's head located in his upper abdomen, directly behind his xiphoid process. He tossed some bills on the table. "Okay. I got it. I think I'll go back to the hotel. Are you coming along?"

Delia nodded.

In the hotel lobby Longstreet said, "So. What do you want to do now?"

"Well, it's been a lot of fun—even with that goat on the boat and that English squid-fucker with the nasal sound effects—but I think I'd better go home. I have clients to take care of."

"Okay. I'll book your ticket tomorrow."

"No. You don't have to. Van Dusen offered to fly me back in the Albatross. I accepted. It would be fun."

"Ah-hah! That's the way it goes? Van Dusen, eh? Big Ipana smile and all?" The Turk's head spun viciously to produce spikes of pain in Longstreet's belly.

"Oh, come on, Longstreet. Leave it alone. Don't get snarky. Please, we've had a good time. Let it go."

Chapter Seven

Van Dusen himself arrived three days later. He landed the Albatross in the channel and picked up one of the moorings at the yacht club. He blew the horn for a water taxi. He shut and locked the Albatross securely. When he arrived at Sweet Fanny Adams he asked the water taxi to wait. He passed up an equipment case and a long, slender package.

Longstreet asked him, "What's that, Van?"

"That's a battery-powered, nondirectional beacon so I can locate you with my automatic direction finder. I'll need you to mount it on the ship's radio mast. When you get to the island, mount it on a tree."

"Okay. What are you carrying? The Albatross is low in the water."

"I'm on a freight run. The ferry tanks, remember? They're full. What happened with the three Englishmen?"

"Correction: two Englishmen and a Canadian prospector who might be a human being. The two Englishmen? Maybe human, but I doubt it. Anyway, they arrived, dumped their baggage on us, and took the plane for San Jose."

"San Jose? What for?"

"Mister RAF-peanut-head Spatchcocker said he wanted

to make everything 'tickety-boo' with the Costa Rican government. I tried to warn him, but he didn't listen. He thought they could do it in a day, but it's been three days now and I haven't heard one squeak from them."

"Damn! What a pain in the neck! That's all we need. Central American politics." Van Dusen chewed his underlip a minute. "For the time being, I'll have to dump the whole load on you and MacTavish. I've got to finish this freight run before I can do anything else." He passed Longstreet a fat envelope and a plug-in crystal for the shortwave radio. "We have our own high-frequency radio channel now. It will get me in the office or on the Albatross and it will work a lot better than the telephone.

"See if you can pick up some kind of a digging machine like a hy-hoe and get it on board. And get the boat fueled, watered, and enough provisions to last us a month or so. Oh yeah, and see if you can get some drums of aviation gas, five hundred gallons at a minimum, but as many as you think you can cram on board, and I'll need a drum of thirty-weight engine oil too."

"Aviation gasoline! What a treat! One little spark in the hold and ka-bluey! There we are, blown to rat-shit and burning to death out in the middle of the Pacific Ocean. More fun than a barrel of deep-fried monkeys!"

"Yeah, I know, I know. I hear you. It's a risk, but we need the gas to do the magnetometer survey. You could unload the barrels and float them to shore as soon as you get to the island. Oh, by the way, I promised Delia a ride home. Where is she?"

"Oh, 'by the way,' she can't take the sun, and 'by the way,' we're not all that tight with each other right now. She's up in the clubhouse drinking soda water."

"Not all that tight, eh? I thought you were a couple."

"You would have been right once. Not now."

"That's too bad, but I guess it can't be helped. I should leave as soon as I can. Could you get Delia and her gear down here right away?"

"I guess so. How are you going? What will be your route?"

"First we have to pick up our freight in Ecuador and we'll fill every fuel tank, ferry tanks and all, to the brim, enough to make it to Ensenada in Mexico, but that's cutting it damned close. We'll fuel up in Ensenada, catch a sleep and a couple of meals. Then we'll be able to carry on to Vancouver nonstop. I don't like landing anywhere during a freight run, especially in the United States. Mexico is bad enough, but I have some pull in Ensenada. We can slip through with bribes to customs, bribes to immigration, bribes to the port captain, bribes to cops, and more bribes."

"That's a lot of bribes. What kind of freight are you carrying, anyway?"

"Gourmet foodstuff."

"What kind of foodstuff?"

"Special seasonings. Sea salt for the most part."

"Sea salt! You're airlifting sea salt? Who the hell can afford airlifted sea salt?"

"You'd be surprised at the food-fads of the rich."

The driver of the water taxi tooted his horn and shouted, "Are you going to be much longer? I could always come back later."

"No, I want to go to the dock. We'll go right now."

When they arrived at the dock, Delia met them with her suitcase in her hand. She was ready to leave Panama.

Van Dusen said, "My goodness, Delia, a sunburn makes you even more gorgeous."

Longstreet waited for Delia's inevitable put-down. It didn't turn out to be inevitable.

"Really, Van? I must look like a boiled lobster."

"A lobster should be that lucky."

Delia blushed through her sunburn. She gave Longstreet a quick hug and a peck on the cheek and hopped into the water taxi with Van Dusen. They both twiddled their fingers to Longstreet as they motored out to the Albatross.

The aircraft engines coughed into life. Delia popped out of the forward hatch and cast off the mooring. There was a north wind blowing. The Albatross taxied away to the south and out of Longstreet's sight. He heard the engines smoothly accelerate to full throttle, three thousand horsepower, an overpowering, trombone-like snarl. When the Albatross came into view again it was up on the step, lightly skipping over the water. It popped up and climbed smoothly.

Longstreet's multicolored Turk's head writhed nastily behind his xiphoid process. "Goodbye, Delia," he muttered.

Longstreet took the water taxi to *Sweet Fanny Adams* when it returned. He counted the wad of money. Van Dusen had passed him about sixty thousand American dollars. "Huh! Ain't that something!"

MacTavish was at his usual post, sitting on the after-sundeck under the awning, reading a girlie magazine and dressed in his sailor hat and a wristwatch.

"Better put on some duds, Mac. We've chores to do."

"No rest for the wicked. I knew this easy life couldn't go on forever. What's up? What happened with that redheaded broad with the big tits?"

"She flew away with Van Dusen. And they're not all that big."

"Big enough. And they climbed into that airplane with Van Dusen? Oh well, goodbye, tits."

"Don't rub it in. But like I said, put on pants and shoes anyway, maybe even a shirt? We have chores."

"Let's hear the bad news."

"We rig this beacon on the radio mast and shove this crystal into the shortwave. Then we provision the ship, get her fueled up and ready for sea."

"That's a lot."

"There's more. Van Dusen wants us to find some kind of a digging machine and get it on board."

"That's going to take a lot of running around. What do you say we get that Moke out of the hold?"

They dropped the mooring and motored to the fuel dock. High noon and business was slow, so the fuel jockey allowed a stay at the dock. The Moke had been fitted with lifting eyes. Mokes are light and the cargo boom and winch did the job.

Unloading the Moke was easy.

Fueling was easy.

However, finding a digging machine was not easy. They checked the Canal Zone weekly English paper. No backhoes or anything like it. They hopped into the Moke and drove out of town. They found a farm feed store. Tacked on the bulletin board was a photo and a brief description: "Like new, tractor with plow and backhoe attachment." The picture looked alright, but it had been clipped from a catalogue.

Half an hour out of the City of Panama and down a rutted country road they found the residence of an expatriate American, long on inspiration but short on accomplishment. He was sitting on his rickety front porch, reading a newspaper in his undershirt. His face sported a stubble beard and an unlit cigar. Clouds of smoke billowed from the kitchen where a frazzled, sweating woman fried something disgusting in rancid grease. Several grubby urchins lurked under the porch playing with sardine cans and battered toy cars to an accompaniment of appropriate noises. When they caught sight of Longstreet and MacTavish, they stopped the sound effects and glared at the intruders.

Longstreet said, "Are you the guy with the backhoe for sale?"

"Yeah. Man-oh-man, are you lucky you arrived today! Lots of guys want it and they're going to give me more money than I asked for, but they can't get here until tomorrow. I'll have to tell them, 'Tough shit. First come, first served.' I'm too honest for my own good."

"Where is it?"

"Out in back behind the chicken house. I used to keep chickens but there's no money in it. It's a little dirty, but nothing that couldn't be fixed with a damp rag or maybe a steam-cleaner or something like that."

"Show it to us."

"Naw. Gotta stay here. I have to keep track of my important investments. Anyway it's easy to find. Go for it. Did you bring cash? It's dirt cheap. I need twenty grand, cash money for it. No dickering. That's my bottom dollar."

The chickens might have moved on but their odor remained. Longstreet and MacTavish found the chicken house by following their noses. They clawed their way through scrub trees, tough tropical vines entwined with barbed-wire fences, and islands of junk. One corner of the chicken house had rotted away. The roof had been propped up by parking the backhoe under it. They pulled away a blanket of vines, complete with thorns and a vacant wasp nest, to reveal a tractor hitched to a farm backhoe mounting a manure scoop, so rusted that spots of light shone through the holes. They scraped off the chicken shit and feathers to find the control valves and most of the hydraulic hoses had been removed.

"Do you think we could fix it?" Longstreet asked.

MacTavish snorted. "Are you kidding? The tractor's name tag says 'Isthmus Invincible Motors.' But who are they kidding? It's only one of those damned three-wheeled McCormick-Deerings that rear up and fall over on their backs. Farmer-killers, every one of them. The engine is probably frozen and that backhoe?" MacTavish used his pocketknife to scrape the chicken shit off a nameplate. "The 'Arkadelphia Earthmoving Company.' Arkadelphia Earthmoving Company? Gimme a break! With a name like that they must have gone tits-up the same day they opened. And parts? Don't make me laugh. Forget it." MacTavish wiped the sweat from over his eyes and dried his hand on his pants.

"Let's move on."

They returned to the front yard. The seller lowered his paper and removed the cigar. "Neat, huh? You like it?"

"No. It's out of the question."

"Hey! You got the wrong idea. Like I still got the hoses and valves. I used them when I built my sawmill. Good as new."

"Where's your sawmill?"

"Well, I had to sell it for scrap after the lumber price hit the basement. But I still got the hoses and valves. They're right there on the ground somewhere in the bushes behind the chicken-house."

Longstreet laughed, "Sorry. No deal. We'll see you later."

"Tell you what I'm gonna do." the farmer said. "I got a soft spot in my heart for that backhoe. I'd like to see it go to a good home. For you, I'd take fifteen grand."

"No." Longstreet laughed harder. MacTavish joined him.

"Aw, come on, have a heart. How about ten grand?" He began to sniffle.

"Sorry. No deal. Don't cry. Things will get better."

They climbed into the Moke and drove back to the outskirts of Panama.

"That would have been a pain in the ass if it wasn't so pitiful. How about we stop for a cold beer?" MacTavish said. "There's a real classy-looking joint over there."

"You mean that one there? Looks clean and the veranda looks cool. And I can see why you like it. That blonde waitress is something else. Built like a brick shit-house."

"Yes! Yes! That one! Five axe-handles wide!"

They parked the Moke on the sidewalk and stepped up onto the thatched veranda. "Boo-nus dee-ass, seenoreet-er," MacTavish oozed, his bulging eyes fixed firmly on the waitress's bust. He hadn't blinked once since he got out of the Moke.

"I suspect what you probably mean is '*Buenos dias, señori-ta.*' You've managed to speak the worst Spanish I've heard this

72

month. And it's not '*dias*,' which means the morning, it's '*tardes*,' afternoon, and damned close to '*noches*,' night."

"Oh, you can speak English, too?" MacTavish's eyes never wavered.

"Yes, I do. And so does my husband, the cook. We're from Medicine Hat, Alberta. And, just by the way, I hate to disappoint you, but they're falsies. I had a double mastectomy. Would you like to see my scars?"

MacTavish squirmed.

Longstreet guffawed.

The waitress acknowledged with a low bow, swishing her magnificent blonde tresses over her shoulders. "What can I bring you fellows?"

"Well, we're looking for a small hydraulic excavator, but we'd settle for a couple of cold beers."

"You're in luck. I'll bring the beers and send my husband out to discuss our hy-hoe."

"What's that again?"

"Something wrong with your ears? Listen up! I said, I'll bring the beers and send my husband out to discuss our hydraulic excavator."

"Holy Smoke! You have a hy-hoe?"

"Yes, and for a princely sum we might possibly be persuaded to sell the dickey-doo little son of a bitch."

"What were you doing with a hy-hoe?"

"My gullible husband and I were minding our own business, running our diner in Medicine Hat. A bearded bum—he said he was a sailor—ate our blue plate special, then broke the news that he didn't have any money. He never gave us his name so we called him Popeye. Popeye washed dishes, packed out the garbage, and mopped up for his dinner, talking all the time. He had the gift of gab. And funny! He really was funny as hell. He kept us in stitches. Roger, that's my husband, took a shine to him, had him work in the kitchen and let him sleep on our back porch. After a month, Popeye's bullshit started to get thin. His jokes weren't all that funny the third time around and I think he was getting warmed up for some serious drinking. When he left, he sold us a 'treasure map' as a 'special thank you.' Cost us five hundred bucks. He said he hated to part with it but he needed the money for a cancer operation for his ex-wife.

"Roger may be one hell of a cook, but he's hopeless in business. He bought the map. We sold the diner. We sold the car. We ordered, at ruinous expense I may add, a Japanese miniature hydraulic excavator. We had it shipped to Panama, also at ruinous expense. We followed the 'treasure map' to a location up a creek in the peninsula near Punta Mala. We dug and we dug and we dug. Of course there's nothing there. Thank God Roger can cook or we'd be in the gutter." She shouted: "Roger! Roger! Come out of the kitchen. Bring a couple of cold ones. These guys are looking for a hy-hoe."

Roger came out of the kitchen, wiped his hands on his apron, and reefed two bottles of beer from the fridge. "But Wren, we haven't given up. We still have a couple places to try."

"I've given up. Let's sell the backhoe. Let's go back to Medicine Hat and buy back the diner. That guy who bought it? He wasn't up to slinging professional hash, just a fool who'd fallen in love with the idea of running a diner. It's not a fancy restaurant where you can feed the customers loud music and dog shit so long as the booze flows. It's a diner. In the diner business, you have to sling steady good hash. One bum meal and the customers are gone. By now, the joint is closed and he must be flat broke. I bet we could get the diner back for a song."

"Yes, dear. You're right. Let's go back to Medicine Hat. You guys want to look at that hy-hoe? It's out in the back yard."

Longstreet and MacTavish fisted their beers and followed Roger through the kitchen and out. There they found a miniature, Japanese-built hy-hoe, a little dusty but intact. "You got the keys?" MacTavish said.

"Do you know anything about hy-hoes?" Longstreet asked.

"Is the Pope Catholic? Not only yes, but hell yes. Roger, gimme the keys. Longstreet, hold my beer, will you?"

MacTavish stepped up on the tracks and climbed into the operator seat. The machine started easily. He gave the motor half throttle and ran it a minute or two to warm up the oil in the engine and the hydraulic tank. Then he spun the machine neatly, first the cab, then the whole machine on its tracks. He cycled the boom and the bucket. He dropped the dozer blade and pushed some dirt. He shut the machine down and checked the level in the hydraulic oil reservoir and the engine oil. He inspected the hoses and pipes for hydraulic leaks. "She's okay. She's almost brand new."

"I guess he knows something about hy-hoes," Roger said. "And the Pope is Catholic, last time I looked."

"Okay, Roger, let's make a deal. You speak how much."

"Thirty grand and that's dirt cheap."

"Fifteen grand. American cash money on the barrelhead."

"I'll split the difference. Twenty-five grand."

"Twenty grand. And that's my last word."

"How about twenty-two fifty?"

"Done deal," Longstreet said.

"Done deal," Roger answered. "I'll even throw in a good dinner."

Longstreet counted out twenty-two thousand five hundred American dollars into Roger's hand while Wren brought in the chairs from the sidewalk and hung a sign, "Closed—Cerrado," on the front door. She slipped into the restroom, wiped off the excess makeup, and emerged minus the blonde wig and the falsies. What a transformation! From a long-in-the-tooth seductress to a human being in the blink of an eye.

When they all sat down to dinner it was obvious that Roger was an exceptional cook: roast pork with cracklings, hot cowboy-style biscuits with butter and honey, fluffy potato balls, savory gravy, beets cooked with their greens.

"Damn!" MacTavish said. "This is real, honest-to-God chow!"

"Not bad if I do say so myself," Roger said.

Longstreet thought quickly. "Did you ever cook at sea, Roger?"

"I can cook anywhere there's a stove and groceries."

"I've got to ask the boss, but maybe we might make another deal. How would you feel about staying down in these parts for another couple of months? Maybe making a boat trip to Cocos Island?"

"Hey! That's where the Loot of Lima is buried! Man alive! That would be my dream. I've read all about it."

Wren said, "Yes, you have, in that damned book that caused all the trouble. That book with the pirate, the octopus, and the blonde with big tits on the cover."

"Big tits? Big tits! Where?" MacTavish said.

"Aha! So, I got your attention." Wren said. "The tits were on the cover of that treasure book."

"Oh yeah," MacTavish said. "And your name, Wren? Were you named after a bird?"

Wren heaved a sigh. "Okay, we'll do it now. It will save time later. I wasn't named after a bird. I was named after a flower, Ranunculus. Wren for short. 'Ranunculus' is Latin for 'little frog,' from rana 'frog' and a diminutive ending."

MacTavish guffawed. "I never heard of a Ranunculus. A flower, eh? How come not 'Rose,' or 'Daisy,' or 'Violet'? Maybe 'Buttercup'?"

"Those names were all used up on my older sisters. My dad was a grotesque son of a bitch with a screwed-up sense of humor. His name was Leo, so of course he wanted to name a son 'Dandelion.' Dandy Lion, get it? But all Mom could produce was daughters, one right after the other. So they kept trying. Eight of us. All girls. All named after vegetables. Dad thought it was funny. I don't. My sisters don't either. Now that you know, let's drop the matter for good. Call me Wren."

MacTavish said. "Okay. Wren it is."

"Good." Wren turned to Roger. "So, these guys need a sea cook. That's fine. It sounds like fun, but they don't get you without taking me along as a sea-waitress or a sea-bull cook or even a sea-housekeeper."

"Certainly, sweetheart. Not without you I wouldn't go."

"And I damned well will *not* wear all that makeup, those stupid falsies, or that ridiculous blonde wig, either."

"Why should you? You won't have to be a decoy at sea. We all know who you are."

Longstreet said, "The falsies and wig would be too damned hot, anyway, and the makeup would run in the heat. But easy does it. I still have to get an okay from Van Dusen. He's the boss."

"Yeah, and something else," Wren said. "You're the one who needs the sea cook. It's your turn now. You speak how much."

"Shares," Longstreet said. "Nobody gets paid. We're all on shares. How about one share for the two of you?"

"Shares of what?"

"The Loot of Lima and maybe some other stuff."

"Done deal."

Chapter Eight

On *Sweet Fanny Adams*, Longstreet thumbed the mike on the shortwave radio. "Historical Salvage, this is *Sweet Fanny Adams*."

Hisses and static.

"Historical Salvage center, this is *Sweet Fanny Adams*."

More hisses. More static.

"Historical Salvage center, this is *Sweet Fanny Adams*."

The loudspeaker answered: "*Sweet Fanny Adams*, this is Van Dusen. Over."

"Hey there, Van, this is Longstreet. Where are you? Over."

"I'm in the office but I'll be flying down soon. Over."

"Things here are going pretty good. We've got a neat little hy-hoe."

"Good going! How did you manage that? Over."

"It's a long story. Suppose we save it for later? We found a good cook and a housekeeper into the bargain. We're going to need them. They'll come for one share for the two of them. Is that okay? Over."

"That's okay by me. Spatchcocker will whine, though. I almost had to beat him with a club to get him to accept you and MacTavish. Over."

"That figures. Where the hell are those guys, anyway? I haven't heard peep one out of them since they left for San Jose. Over."

"I've been hearing altogether too many peeps, over the telephone, collect. Spatchcocker has been peeping into my ear every evening. They've been roosting in San Jose getting passed from one government office to the next. It seems Costa Rica doesn't measure up to the 'jolly old RAF.' And I've had to shut Ratcliffe off, too. 'I'll never forget the Taj Mahal in the moonlight' and so on and so forth over the expensive telephone. I'll be flying down to San Jose in a couple of days and picking them up. Over."

"Goody, goody. I can't wait to see them. All three of them. Over."

"All four of them. The politicos are making them bring a Costa Rican cop with them. A Guardia Civil. The Costa Ricans want to make sure they get their share. Over."

"That will make six of us so far, not counting you. What do you say we add that cook and his wife. We're really going to need them. Over."

"Yes. Sign that pair on. Over."

"Will do. Is there any way you can get Spatchcocker and Ratcliffe to shut up? Over."

"I'll try. God knows I'll try. Over."

"Okay. Now I've got to get to work. Roger and Wren, that's our new cook and housekeeper, are helping us with the grub. They know every supplier in town. Over."

"That's a blessing. Anything more? Over."

"That's it for now. Over."

"Van Dusen, over and out."

"*Sweet Fanny Adams*, over and out." Longstreet turned off the radio.

On the main deck, Longstreet and MacTavish studied the winch. "What about it, Mac?"

"We lifted the Moke easily enough, but it weighed only nine hundred pounds. That hy-hoe weighs four thousand, too much for the clutch on the winch. I think the boom can take the compression load, but we're going to have to do something about the winch."

They visited a ship's chandlery and bought two blocks and a hundred feet of wire rope. MacTavish long-spliced the wire on the end of the existing winch line. Longstreet shackled a double block to the end of the boom and a single block with a becket to the headache ball and hook. They rigged the new winch line through the blocks.

"Maybe that'll do it," MacTavish said.

They tied up to the fuel dock.

Roger had rented a truck and lowboy trailer and moved the hy-hoe down to the fuel dock. He cast off the chains and started the hoe.

The manager came out of the pump house. "You ain't going to load that thing here. Stop right now."

Longstreet said, "Hey man, we're here to buy fifteen drums of aviation-gas and a drum of oil from you. Give us a break. Couldn't you let us load the hoe? Please, pretty please with cream and sugar on it?"

"Well, okay, maybe, but we're expecting a couple of tugs any minute now. When those tugs show up you have to be gone."

They rigged the hook to the lifting eyes on the hy-hoe. MacTavish took a strain on the winch line. *Sweet Fanny Adams* heeled over almost thirty degrees before the hy-hoe lifted. When it was high enough to clear the rail, it took all of MacTavish's weight to lock the brake. Longstreet took a strain on a tag line with the gypsyhead and managed to swing the boom over the hold. "Careful, man! Down real easy. If that goddamned thing gets away from us it'll keep right on going, right out through the bottom."

"Do tell," MacTavish grunted. "Shaddap. Don't bug me." He eased the brake and slowly lowered the hy-hoe into the hold.

The fuel jockey shouted, "Those tugs will be here in a few minutes."

Longstreet yelled back, "We ordered fifteen drums of avgas. If you want to sell it, bring it on out."

The fuel jockeys rolled out the drums. Longstreet slapped a rope strap around a drum and hooked it up. MacTavish swung it into the hold with the winch. Longstreet ran on board, down the hatch to cast off the rigging, then back to the dock to rig another drum. By the time all the drums of avgas and engine oil were loaded, Longstreet was sweating rivers and panting.

MacTavish threw him a big grin. "Treasure hunting! How romantic! More fun than a barrel—"

"Shaddap, Mac."

The first tug had arrived and blew a sharp, demanding blast on its horn.

MacTavish said, "You better cast off, I'll take the con."

"Your ass!" Longstreet panted. "I'm bushed. You cast off. I'll take the con."

"Okay, okay, but only this one time," MacTavish chuckled.

"Someday, Mac, you're going to be too funny. Cast off, god-dammit." Longstreet limped up the companionway to the bridge.

The second tug arrived and joined the first to blast on their horns. Longstreet started the engine while MacTavish cast off the mooring lines. They slid away from the fuel dock and back across the channel to the yacht club.

"Goddammit," MacTavish said. "The brake on that winch has had the bun. We'll have to reline it before we sail."

At the ship's chandlery they found some asbestos brake lining for the winch. Longstreet added a gasoline powered fire pump with a few hundred feet of forestry hose and three large, dry-chemical fire extinguishers. "Fire insurance."

The next morning Roger and Wren arrived with a van from the Canal Zone commissary. They stuffed the ship's re-frigerator and freezer full of perishables. They loaded sacks of rice, beans, and flour, cans of powdered eggs, powdered milk, olive oil and case after case of smaller items into the store-room. Roger said, "We have onions, spuds and other vegetables enough for a couple of weeks but they won't last longer in this heat. We have a couple of sacks of dried hot peppers. That's going to help a lot. Nothing like a little hot stuff to make bland food interesting. We're going to have to eat a lot of fish. I'd like to suggest we slow down to about five knots for a couple hours a day so we can troll."

Longstreet said, "You're the boss of the food. What you say goes. Now we have to figure out where you and Wren are going to bunk down." They looked at the old owner's cabin, now half full of stores and the Brits' duffel bags. The round black bed and mirror were long gone. The portholes had been open for a couple weeks and they'd burned a lot of coffee so the smell was bearable.

Roger said. "Great for sea stores, but it's going to be too close and crowded for us."

Longstreet said. "Yeah, I think you're right. Besides the grub we have a lot more gear to load: picks, shovels, the backpack magnetometer, the metal detectors. The list goes on. What do you say MacTavish and I move down to the pilot berths in the deckhouse? That would free up those two little cabins in back of the bridge. Would you and Wren mind separate cabins?"

"That would suit us fine. We could visit any time we felt like it and a double bunk doesn't work at sea. We would bash into each other all night long."

Chapter Nine

The radio in the pilothouse chattered, *"Sweet Fanny Adams, this is Albatross. Sweet Fanny Adams, this is Albatross. Sweet Fanny Adams, this is Albatross."*

Longstreet grabbed the mike. "Albatross, this is *Sweet Fanny Adams*."

"Hey there, Longstreet. I'm about two hours out with passengers and freight. Over."

"Have you gotten Ratcliffe and Spatchcocker to shut up yet? Over."

"That's negative. But the Costa Rican Guardia Civil seems to be a nice young fella. His name is Pedro. He's a fighter jockey. It seems the Guardia Civil has a couple of P-Fifty-Ones. Over."

"What do the cops need with a P-Fifty-One? I thought Costa Rica got rid of the Army. Over."

"Sometimes those football riots can get pretty fierce. Over."

"Got it. I'll tell Roger there's going to be five more for dinner. Over."

"Six with Delia. She is flying copilot. Over."

That was a low blow. Longstreet's Turk's head twisted, jabbed, and burned, hot and bright behind his xiphoid process. So, Delia had, in fact, hooked up with Van Dusen. The man with the big Ipana smile. The mover and shaker. The big-time operator.

"*Sweet Fanny Adams.* Over and out."

Longstreet thought long and hard. "So. I tell Van Dusen and Delia to stuff it. I dump this whole mess and go someplace else. Sit on the beach. Drink cold beer. Soak up the sun. What does that do for me? Does it get me back together with Delia? No. Does it fix Van Dusen's little red wagon? No. What does it do? It leaves some folks in the lurch. I'm beginning to like MacTavish, and Wren, and Roger. I think those Brits are going to be funny and I suspect Houlihan might be a decent guy. This Cocos Island caper is going to be fun, maybe, an adventure for sure—if you count all the good stuff and the ridiculous fuck-ups and blunders. Treasure? Getting filthy rich? Slim chance, but there is a chance. I guess I'll stay on board. I don't want to miss this."

About four o'clock in the afternoon, the Albatross flew a downwind leg over the channel. Longstreet and MacTavish watched from the bridge. The Albatross turned over Miraflores Locks, dropped down to the channel to make a beautiful landing.

The Albatross turned into the current and drifted to come dead in the water at a mooring at the yacht club. Delia popped out of the forward hatch with a boat hook and picked up the mooring neatly. "That son of a bitch can handle an airplane, dammit. No doubt about it," Longstreet grumbled.

"Yup. He can fly," MacTavish agreed. "And you're right about the son of a bitch part, too. No doubt about that either. But he's our son of a bitch and my rice bowl. I know he's long-cocked you, but straighten up and fly right. Show some class."

86

"Don't worry about that. I'm already there."

"Good on you, pal. Good on you."

The water taxi picked up the party and several bundles from the Albatross and brought them to *Sweet Fanny Adams*. Van Dusen was his usual self, Mister mover-and-shaker, great big Ipana smile and all. He climbed on first and gave Delia a hand up. Delia carried her entrance off, too, only a slight blush and a weak smile and nod to Longstreet. She looked gorgeous, flaming red pigtail under a flyer's ball cap. Even in dungarees and a loose work shirt she was a real showstopper. MacTavish was so impressed he quit smirking and began to wheeze.

The treasure hunters followed. Joe Houlihan bounced on board, clean-shaven, fresh as a daisy. Kevin Ratcliffe had started a sparse beard but was otherwise neat enough. He had washed his loose, embroidered clothing in a hotel sink because it was rumpled but reasonably clean.

Ian Spatchcocker, on the other hand, looked like the ass-end of creation with a dry shave. Sherlock Holmes could have deduced the precise contents of every meal he had eaten from the stains on his bulletproof tweeds, liberally soaked with sweat and worn for ten days. His old-school tie sported egg yolk and a solitary bean, among other things. His whiskers had grown into islands scattered about on his face. He didn't carry a stubble beard well. He pulled a wilted Woodbine cigarette from the pack in his shirt pocket and reefed a lighter from his baggy pants.

MacTavish grabbed his wrist before he could use the lighter. "Smoking only to windward of the hold or on the foredeck. We have aviation gasoline on board."

"Oh, I say! Get your hands off me! I don't smell any gasoline."

"Whatever," Longstreet said. "Smoking only a long way to windward of the hold or on the foredeck."

"I'm not in the custom of taking orders from bloody boat drivers."

Van Dusen barked at him, "Get used to it. We're not in the custom of burning to death. Now hear this! Now hear this! Longstreet and MacTavish run this ship and what they say goes. Nobody is a servant here. We are all shareholders."

"That cook and his wife too?"

Longstreet nodded. "Yup. That cook and his wife too."

"Outrageous. Bloody outrageous. Sniff-sniff."

"Get used to it. It won't hurt so much after a few days."

Spatchcocker muttered but put away the lighter and slipped the Woodbine into his pocket.

The Costa Rican watchdog introduced himself: "Pedro Rivas, is I," and shook hands with Longstreet and MacTavish. He wore lieutenant's bars and a nametag on his neatly pressed fatigues, a Guardia Civil patch on the shoulder. Around his waist was belted a military webbing belt and holster, from which gleamed the butt of a forty-five, government issue, automatic pistol, slightly worn. He probably knew how to use it.

Spatchcocker said, "Show me to my cabin, please. I require a bath and a change of linen."

"No cabins," Longstreet said. "This is a converted tuna clipper, not a cruise ship, but you can have the forward lower bunk on the starboard side in the main cabin. The head and showers are in the main cabin, too. Your duffel bag is in the storage room, one deck down. Go easy on the hot water. Don't shave in the shower."

"What about me?" said Ratcliffe.

"Why don't you take the upper bunk over Spatchcocker?"

"Jolly good!" Ratcliffe said. "Quite reminiscent of the crew quarters on those Foochow pole jokes that once plied the China coast. It was on the deck of the Kow Loon ferry. I was on my way to Portuguese Macau for recreation, don't you know, a game of roulette. It was there that I first saw one of the magnificent Foochow pole junks. Only a glimpse before she disappeared into the mist. I reached into my binocular case for a closer look but encountered the hand of one of the ferry crew. The rascal was trying to steal them. A slippery devil he was. He maintained he was only catching his balance. Of course, he said this in Cantonese, of which I have a smattering. I was a dishwasher in a Chinese restaurant, working my way through college, don't y'know, and I picked up a few Cantonese phrases like you know, 'Where is the toilet,' 'another beer, please,' only enough to be useful."

"Yes, yes. Fascinating, utterly fascinating—and I suppose I take the next bunk back?" Houlihan said.

"You got it," Longstreet answered. "And there's several showers. You don't have to wait for Spatchcocker. These old tuna clippers carried a big crew. But, like I said, go easy on the hot water."

"Good. When's dinner? Van Dusen tells me you've shipped a good cook and a bull cook. That's really important. Good food makes a happy camp."

"And I really do think you could've hired them without

giving them a share. Sniff-sniff. Kerchuckle-snerk, Sniff-sniff," Spatchcocker said.

"Well, that's the way it is," Longstreet said.

Joe Houlihan said, "You know, Ian, if we find anything and it's half as big as you read about, there'll be plenty for all of us. And we don't find anything, at least we'll have eaten well."

Van Dusen said, "We'll be taking the water taxi right after supper. We're on another freight run."

MacTavish could make the Twenty-Third Psalm sound like a punchline in a burlesque show. He wiggled his eyebrows suggestively at Delia. "I'll row you over in the *Cunning Punt*. You won't need the water taxi."

"You'll row us over in *what*?" Delia squawked.

"The *Cunning Punt*. One of our skiffs. That's her name."

"And I'll bet you gave her that name, Whisker-Snot."

"No, Angel-Tits, I would've called her the *Punning*—"

"So, Delia, you're a copilot these days?" Longstreet said quickly.

"Yes. It's fascinating. Van has been teaching me to fly. With the autopilot I can manage while Van takes a nap." She stared stonily at MacTavish.

"Isn't that sweet," MacTavish said. "And what are your other duties? Like—"

"Shaddap, Mac!" Longstreet snarled.

Wren popped out of the main cabin and whistled piercingly through her fingers. She shouted, "Dinner will be on in half an hour, kiddies. Get yourselves cleaned up. We don't dish up for slobs."

The group filed up the deck and into the main cabin.

Longstreet grabbed MacTavish's shirttail and held him back. "Mac, this is one of those times we talked about. Remember? Please don't start a fight, particularly with Delia."

"I was having a little fun."

"Fun, my ass. As a special favor to me, lay off Delia. Let's get through dinner with minimum fuss and get them on their merry way. That goes for all the rest of these flakes, too. You know damn good and well that you don't stir up friction at sea. We have to ride herd on this bunch for a month or so, maybe more."

"Okay, okay, okay. I got it."

They looked quite a lot better when they sat down at the table. Spatchcocker had showered, shaved, and put on a clean khaki shirt and shorts. He must have had another old-school tie in his duffel bag because he was wearing it, cinched up in a small, hard knot. Kevin Ratcliffe had shrugged out of his embroidered garments and put on a nearly identical set from his duffel bag. Only an expert in Oriental religions would have noticed that the symbolism was now Sufi, no longer Tantric Buddhist. Houlihan had washed and shaved. Pedro Rivas had taken off his gun belt. Van Dusen was spruce enough, great big Ipana smile and all, but then, Van Dusen was always spruce enough. Longstreet had never seen him looking sloppy. Delia had squared away her makeup and combed out and re-braided her red pigtail.

Wren and Roger carried platters and bowls from the galley and plunked them down on the table: some big corvinas, flash-broiled to perfection, garnished with chopped green onions and a savory lemon sauce, steamed broccoli, dishes of hollandaise, bowls of dark-brown potato balls, and plates of hot biscuits covered with tea towels to keep them warm. Some pitchers of lemonade, tinkling with ice, filled out the setting.

Everyone poured themselves glasses of lemonade. From his place at the head of the table, Van Dusen rapped on his glass, rose, and said, "Well, people, here we are at the beginning of the venture. Let's toast to smooth sailing and a successful enterprise. Here's to the Loot of Lima." Glasses clinked.

Roger came out of the galley, wiped his hands on his apron, and hung it over the back of his chair. "I think the fish is okay. I know the fisherman. The broccoli? Well, it will pass, but fresh vegetables don't thrive in the tropics. The spuds are one of my specialties, a quick variation on *pommes de terre Lorette*. Eat hearty."

Everybody passed the platters around and helped themselves. For a few minutes nothing was heard but the clatter and squeak of cutlery and chewing.

"Goddammit!" MacTavish said. "You've done it again, Roger!"

"Yes indeed," Van Dusen agreed. "These potatoes in particular. Quite unique. Absolutely superb."

Delia fancied herself an epicure. "The hollandaise, too. Roger, I'll bet you make it from scratch, not from a mix."

"Mix! What do you think I am, an amateur? A snot-nose graduate from cooking school? You bet I make it from scratch."

Wren said, "Careful, sweetie. About the only way you can get a rise out of Roger is to insult his cooking."

"How do you like the food?" Longstreet asked Pedro.

"I do not speak the English too good," Pedro said.

"*Le gusta las comidas?*"

"*Jue puta! Muy bien!* I like. Much. *Jue puta!*" In Costa Rica, '*jue puta*' expresses everything from rapturous enthusiasm to nauseating disgust. In this particular case it was enthusiasm.

For dessert Roger and Wren brought out a couple of fresh, steaming apple pies and a bowl of whipped cream. They dished everybody up a generous slice and an ample scoop of cream. For a few minutes nothing was heard but the rattle of forks against plates, smacking of lips, and deep, satisfied sighs.

"All right," Van Dusen said, "we've had a very good dinner and we're all here. It's time to put our cards on the table. I guess I'm the big cheese, so me first. I sold the stock and raised the money. I run the company and I fly the airplane. Longstreet and MacTavish handle the boat and the cargo and generally make sure that everything works. Pedro represents Costa Rica and makes sure we behave ourselves. Let's hope he never has to take that howitzer out of the holster."

Everybody snickered, even Pedro.

"After that meal I don't think I have to tell anybody what Roger and Wren do. We're all on shares. Everybody works. Everybody contributes. We cooperate, and no independent ventures. No whispering. No cliques, and most of all, no secrets. Cards on the table, folks. You first, Joe."

Houlihan got to his feet. "Okay. I financed Spatchcocker's and Ratcliffe's travel. I am also an experienced geologist and I've done a lot of prospecting. I know quite a lot about digging and finding what's underground. I can operate a magnetometer and interpret the results." Houlihan sat down.

"Okay, Joe. You next, Spatchcocker."

Spatchcocker pulled a Woodbine cigarettes from his pocket and got his lighter out.

"Ian, let's make a deal," Houlihan said. "If you have to smoke, please do it out on the foredeck, never in the cabin."

"Sniff-sniff-sniff. Kerchuckle-snerk, sniff-sniff. You can't stand a little cigarette smoke? In the jolly old RAF we all smoked like furnaces in the mess and nobody complained about it."

"This isn't the jolly old RAF, Ian. Don't smoke in the cabin."

"Well, sniff-sniff-sniff. We'll see about that." Spatchcocker looked around for a bit of sympathy. He didn't find any.

"Let's stick to business," Van Dusen said.

Spatchcocker put the cigarette back in his pocket. "Well, while I was rummaging in the Museum library, I found a copy of Sir John Seede's book, *Personal Encounters with Noted Pirates of the Spanish Main*. That got me interested. When they auctioned the effects of the Seede estate—the family died out, don't y'know—I acquired the original manuscript and a few sketch maps. All in all, I have a great deal more information than was printed in the popular version—you know, that one with the octopus and the blonde. I also have a clear copy of Captain Colnet's notes on Cocos Island to give us some idea of what the topography was in those days. However, I don't feel comfortable with exposing this information to everyone. I would prefer to reveal such of it as I feel is relevant when the occasion arises."

"No," Van Dusen snapped. "All of it is relevant and right now. You either produce your book and your notes to the entire group for reference or you can fly back to jolly old England—at your own expense, I may add."

"This is most irregular. I must insist—"

"You don't insist anything. Produce your book and your notes or leave."

"You won't have to swim," MacTavish said. "I'll row you over to the dock in the *Punning*—Oops! I mean the *Cunning Punt*."

"Kerchuckle-snerk, well if you put it that way, I have really no choice in the matter, do I?"

"No, you don't."

Spatchcocker frowned. "All right, I'll go fetch my notes." He left the table.

Longstreet thought that Van Dusen had handled that situation well, just like a real big-time operator, captain of industry. Longstreet glanced at Delia. His multicolored Turk's head spun rapidly at white heat, seeing Delia's look of stunned-haddock admiration.

Van Dusen said, "I guess it's your turn, Ratcliffe. But before you start, how did you manage in Costa Rica?"

"Well, at first we got nowhere. Any official we needed to see was either at lunch, out of his office, on vacation, or hadn't come in yet and so forth. If we insisted, it turned out that nobody spoke English. Then, on Sunday, Joe went to mass at the Cathedral in San Jose. He was gone all day. On Monday—surprise, surprise! It turned out that everybody was back in their office. Everyone spoke English. Everything worked."

"What did you do, Joe?" Van Dusen asked.

"We were in luck," Houlihan said. "It turns out that the Archbishop of Costa Rica's mother was my mother's second cousin. We had a nice long talk. He said he'd call the president and see what he could do for us."

"Talk about lucky!" Van Dusen said. "You can't beat the old-boy network, especially the Church. Now, Ratcliff, tell us what you're going to put on the table."

"Jolly good! I'm included because of kismet—fate, that is. For one reason or another the Ratcliffe family have occupied the same building for many generations. We own an ordinary public house in South Shields—it's near Newcastle On Tyne. It's a comfortable, rambling jumble of roofs. A year or so ago, when I wasn't traveling—I travel a great deal, you know. Why, last winter in Kathmandu, I was on a pilgrimage. The Nepalese Buddhists have a custom of—"

"Kevin! Stick to the point," Houlihan said.

"Oh, all right. As I was saying, I was rummaging in the attic, amusing myself on a rainy day, when I came across an old leather trunk. Within it I found some clothes, almost completely rotted away, a snuffbox—it stunk to high heaven—and several journals. It turned out that these items had belonged to an ancestor, a Ratcliffe who was secretary to Governor Seede of Jamaica. Ratcliffe wrote an excellent hand, of course; as a secretary he had to. His journals are easy to read. He did most of the primary interrogation of prisoners and kept precise notes adding considerable substance to Seede's manuscript, and even provided details of pirate escapades that escaped Seede's notice. In particular, one Benito Bonito, or Bonito of the Bloody Sword—he was reputed to have been a Royal Navy officer named Bennett Graham—they say he served under Nelson at Trafalgar, the decisive naval battle of the Napoleonic wars. Nelson had devised a new strategy. It was risky, but—"

"The point, Kevin," Houlihan said.

"Yes. Alright. Alright. Graham turned to piracy and became Benito Bonito. After capturing loot in the Caribbean, he rounded Cape Horn to avoid capture. In Acapulco he seized a mule train of silver and some Church valuables: gold chalices, thuribles, candlesticks, things like that. He stashed his loot in a cave in the Cocos Island mountains. To seal the secret, Bonito shut one of the two crewmen who witnessed the deposit into the cave after it was closed up. The other crewman was a fellow named Cangrejo. I suspect that wasn't his real name. 'Cangrejo' means 'crab' in the Spanish, a fascinating language, a mixture of Arabic, Latin—"

Houlihan slapped the table. "Ratcliffe!"

"As I was saying, Cangrejo managed to avoid capture when Bonito was caught and hanged. He joined Thompson and was captured in Jamaica. My ancestor, Ratcliffe, managed to convince him that he could be set free if he revealed the location of Bonito's treasures. Ratcliffe seemed to have omitted to mention this to Governor Seede. The Governor didn't include these details. I suspect Ratcliffe might have had visions of going into business for himself, but he never got the chance. He was killed when Thompson attempted to escape. Shot with one of Governor Seede's dueling pistols—pure bravado, don't y'know. I don't fancy the governor ever fought a duel or intended to. Damned accurate, those pistols were. Very carefully made by the best gunsmiths. They were rifled, too, unlike the military muskets of those days. I shall never forget when I tried one out. I was visiting the Highlands. My Aunt Bessie ran a laundry in Inverness—"

"Kevin!" Houlihan said.

"The point. Yes, yes. Alright. I found Ratcliffe's notes in that trunk. They can lead us to some rather juicy little caches. Going into business for oneself was quite common in those days. I am happy to contribute those notes to the general knowledge. Should I get them now?"

"Yes," Van Dusen said. "That would be an excellent idea. I'd like to say a few words about 'going into business for oneself.' We have to avoid that at all costs. Nothing could spoil our venture quicker than secrecy and cliques. I must emphasize again that all information must be shared openly. No private expeditions. Now Delia and I must leave to complete our freight run. I have a suggestion. Right after MacTavish runs us back to the Albatross in the skiff—*Cunning Punt*, you said? Great name for a boat." Delia winced but retained her stunned-haddock-in-heat gaze at Van Dusen. "I suggest you drop your mooring and put to sea tonight. You have all your gear and all your people and, now that the cards are on the table and in the interest of security, the sooner you put to sea the better."

Houlihan said, "Suits me."

Longstreet said, "No problem. But what about the Moke?"

"Leave it on the dock. We can do something about it when we come back."

"But I want to do some shopping in Panama. Pick up a few items for my kit, don't y'know," Spatchcocker protested.

Houlihan said, "Anything you need we probably have already between us. I think we can fill out your 'kit.' Security is important. Let's go to sea now."

"Yeah," MacTavish agreed. "You guys are pretty talkative. Yapita-yapita-yap—"

"Easy does it, Mac," Longstreet said. "But I think Van Dusen is right. The less chances we take with security, the better."

"All right, that's settled," Van Dusen said. "Delia and I must leave. Mac, how about you run us over to the Albatross?"

"Righto, chief."

Chapter Ten

By the time MacTavish had returned and nested the *Cunning Punt* in her cradle, Longstreet had the engine warm and purring. He had extinguished the anchor light and lit the running lights. Longstreet dropped the mooring. With MacTavish at the wheel, *Sweet Fanny Adams* slipped down the channel and out into Panama Bay.

Longstreet joined MacTavish on the bridge. Spatchcocker and Ratcliffe stood on the deck, chattering excitedly and watching the lights slip by. The night was hot, as are all nights in Panama, but their motion and a light sea breeze tempered the heat and made the evening pleasant. Dishes and pots clattered in the galley. Wren and Roger were cleaning up and doing the dishes. Houlihan tried to help but was chased out of the galley by Wren. "What the hell! Are you after our jobs? Light a rag."

At the wheel, MacTavish said, "I'm familiar with this channel and the harbor. I'll take the con from eight to twelve. How about you take the graveyard watch, twelve to four?"

Longstreet said, "That sounds about right. I'll grab forty winks after we clear the channel."

Houlihan joined them on the bridge. "I can steer a boat. I could take a watch."

"Good stuff," Longstreet said. "You can take early morning watch, four to eight. After we clear Punta Mala we can probably let Iron Mike do the steering, but we have to keep a watch. There's a lot of shipping around here. How about the rest of your gang?"

Houlihan scratched his chin. "I don't think they have had any experience with boats. We'll see when we get farther out."

On half throttle, *Sweet Fanny Adams* made about six knots down the channel on the outgoing tide. They passed Rodman Naval Station, then Fort Amador and moved into the outer harbor. By the time Longstreet took the con at midnight they were clear of most of the shipping. When Houlihan took over at four, Longstreet had increased speed to ten knots, and the ship was on autopilot. They didn't sight any more shipping except for a tug and two scows loaded to the gunwales with gravel.

After breakfast in the main cabin, Spatchcocker lectured at great length on the magnificence of the jolly old Royal Air Force, comparing it unfavorably to all the other air forces in the world, particularly the small ones of small countries and most particularly the smaller ones of Central American states.

"For instance, Pedro, you are flying a P-Fifty-One, an interesting machine, and the engine, a Packard, is only a variation of the great Rolls-Royce Merlin engine, built under license, don't y'know."

"*Jue puta.*"

"Our Spitfire, however, was the only airframe that could really carry the Merlin properly. Plus which the Spitfire had many, many advantages over the P-Fifty-One, which was, in actuality, a machine designed to facilitate mass production."

"*Jue puta!*" Pedro glanced around, looking for an exit.

"Yes indeed. Another rather unforeseen advantage of the Spitfire was its wooden propeller."

"*Jue puta!* I tink I get air." Pedro stood and headed for the door.

"Yes indeed. I would if I were you. You're looking a bit green about the gills."

Sweet Fanny Adams had picked up the long, slow, Pacific swell and was rolling rhythmically. "I say, leave the door open. Every breath of fresh air is a penny in the bank of health."

"*Jue puta!*" Pedro disappeared onto the deck.

"Poor chap," Spatchcocker said. "Hasn't got his sea legs yet, I'll warrant."

"Quite so," said Ratcliffe. "I'll never forget the time I first hit the Indian Ocean swell after emerging from the Red Sea. Like no other swell in the world. I myself tossed my cookies for three days. Speaking of green about the gills, you yourself are looking a bit pasty, Ian."

"Not at all. I think there was something in the breakfast, don't y'know. I do believe I'll lie down for a while."

Dinner that evening was not a triumph. Both Wren and Roger had succumbed to the swell and retired to their cabins on the bridge deck. Roger had held off seasickness long enough to cut some ham sandwiches with sliced pickles and the right smattering of hot mustard. He'd made a big pot of coffee, too. Longstreet, MacTavish, and Houlihan munched their sandwiches and drank their coffee in the open air on the bridge deck, avoiding the occasional retching sounds from Wren and Roger in the cabins behind. Below, in the main cabin, the sound effects and smell were of epic proportions. Spatchcocker had been facing the wall so that most of his dinner stayed in his bunk, but from his elevated upper berth, Ratcliffe had managed to spew his dinner on the world at large.

Chapter Eleven

After another day at sea, the sound effects had been brought under control and burning coffee and fresh sea air had managed to dissipate the stench. Wren and Roger had recovered. Once again, the meals were excellent. Wren, like the true heroine she was, had broken out the bucket, the mop, and Clorox. MacTavish, Houlihan, and Longstreet had pitched in with her. This time she had not accused anyone of trying to steal her job.

In midafternoon, they had reduced speed to five knots. MacTavish, Roger, and Wren were trolling from the afterdeck. Pedro looked on. Not that he was that excited about fishing; he was avoiding another 'Jolly old RAF' lecture from Spatchcocker.

Sweet Fanny Adams was steering on Iron Mike. Houlihan had the con. On the wing of the bridge deck Longstreet was taking a sun sight. Spatchcocker, wearing his most supercilious RAF smirk, watched: "By George, skipper, it would appear we are in the nave of Westminster Abbey. Boo-haw, sniff-sniff. Kerchuckle-snerk." He fished a Woodbine cigarette out of his pocket and lit it with his lighter.

Houlihan took Spatchcocker's elbow. "You know, Ian,

Longstreet is learning celestial navigation. If we want to find Cocos Island, what do you say we leave him alone?"

"I was having a bit of fun, don't y'know."

"Yes, I know. When Longstreet bites your head off that would be a bit of fun too, eh? Supposing you and I leave him alone? Perhaps finish your smoke?" Houlihan led him through the bridge and out onto the deck at the other side. Spatch-cocker kept his head on his shoulders for the time being.

Longstreet stopped gritting his teeth and focused again through the scope and the smoked filters to bring the lower limb of the Sun neatly down to touch the horizon. He pushed the button to stop the watch. At the chart table he muttered, "C minus W—height of eye—lower limb. What the hell are those other corrections? Yeah. Here they are." His pencil scratched furiously on the scratchpad, doing column after column of careful arithmetic. He opened a volume of HO-214 and extrapolated an appropriate assumed position. His pencil scratched some more. He drew a line on the chart and heaved a sigh of relief. "Okay. I have a running fix. If we steer sou'west by west we should raise the island tomorrow afternoon."

"Oh, I say! Jolly good!" Spatchcocker said.

Houlihan nodded and changed the course on the autopilot. *Sweet Fanny Adams* veered a few degrees to the south.

Wren shouted, "I got one! A fish! A fish!"

Houlihan yanked the throttle back to idle and popped the twin-disc gearbox to neutral.

MacTavish stood ready on one of the fishing platforms, gaff in hand. "A humdinger, Wren. A big dorado! Hot damn." He gaffed the fish and swung it up onto the deck.

Roger said, "That's one beautiful fish."

Pedro nodded. *"Jue puta!"*

Wren shouted again, "Hey! I have another one! Damn! Ready with that gaff, Mac!"

"Right you are. We eat tonight!"

Chapter Twelve

Because the breeze had backed to west-southwest, it was quite late in the afternoon before they raised Cocos Island's green peaks looming ahead through a rain shower. Longstreet had the con. He turned off Iron Mike and steered by hand. The two Brits stood on the forward deck, pointing and chattering excitedly. Houlihan and Pedro were on the bridge with Longstreet.

"Not bad navigation, old man. Not bad at all. We hit the island right on the nose." This was as much excitement as Longstreet had ever heard from Houlihan.

"Blind luck, Joe." Longstreet didn't mean it. He was quite pleased with his beginner's celestial navigation. It was, indeed, quite a thrill to find that a sextant, a watch, some books, and arithmetic will actually produce terra firma in the middle of the trackless ocean. "That would be Chatham Bay dead ahead. It's on the northeast side of the island. I think we'd better steer to starboard, round the point, and come into Wafer Bay. Deeper water. Better anchorage—I think."

"You think?"

"Yeah. I think. The only chart we have is old and large-scale. I don't know what it's really like in there."

Houlihan said, "Spatchcocker had a copy of Colnet's notes. You remember? The Royal Navy skipper who took *Rattler* into Cocos a couple of hundred years ago."

Longstreet shook his head. "I read them. Colnet reported the anchorages are difficult—foul ground, shallow. He also said the island was hotter than hell, it rains every afternoon, and the clothes rot on your back. I think maybe we better put a skiff in the water. Scope it out before we risk the ship." Longstreet cut power and put the engine out of gear.

MacTavish climbed up to the bridge. "What gives? We're hove to."

"I'd like to take a boat in and look stuff over."

"Good by me. How about we use the seine skiff, *Waltzing Matilda*? It's choppy out here for *Cunning Punt* or *Chicken S*."

They took the lashings off *Waltzing Matilda* and the cargo boom. A light breeze had kicked up a bit of chop but they had no trouble launching her to leeward. *Waltzing Matilda*'s engine, a marine conversion on a Ford V-8, was persnickety, but they got it started after they drained and refilled the carburetor and dried out the wiring.

Houlihan said, "You and MacTavish are the seamen. Why don't you go? I'll take the con."

MacTavish and Longstreet climbed in. They cruised across the north end of the island, around the point, and into Wafer Bay. The point shut out the sea breeze and the heat dropped onto them like a blanket.

"I thought I knew something about hot," MacTavish said and wiped a river of sweat from his face, "but this takes the cake."

Longstreet peeled off his shirt, already soaked. "It's beautiful, though."

The hills were covered with lush green foliage. The afternoon rains had ceased and here and there, horsetail waterfalls gushed. Ahead of them on the beach stood a forest of coconut palms and, on the right, a creek emptied into the bay over a low rock ridge. Through the water they could see the bottom clearly, level and sandy but studded with coral heads and boulders waiting to snag their anchor chains. And sharks! They had never before seen such a flotilla of sharks of so many species, and big ones at that.

MacTavish said, "I guess we do our swimming in that creek."

Longstreet said, "Look at that big bastard over there!" He pointed. "Is that a hammerhead?"

MacTavish nodded. "Sure is. The last one of those I saw ate two of our ship's cooks when we were in the Solomons. This one is even bigger. He might look slow and lazy but don't you believe it. He'll move like greased lightning when he sees something to eat."

"You said 'he' instead of 'her.' How do you know it's a he-shark, not a her-shark?"

"No tits."

"Fish are cold-blooded. They don't have tits, Mac, or do they? You wouldn't bullshit me, would you?"

"I might. About the tits, I might. But, no bullshit, all sharks aren't cold-blooded. There's the mako shark. He's warm-blooded. That's why he's so damned fast."

"So you don't really know if it's a him or a her, do you?"

"No, I guess not. And I'm not bullshitting about those poor cooks. These sharks are hungry. Don't go swimming."

"Do you think it's deep enough for an anchorage?"

MacTavish shrugged. "The bottom is so damned clear it looks shallow. Try the sounding lead."

Longstreet dropped the lead over the side and whistled. "Five and a half fathoms. I'll be damned. I'd have sworn it was only about ten feet. We can anchor right here in the bay."

They returned to *Sweet Fanny Adams* and hoisted the seine-skiff back into her cradle. They took the ship into Wafer Bay, dead slow. It was sunset before *Sweet Fanny Adams* was anchored to their satisfaction. They used mudhooks fore and aft with as little scope as possible to keep from snagging on the coral heads. This was not easy: dragging lengths of anchor chain, backing and filling with the ship: gypsyhead-windless work, anchor-windless work, safety-wired shackles, rust, bruised fingers. They rigged deadmen on the anchor chains. By the time Longstreet, MacTavish, and Houlihan finished they were running sweat in rivers.

Spatchcocker helped by giving advice: "Oh, I say, now. A simple square knot would do. In the jolly old RAF we always used a simple square knot when we had to drag a Spit out of the muck."

"Why are we using two bloody anchors? It's quite calm in here. One would do."

Ratcliffe was noticeably absent. He'd disappeared below decks. When he emerged he was no longer Namaste Ratcliffe, the Sufi mystic, but had transformed himself into Sargent Gaspard Le Ratcliffe of the Foreign Legion, complete with kepi, boots, baggy pants, and khaki military shirt. He had a pack on his back and a Winchester lever-action 30-30 hung on its sling over his shoulder. "Sacre bleu! I shall spend my first night onshore alone."

Pedro laughed. "*Jue puta! Con los chinchos, sancudos, moscas, hormigas, avispas, abejas—*"

"*Merde!* What did that Dago say?"

Houlihan said, "The Costa Rican Lieutenant of the Guardia Civil with the loaded forty-five automatic pistol which he obviously knows how to use and who is the law here said 'With the bugs, mosquitos, flies, ants, wasps, bees.' He's right. The bugs on the beach will eat you alive. But don't worry. If you continue to insult the Lieutenant, he would be within his rights to take care of you long before you hit the beach."

Pedro laughed again. "*Jue puta.* It is nothing of importance. I not hear never insults from *bobos.*"

Cracks appeared in the invincible Sargent Gaspard Le Ratcliffe. His eyes puddled up. "What's he mean, '*bobo*'? Is he being sarcastic?"

Longstreet said, "There, there. Don't cry. '*Bobo*' is Spanish slang for 'friend.' Pedro wouldn't dream of being sarcastic. Would you, Pedro?"

"Not understand the word 'sorkrasic.' No can be something I understand not." Pedro folded his arms.

"So you see?" Longstreet said. "But the bugs will eat you alive."

"No. I have my tent. Bugs? *Merde!* That won't bother me. I shall cover my face with my blanket."

"In this heat? Jesus!"

"I shall get some game with my gun. Some fresh meat would be good."

MacTavish said, "Where did you get that antique shooting iron? The 30-30 was a black powder cartridge and that cowboy carbine was out of date fifty years ago."

Spatchcocker chimed in, "You Amiddicans have no respect for tradition. You throw away what few items actually have historical significance without a second thought. I've read a great deal about the 30-30 Winchester. It was the mainstay of the Amiddican westward migration."

"Maybe," MacTavish said, "but it's still an out-of-date cartridge and that lever action is loose and sloppy. Wouldn't hit a bull's ass at fifty feet."

Houlihan said, "Hey, Kevin, think about it. Why not spend the night on board? Have some dinner. Tomorrow morning is soon enough. We have plenty of time."

But Ratcliffe wasn't about to abandon his Foreign Legion persona. He thrust out his jaw and pulled his kepi lower over his eyes. "Sacre Bleu! No! I intend to spend my first night on Cocos Island alone on shore. I must reconnoiter. Get the lay of the land." He dragged the small dingy, *Chicken S.*, out of her cradle, carried her aft and dropped her into the water by the fishing platforms. He dropped his pack into the boat and rowed away toward the beach in the last of the light.

"I hope he'll be alright," Wren said.

"No bloody worry," Spatchcocker said. "We Brits are resourceful. We can adapt. We can take care of ourselves. Why, back in the jolly old RAF, a Stuka dive-bomber made an emergency landing in a farmer's field near our strip. Had to, don't y'know. Those Stukas weren't carefully constructed, don't y'know. Not like the Spits. We—"

"Dinnertime," Roger shouted. He had cooked another do-rado, rice, and some canned spinach for dinner. By the time they finished it was pitch-dark. Happily, bugs don't usually come offshore but the still, evening air was sweltering.

"Bang, bang, bang, bangity-bang," rang shots from the beach.

"*Jue puta!*" Pedro said.

"Good Heavens!" Spatchcocker squawked. "I certainly hope Kevin hasn't run into trouble."

MacTavish said, "More likely he's 'getting us some game' with that 30-30. They say this island swarms with wild pigs. If he got one, he's going to have a tough time cleaning it in the dark, and with those damn mosquitos sucking away at his blood."

No more gunfire. The only sounds that came from the beach that night were loud slaps of hand on skin that signified mosquitoes, and a great many of them.

Next morning, Longstreet, Pedro, Houlihan, and Mac-Tavish rowed *Cunning Punt* to the beach. The morning air was cooler, almost fresh. The line of coconut palms rustled softly. The tide was out. The dinghy *Chicken S.* was high on the beach. Ratcliffe still snored in his pup tent and a very big, very dead pig bloated and stank in the sunshine, leaking gastric juices and pestilent serum from several bullet holes. An army of flies clustered around the pig. A jet of aromatic gas whistled from one of the holes. "Eeeeeeeee." Mad with rapturous excitement, the flies circled the jet and buzzed their approval.

Longstreet held his nose.

Houlihan said, "I believe that pork might be past its prime."

Pedro said, "*Jue puta!*"

"Good morning, chaps." Ratcliffe stuck his head out of the pup tent. His face was puffy from multiple bites. "I got a topping, great pig last night for our larder. It was too dark to clean it and I had no knife. I suppose we should clean it now, yes?"

Houlihan said, "Now? No. It's much too late."

Longstreet said, "If we put a rope on it and drag it down the beach the tide will take it away. There are enough sharks in the bay to take care of it."

MacTavish got a length of line and, circling to windward, dropped a clove hitch over one of the pig's hind legs. With Longstreet and Houlihan helping, the pig was dragged down to the water's edge. "Couldn't some of the meat be saved?" Spatch-cocker called from the shade of the coconut palms. "Seems a dreadful waste. Perhaps with some strong spices we could make bangers? In the jolly old RAF we loved bangers and mash."

"Yes, indeed," Ratcliffe echoed. "In hot weather, hot, highly spiced food is the thing. In Calcutta, I always had a good, hot curry for breakfast. I will never forget the time—it was before the monsoon set in. The heat was appalling. We had sat down to our lamb curry and rice when an elephant came around the corner with the Maharaja of Prawntang and the Commandant of the Brigade of Prawntang Grenadier Guards rocking around in the howdah. Those howdahs are like a ship at sea, y'know. Seasickness takes over, and—"

"Well and good, but this pig is way beyond that, even for the Maharaja, perhaps even for the jolly old RAF," Houlihan said.

"You Amiddicans are so quick to waste things. Why, in the

jolly old RAF we had to make do with whatever we had. We were all alone to stop the bloody Boche."

MacTavish went up the beach to where Spatchcocker and Ratcliffe sat in the shade. "Come with me." He pulled Spatchcocker to his feet and guided him down the beach and to leeward of the porcine corpse. Another gusher of fluid and gas erupted. MacTavish smacked his lips. "Yum, yum! I think you're right, Ian. Get a whiff of that. Bangers and mash coming right up."

Spatchcocker shook off MacTavish's hand. "It would seem that you might be correct. It might be a bit too far on the gamey side. Let the tide take it away."

Houlihan studied Ratcliffe's swollen face. "I think you should take the dinghy back and have a good wash. Those bites could become infected. Perhaps you'd like some breakfast?"

"Yes! Now that you mention it, I'm famished. I haven't been so hungry since the time the Maharaja of Prawntang took us on a tiger hunt with that elephant of his. I was telling you about that. We had to get up very early, after the elephant was fed his grass and vegetables. An elephant is very, very choosey about his food and must eat before traveling—"

"Like that elephant, you'll feel better with some breakfast in your gut. Then you could tell us all about hunting tigers with the Maharaja of Poontang. I can hardly wait to hear all about it."

"That district was called Prawntang, not Poontang. You're being sarcastic with me."

"Sarcastic? Wouldn't think of it. Your tough night with the mosquitos is doing the talking. Hop in the dinghy. Row back to the ship. Take a hot shower. We'll be right behind. Roger and Wren are making a good breakfast. Everything will get better after you've eaten."

"Oh, all right, so long as you didn't intend any sarcasm." Ratcliffe scratched the stubble on his face. He dragged *Chicken S.* down to the water, plumped himself amidships, and took the oars. "Ian, come along."

Spatchcocker gave the putrefying pig a wide berth, walked to the dinghy, and climbed into the stern sheets. Ratcliffe splashed the oars in the ankle-deep water with no effect. The dingy was firmly aground.

"You kiddies waiting for the tide?" MacTavish said. "We're going to beat you back if you don't shove that dingy into deeper water."

"But I'll get my bloody feet wet," Spatchcocker whined.

"Suit yourself."

"Fucking hell!" Spatchcocker snarled. He climbed out of the dinghy and pushed feebly on the stern. Ratcliffe stayed in and splashed with the oars. "Damn it, Kevin, you're going to have to get out, too."

"But I'd get water on my socks. That would make the bites on my ankles itch like fury. Can't you push harder?"

"No! I bloody well *can't* push harder."

"Pitiful. Just fucking pitiful," MacTavish said. "Spatchcocker, why don't you get back in. I'll shove you off."

"Roger, that. Wilco. Proceed." Spatchcocker climbed in over the stern. MacTavish put his hands under the stern of *Chicken S.*, lifted her a bit, and gave a mighty heave. The dingy shot away from the beach. Ratcliffe fell forward into the bilges of the dingy and Spatchcocker tumbled back, over the stern, and into the shallow water.

"Bloody hell!" Spatchcocker shouted, then got to his feet and threatened MacTavish with his fists.

MacTavish laughed. "There, there. Let's put the fight off for another day, shall we? I'm awfully sorry to have dumped you into the drink. Now, if you'll put your dainty ass back into the dinghy you could row back to the ship and get into some dry clothes."

"You _bah_-stad!" Spatchcocker shouted. "Why, for tuppence I'd—I'd—I'd—"

MacTavish felt in his pocket. "Hey! This I gotta see! I'm sure I've got tuppence somewhere—oops. Awfully sorry. I seem to have left all my small change in my other pants."

Houlihan stepped between them. "Dammit, Mac, quit it. And you two"—he glared at Spatchcocker and Ratcliffe— "this has gone on long enough. Too long, in fact. Get back to the ship. Put on some dry clothes. Get some breakfast. You'll feel better."

"_Nev_-ah! In all my life! Have I—"

"Put a sock in it, Ian. We can't have fights on this expedition."

"Alright for now, but I'll not forget—"

"Forget, don't forget," Houlihan said. "Whatever. Row, Kevin."

"But mark my words—"

"Row, Kevin."

Ratcliffe dug in with his oars and moved away from the beach.

Longstreet turned to MacTavish. "And you, Mac, for God's sake, please keep your sense of humor under your hat. We can't have scraps."

"Okay, okay, okay."

Ratcliffe rowed. Spatchcocker muttered. "That bloody bah-stad is lucky that Houlihan intervened. Sometimes I can't control myself when I get angry. No telling what might have happened—"

"Fortunate indeed," Ratcliffe said. "The Maharaja was furious with his hunter-wallah when we found no tigers that day, but later on, in a remote village up in the hills, the village head woman said—you may not know about this interesting anthropological fact, but in those hills, it's the women who run the show. It's a matriarchal society in the hills—"

"—let me tell you, Spatchcocker continued. "The last time I was so angry was back when I was with the jolly old R.A.F. The Boche had dropped a bloody great bomb from a Stuka on the end of the runway—"

"—they can be quite stunning, you know. They're not bashful at all either, those hill-women. Why, if they fancy you, they come right out and—"

"—which shortened it quite a bit. The chaps had to land. Almost out of fuel, don't y'know. One of our Hurricanes wasn't—"

"—invite you to bed. Why, I'll never forget the time this strapping wench went ahead and grabbed my John-Thomas—"

"—so lucky. He slid right off the end of the runway and into the bomb crater—"

Still chatting in unison, the two drifted out of hearing. The others rowed back to the ship in the *Cunning Punt*.

Wren was on the afterdeck of the ship fishing. One after another, she pulled in flatfish a little bigger than the palm of her hand. She already had a pile of them on deck. They grunted, "Oink! Oink!" like little pigs.

"Grunts! That's what I call them. Listen to them!" She giggled with pleasure and Roger laughed along with her. Roger cleaned them as fast as Wren landed them. Their abdominal cavity was a small pocket in front that sliced off easily. After Roger had removed the fins, the heavy skin was easy to rip off. They made a delicious breakfast. Roger dredged them with cornmeal and pepper and quick-fried them in butter and a touch of paprika. He made a pile of them on each plate, like flapjacks. He served them with a sauce of butter, lime juice, and a few hot peppers.

This magnificent breakfast soothed the frayed tempers. Roger made a fresh pot of coffee. Spatchcocker continued his tale of the Stuka crater and the hurricane. Ratcliffe's story had gone off on an acute tangent so they never did find out what that hill-woman had done with his 'John-Thomas.' The others sipped their coffee in tranquil silence.

Longstreet interrupted, "Hey, We've got to get our asses into gear. Good food, but if we're going to get anything done today we've got to get started."

Spatchcocker pulled a Woodbine cigarette from his shirt pocket and groped for his lighter.

"Please don't," Houlihan said. "Let's get that gasoline off the ship before you smoke."

Spatchcocker put away his unlit smoke. "Bloody hell! Yes, let's do that so you Nervous Nellies can leave me alone."

One drum at a time, Longstreet and MacTavish hoisted the avgas out of the hold with the winch. Fifty gallons of gasoline plus a steel drum may weigh over four hundred pounds, but it still floats. When the drums were all in the water, MacTavish roped them together and towed them to shore with *Waltzing Matilda*.

"What a bloody waste of time," Spatchcocker said. "We could be uncovering the treasure." He reefed a Woodbine from his shirt pocket and lit it.

"Not a waste of time," Houlihan said. "The farther that gasoline is from your cigarette lighter, the better I feel."

"Oh, pish. You chaps are over cautious. Why, in the jolly old RAF we handled aviation gasoline all the time. We were much braver than—"

"—and died like toasted flies. Yeah, yeah, yeah," Longstreet said. "Tell me all about it, but on second thought, maybe I could wait until later to hear about it."

MacTavish cast off the string of drums in the shallows and motored back to the ship. They hoisted *Waltzing Matilda* back on board and into its cradle.

Houlihan said, "About digging for treasure, where do you think we ought to start?"

Spatchcocker said, "The large cache, the Loot of Lima."

Longstreet said, "Treasure hunting will have to wait. Today's activities will begin by rolling those drums high and dry."

They rowed ashore in *Cunning Punt*.

Spatchcocker and Ratcliffe had brought a metal detector along. Houlihan asked, "What are you going to do with that?"

Ratcliffe said, "We thought we might search the beach and the coconut grove. According to my ancestor's notes, Thompson's crew spent the night ferreting away small items during that night of drinking and carousing. They should be all over the beach."

While Longstreet, MacTavish, and Houlihan waded in the shallows to untie the drums and roll them up to the coconut palms, Spatchcocker and Ratcliffe wandered off.

"I say, Kevin, if we should find something, I don't feel we need to tell those bloody Amiddican bastards anything. Nevah, in all my life, have I been subjected to such rudeness."

"I quite agree, Ian. They have been sarcastic with me. They deny it, but I can tell. I simply cannot abide sarcasm."

"Rah-ther! Why for tuppence I'd—well—there's no telling what would happen if I lost control of my temper." He put on the earphones of the metal detector. Waving the instrument from side to side, he wandered through the coconut grove

Ratcliffe followed. "This is rather reminiscent of the time I dropped my gold watch in an outdoor privy on Easter Island. We were investigating those monstrous stone idols they have there. I've told you about that watch, haven't I? The one I inherited from my Uncle Tobias, you know? Died in poverty. He drank. He had put that poor watch through pure hell. You can't imagine how many times he pawned it. I finally found a watchmaker in Inverness who managed to remove the last vestige of that odalisque's ooze from the works, sticky, pernicious stuff it was. I told you about her, remember? Port Said? Anyway, it was not injured by the contents of that Easter Island privy, quite petrified, you know. Only dusty. No smell, either. Petrified shit doesn't smell at all. The islanders were long gone. But I had the devil's own time climbing down into the pit to retrieve it. Quite deep, that pit, but not near as deep as the ones they had to dig to uncover the latrines of Troy. Fascinating how they discovered Troy. This German chap found it from the instructions contained in the *Iliad*—in the original Greek, of course. Not at all like Modern Greek. Speaking of Modern Greek, I'll never forget that time in Athens. I had ordered a slice of baklava and yet another shot of Metaxa from this villainous waiter who spoke nothing but Modern Greek. Metaxa goes down so smoothly one tends to forget how many one has had until it's too late. Then, I was so sick, so very sick. The waiter said—"

Spatchcocker stopped short and whipped the earphones off his head. "By George, Kevin, I do believe I have a bloody echo! Right here! Did you bring the shovel?"

"No, I didn't. I thought you would bring it."

"Look at me. Do you see a bloody shovel?"

"No, Ian. I thought—"

"Dammit, Kevin, what a bonehead you are! How could you be so bloody obtuse!"

Ratcliffe began to sniffle. "Ian, you're being sarcastic. I can tell."

"Don't bloody well go on about bloody sarcasm. We need a bloody shovel."

"*Jue puta!*" Pedro said, stepping forward from his observation post. "Wanting shovel? I have." He held out a shovel. "Here is shovel. You dig. I watch."

They dug. A previous treasure hunting expedition had been conscientious with their garbage. In addition to the tomato, bean, and vegetable cans, they uncovered a cache of chicken and pig bones and several tin boxes which had once contained those neat little cigars so popular with operagoers and some treasure hunters.

"*Jue puta!*" Pedro said. "Costa Rica be very generous. Insist not in our share. You keep all."

"He's being sarcastic, Ian."

Spatchcocker mumbled, "Bloody Spic bah-stad."

Pedro's smile faded and he undid the flap of his holster. "What that you say?"

"I said, 'Big disappointment.' That's all. No insult was intended." Spatchcocker giggled nervously.

The afternoon deluge was early that day, and what a deluge. By the time the party arrived at the ship, the shore was no longer visible through the sheets of water. For lunch, Roger had baked several fresh loaves of bread and prepared a platter of corned-beef sandwiches with sliced onions and pickles. A jar of hot mustard stood on the table.

Nobody talked. They ate.

Roger brought out a pot of fresh coffee.

"Back to business," Ratcliffe said, over his second cup. "According to my ancestor's notes, the pirate, Cangrejo, was quite specific about the cave where Captain Graham, also known as Benito Bonito of the Bloody Sword, cached that mule train load of silver. Twenty tons of silver would be a decent beginning. Imagine how many teeth could be filled with that. Amalgam fillings have a long history. The first recorded use was during the Tang Dynasty in about eight hundred A.D. Amalgam fillings have always been controversial because of the amount of mercury used. Mercury can be quite deadly, don't y'know. I will never forget my first amalgam filling. When I was a child, there was a dentist that traveled from house to house in a wagon drawn by two beautiful white mules. Mules are hybrids, you know, and these—"

Houlihan said, "Yes, yes. Utterly fascinating, but if we should happen to find this silver trove, I'll bet it's closer to two tons, not twenty. These quantities have a way of growing over time, but let's give it a try. Tell us more about it. But maybe you could save your teeth for later, huh? The white mules, too?"

"Oh all right! Have it your own way." Ratcliffe opened his portfolio and read: "'In the west end of Wafer Bay stands a creek which appears to flow inland at high tide. Walk up this creek until you see the cleft in the northern hills. Walk up the buttress of the opposite hill about fifty fathoms to the door in the rock.' That's clear enough, isn't it?"

"This is bloody stupid," Spatchcocker said. "Why are we discussing trifles? We came for the Loot of Lima. Let's get started. Those landmarks should be easy enough."

Longstreet said, "Those 'landmarks' will be long gone. One was a tree, wasn't it? Three notches carved in the butt? That was two hundred years ago. That tree has rotted away long ago. No tropical tree lasts more than a hundred years. And 'a cleft in the northern hills'? We've seen landslides almost every day and the forests have come and gone. The Loot of Lima will be impossible to find until we have magnetometer data. According to Thompson's story, it was buried 'between the stream and the base of the hill at a depth of a fathom, with dirt and rocks withal and well packed.' Don't forget, a fathom is six feet and that's without landslides."

Houlihan said, "A magnetometer needs magnetic material—iron, steel, something like that. According to the story, the only magnetic material in the cache would be the sword blades and maybe binding on the chests. Gold, silver, gems are not magnetic. The airborne magnetometer might give us a location within fifty yards or so, but the backpack magnetometer will narrow it down. Otherwise we'd have to excavate an acre or so. Metal detectors are useful only within five or six feet and, by this time, landslides and weather will probably have buried the cache deeper. It probably wouldn't do us any good to be trotting around with metal detectors. The terrain here is steep and the vegetation is dense. We'd get nowhere. When is Van Dusen coming? We're going to need that aerial magnetometer survey."

Longstreet said, "The end of the week, he told me. I think he's finishing up one of his 'freight runs.'"

Ratcliffe suggested starting on the Bonito cave while waiting for the Albatross.

"That's going to take a lot of bushwhacking," Houlihan observed. "We'll need machetes and axes."

"Tomorrow," Longstreet proposed. "What do you say we break out the tools tomorrow morning—unless you eager treasure hunters want to blunder around in a flood."

They had the balance of Wren's catch for dinner.

For breakfast Rodger dished up bacon and flapjacks with butter and maple syrup. "I'd like to go with you today. Give us a minute or two to clean up."

The whole gang went to shore.

The creek was easy to find. At low tide a rock ledge dammed it up and made a pool that became freshwater when the creek had displaced the tide. The going was easy through the grove of coconut palms on the border of the beach. Then it became dense jungle. They took turns hacking their trail. The jungle yielded to a grassy patch.

Longstreet was in the lead. "Hey! Look at that. Easy going!"

"I take it you've never seen saw grass before," Houlihan said.

Longstreet pushed on into the patch. "Ouch! Jumping Jesus! This stuff cuts like razors."

"Let me take the lead," Houlihan said. "I have on long pants and a long-sleeved shirt." He shoved into the patch and sunk to his knees in the mud. He backed out. "I think we better give this stuff a wide berth."

They circled the grass patch and continued to hack their way through the trees and vines.

By noon they'd gone only a scant hundred yards from the beach. The air was sticky and stifling and it hummed with hungry insects. They were bathed in sweat, exhausted, and covered with scratches and prickles from the underbrush and bites of the legions of insects. They returned to the beach.

Ratcliffe said, "By George, I do believe I'll take a swim." He peeled off his embroidered shift, his pants, his shoes, and his socks and made a long, shallow dive into the pool that had accumulated behind the rock ledge. Shallow, because the pool was only five feet deep. Lord, that cool fresh water felt good! It swished by him, gurgling in his ears, cleansing him of sticky sweat and dirt, alleviating the smarting of bites, minor cuts, and bruises. His hair eddied freely about his head and freed itself of twigs and dead bugs. Near the end of that delicious dive he opened his eyes. About six inches directly in front of him was another eye, a big one, the size of a teacup. Surrounding that eye was a wall of off-white skin. Below it hung a mouth, half open and well furnished with row upon row of teeth. Ratcliffe froze for a moment. The shark flickered a fin but did nothing else. Its huge eye focused unblinking on Ratcliffe.

"Yaaaah!" Ratcliffe erupted from the pool in an explosive gusher. "Shark! There's an enormous great shark in there!"

"Damn!" MacTavish said. "Wasn't that something! I've heard about walking on water but I never believed it. You walked on water."

Ratcliffe stood, shaking, on the beach. He pointed to the pool. "Shark! Shark! I saw him. I came right up to him. He leered at me. Big, he was. Bigger than me."

Longstreet studied the pool. "I believe you're right, Kevin. He must have been foraging along the edge of the beach. That creek runs inland at high tide. The outgoing tide marooned him. You're lucky. Perhaps he's groggy from the fresh water. It looks like a mako and they're very fast."

MacTavish said, "I do believe I'll take my bath a bit farther upstream."

Ratcliffe's eyes bulged. He continued to shake. "Shark—shark—shark—shark—"

"Easy. Easy," Houlihan soothed. "You're all right. Think what a great story it will make. 'There I was on Cocos Island. I will never forget when I dived into a pool and came eye to eye—'"

"That's not funny. I really did almost bump into a huge shark."

"I don't doubt it for a minute. In fact, I can see it. Ten feet long if it's an inch. Why don't you sit in the shade of these coconut palms and catch your breath. I'm going to go up the creek a bit and have a splash myself."

They returned to the ship for a bite of lunch. Wren caught some more grunts and Roger sautéed them. He made steamed rice and warmed up canned asparagus, too. They topped it off with slices of lemon pie. By the time they finished, the clouds had closed in and the afternoon downpour had begun. Small waterfalls sprung from the surrounding hillsides. The rain had abated the stifling heat a bit.

Ratcliffe said, "I could use a nap. That encounter with the shark exhausted me."

MacTavish snickered. "Yes, but just think about that poor shark. I can hear him now, recounting his adventures to the other sharks." MacTavish's voice assumed a fruity treble. "Nev-ah! In all my life! Will I ev-ah forget the time when I was taking a breather and I came eye-to-eye with the *most* terrifying creature I have ev-ah—"

"Lay off, Mac!" Longstreet snapped.

Ratcliffe's eyes puddled with tears. "He's being sarcastic. I can tell. I can't stand anybody being sarcastic. It's so mean."

Houlihan said, "There, there, Kevin. I'm sure Mac was only joking. Weren't you, Mac?"

MacTavish snickered.

Longstreet snapped, "Goddammit, Mac, you're doing it again! Apologize."

MacTavish said, "Alright, Kevin, I'm sorry. I was only joking."

Houlihan said, "See, Kevin? He apologized. Now, why don't you go take that nap?"

"Alright, I accept—but just this time." Ratcliffe retired to his bunk.

The downpour continued. They would find that an afternoon deluge was the way weather worked on Cocos Island. Bushwhacking was only possible in the morning.

Two more mornings and they reached the spot where they could make out "the cleft in the northern hills." Walking "up the buttress of the southern hills about fifty fathoms" took another morning. Fanning out, they searched for the "door in the rock."

Wren found it. A sow erupted from the underbrush followed by seven of her young. Wren managed to clout one right behind its ear with her shovel. They gutted it and took it back to the ship. Roger was delighted. It would make a fine change from a diet of corned beef hash and grunt-fish. Roasted suckling pig for dinner! Roger spent the afternoon cleaning, scalding, and scraping the bristles from the pig. Then he popped it into a blazing hot oven to make the skin into delicious cracklings. After twenty minutes he reduced the heat and slow roasted it to perfection. The last of the apples had become soft so Roger made a bowl of hot, cinnamon-spiced applesauce. They ate every scrap of the piglet and chewed on the bones. They wiped up the last of the applesauce with Roger's fresh, hot biscuits, dripping with butter.

Next morning Roger stayed on board to improvise a decent dinner, and Wren stayed to help Roger and catch more grunts. The rest rowed toward the beach in the *Cunning Punt*. The day's heat starting to build up but the offshore breeze tempered it and made it bearable.

"I say, there is something washed up on the beach," Ratcliffe said.

"Shit," Longstreet said.

"Shit what?" MacTavish was at the oars. His back was to the beach.

"Ratcliffe's pig is back."

"Shit."

"You can say that again."

"Alright, I will. Shit."

"But it simply cawn't be that bloody pig. I saw it float away on the tide."

Longstreet said, "It floated back on the tide."

"But why didn't the sharks eat it?"

"The sharks around here have discriminating taste," Houlihan said. "I guess they like their meat fresh."

"But it doesn't stink," Ratcliffe said.

"It's to leeward," Longstreet said. "Wait till we get to the beach. It will stink."

When they reach the beach they discovered that Ratcliffe's pig was indeed back, bigger than ever and untouched by sharks. The bloated corpse had been left at high-water mark. The smell, if anything, was more rancid with a bitter, penetrating cast.

"It's a shame we didn't get some of that meat. Should we see if we could salvage a bit? Maybe try a taste?" MacTavish was not a kind man.

The bullet holes appeared to have plugged themselves, but when they dropped a clove hitch over the hind leg and began to drag the pig down to low water: "Eeeeeeee!" A ghastly cloud gushed forth, followed by a yellow-green jet of liquid loaded with squirming maggots. MacTavish was abeam of this jet and was plastered with it.

"Doesn't pay to be a smart-ass." Longstreet, too, could be unkind.

MacTavish spewed his breakfast onto the sand.

The tide was low. Freshwater had filled the tide pool at the mouth of the creek. MacTavish checked carefully for sharks and immersed himself, clothes and all, and was able to wash off the gelatinous, maggot-loaded scum.

"You're all wet, Mac," Longstreet said.

"Makes no difference. Even cools me—give it a try. Let's get that pig afloat."

They dragged the putrid corpse into the water until it floated.

"I'll cast off the line," Longstreet said.

"No, don't. I'll make fast to it with the seine skiff and tow it out of the bay."

Sweet Fanny Adams's horn blew a series of short, insistent blasts. They could see Roger run down to the afterdeck and hop into *Chicken S.*

"What the hell is going on?" MacTavish said.

Roger arrived on the beach. "Van Dusen was on the blower. He says he'll be here in an hour."

"What do you say we tow that pig out to sea?" MacTavish came as close to the beach as he dared in the seine-skiff, *Waltzing Matilda*. Longstreet coiled the pig-rope and threw it to MacTavish, who made it fast on *Waltzing Matilda*'s towing bit. He cruised out of Wafer Bay and into the open ocean. He cast off the pig and returned to the beach.

Half an hour later, the Albatross circled the bay, landed, and taxied up on the beach. The after-hatch opened and Van Dusen appeared. "Lend a hand. I've got some fresh meat and vegetables." He didn't have to repeat that message. They all fell to and bundled the cartons of food out to the boat.

"Magnetometer time?" Houlihan asked.

"Yes. Magnetometer time. I need to fuel up first. Only the main tanks. We'll be doing some low, slow flying. I don't want the weight of full ferry tanks."

They unpacked the magnetometer from its case. The sensor, a yard-long, finned cylinder, they made fast to its cables in the cage under the Albatross's tail. Inside the Albatross they ran the cables to a console mounted on the bulkhead behind the pilots.

Van Dusen said, "Joe, you'll have to read this thing. You're the geologist."

"I'm rusty but I'll give it my best shot."

"Good. Longstreet, I'll need you to fly copilot."

"What about Delia? Isn't she flying copilot these days? Why didn't you bring her along this trip?" Longstreet's multicolored Turk's head was spinning viciously and doing the talking.

Van Dusen took no notice. "She's a quick learner, all right, but she's not up yet to low, slow flying over rough terrain dragging a magnetometer. That job requires someone with more flying experience—you, for instance. And, in point of fact, I did bring her along. She's in San Jose. The climate in San Jose is quite salubrious, as opposed to this hellhole. I'll pick her up when we've finished here. While I'm there I'll fill all fuel tanks chock-full. Then, outbound, we stop off here again and fill the drums from our ferry tanks. On our way back, we can top off our ferry tanks here."

Longstreet's Turk's head spun at supersonic speed. "She's in San Jose, eh? That's a lot of shuffling around and pumping gas—let alone picking up a copilot. On your way back, why not gas up again in Costa Rica or Panama?"

"That's out of our way and I'm not comfortable with stopping on a freight run. It would mean one hell of a lot of useless bribes, delays, and paperwork—Customs, Immigration, all that kind of thing. I think I told you about that, didn't I?"

Longstreet said, "Yes, you did. But this freight, now. Let's talk about freight. Where are you coming from, where are you going, and what are you carrying?"

Van Dusen said, "Look, I've gone through this once before but I'll do it again. Rebuilding that Albatross cost one hell of a lot of money, some of it from our company, but the rest of it came out of my own pocket. I have loan payments to make. I have to take freight jobs to meet those payments and to support you guys while you search for the Loot of Lima. I have to take these jobs where and when I find them. They're my business and they're going to stay my business. So don't snoop, okay?"

Longstreet said, "All right. I'll leave it alone, but I have to admit I'm curious."

Van Dusen said, "So be curious, but don't snoop. Joe, if you'd man that magnetometer console, let's do some preliminary tests."

Houlihan climbed into the Albatross and powered up the magnetometer. As usual with sophisticated, complicated, modern, and very expensive electronic gear, it didn't work. Stone-dead. They cleaned corrosion off the connectors, replaced blown fuses in the reel motor and transmission, disassembled, cleaned, and greased the driving mechanism in the reel winch, unplugged the connecting cable to the readout station, cleaned the corrosion from the contacts, found and spliced two broken wires—and a few more little chores. The magnetometer came to life.

By the time they finished, it was getting dark and they returned to *Sweet Fanny Adams* for dinner, an excellent dinner. The boxes of groceries that had arrived in the Albatross contained a fine rib roast of beef and fresh vegetables. Roger had belted out a hasty pudding, steamed some fresh spinach, roasted some potatoes, and made a crisp green salad. He'd baked a couple of lemon pies, too.

Nobody spoke until the roast beef was rendered into well-gnawed bones and the lemon pies were only a sweet memory.

Spatchcocker lit up a Woodbine cigarette. Houlihan snarled at him. Spatchcocker went out on the deck to smoke but listened from the doorway.

Wren said, "Well, Mister Van Dusen—

"Please! Too formal. Call me Van."

"Okay, Van it is. We might have discovered the entrance to Bonito's cave. Some pigs were living in it and came whizzing out when I started digging. I got one of the piglets, too. We ate him yesterday. It will take some digging before we can get into that cave—if it's a cave, not a mere pig burrow. Probably it will take a couple of days' digging. But at least we've found something."

"Yes. A pig burrow. Not the Loot of Lima. Sniff-sniff-kerchuckle-snerk." Spatchcocker flipped his cigarette butt over the rail and came back into the cabin.

"*Jue puta*, but already you find the hole." Pedro's English had improved.

Spatchcocker said, "Look here. You say 'twenty tons of silver ingots'? At two dollars and a half an ounce, that would be slightly over a million Amiddican dollars. And twenty tons? Bloody likely it would be closer to twenty pounds. That is a long way from the Loot of Lima. And when you get right down to it, all that stuff about 'church treasures' and 'twenty tons of silver ingots' depends only on the accuracy of Ratcliffe's ancestor's information as related by Cangrejo, a scurvy pirate trying to save his own bloody neck. Sniff-sniff."

"Wait a minute," Houlihan said, "every single bit of the information we have was related by 'scurvy pirates trying to save their own bloody necks.'" Houlihan slapped the table sharply. "Spatchcocker, please don't light that damned cigarette in the cabin."

"Very well, if you insist." Spatchcocker slid the Woodbine back into his pocket. "You Amiddican Nervous Nellies complaining about smoking. In the jolly old RAF, we never complained about smoking. Why, we all smoked like furnaces. Helped to keep us awake, don't y'know."

"Surely not around airplanes," Van Dusen said.

"Of course not. We never smoked around airplanes."

"Interesting. How did you stay awake long enough to fly them? Why not pretend that this cabin is an airplane?" Houlihan said. "Now, let's get back to business. The Albatross is here now and we have to use it while we can. Tomorrow we'll do the magnetometer survey. Then we'll get back to that hole in the hill."

"Why not divide our efforts?" Ratcliffe suggested. "Some of us dig out that cave in the hill while the rest of us do the magnetometer stuff?"

"No," Van Dusen insisted. "Stick together. No private expeditions, remember?"

"Oh, well, all right," Ratcliffe said. "This all reminds me of the time I was on an archaeological survey of Angkor Wat. They use a lot of hot peppers in the food in Cambodia—"

"—and the bloody Amiddicans are bombing Cambodia back into the bloody Stone Age. Kerchuckle-snerk-snerk."

"Some of our chaps went off by themselves. We never saw them again. Our best guess was they had strayed too far into the jungle and something—or maybe somebody—ate them after they'd seasoned them highly. They use a lot of hot peppers—"

"Sorry, Ratcliffe. That sounds absolutely fascinating, "Van Dusen said. "I'd like to save that story for tomorrow or maybe later. It's my bedtime. I'll take *Chicken S.* to my bunk in the Albatross."

Longstreet said, "Don't do that. You don't have any screens in the Albatross. On the beach the bugs will eat you alive. The bugs don't come out over open water. We have a spare bunk the main cabin."

"—perhaps one of those wild tribes—cannibals, some of them, that live in the jungle around Angkor Wat. They have these little gardens all full of hot peppers—"

"Hot peppers, eh? You don't say. Marvelous," Van Dusen

said. "Simply marvelous, Ratcliffe, but now if you don't mind I would like to turn in. Tomorrow's going to be one hell of a long day. I can do without bugs, Longstreet. I'll take you up on that bunk, if I may."

Tomorrow did turn out to be one hell of a long day. Van Dusen had Longstreet do most of the flying while he navigated. No problem on takeoff. They cruised up to five thousand feet and out over the sea before they unreeled the magnetometer. It caused a lot of vibration until they established the correct airspeed and attitude. Then they descended to a hundred feet above the treetops and did a series of low-level passes over the island, spaced about fifty yards apart. Houlihan watched the console and made notes. He asked them to repeat several passes that hadn't satisfied him. Toward the afternoon, updrafts from the hills shook them. Then, at about two o'clock, the afternoon storms rolled in. Torrential rains and low scud increased the turbulence and decreased the visibility to dangerous levels.

Houlihan shouted over the grinding engines, "I think that does it. I don't think we'll gain much with any more passes anyway. What do you say we land and get something to eat? I'll need a few hours to get this data into shape before we can draw any conclusions."

"Okay. Longstreet, you flew the patterns. Do you want to land it? No time like the present to learn."

"Why not."

"Okay. Let's do it. You're lined up about right. Don't worry about the visibility. I've picked up our beacon on the automatic direction finder. I'll do the navigating. You fly the airplane. Steer three-ten magnetic. Back off on manifold pressure, props full fine pitch, fuel pumps on. Ease back on the yoke. Slow her down—a little more power-touch of left rudder. That's it!"

The tops of the coconut palms appeared close beneath their hull.

"Half flaps—yes—little more power—nose up a bit—good! Keep that nose up."

Wave tops rattled.

"More power. More. That's it. Keep that nose up."

The albatross settled into the water.

"You're down. Cut power. Keep that nose up. Good. We're there. Good landing, Longstreet."

Longstreet exhaled. Landing is always difficult. "The same as a Super Cub, except heavier."

"You got it. Like all the other airplanes in the world. Exactly like Super Cubs. Any landing you can walk away from is a good landing."

They lowered the wheels and taxied up onto the wet sand of the beach. "Let's grab some lunch," Van Dusen said. "I'll fuel up after. Then I've got to go pick up Delia and be on my way."

"Don't you want to know what we've found—if anything?" Houlihan asked.

"I'll be back to fill the gas drums. We can go over the data then. Do you think you'll have it in shape?"

"Maybe. But I've got a lot of work to do."

They rowed back to the ship. Roger had cut some sandwiches and made some lemonade. Van Dusen grabbed a quick bite and rowed *Chicken S.* back to the beach. The magnetometer runs had used a lot of fuel. He pumped avgas into the Albatross, climbed in, and buttoned all the hatches. The engines coughed into life amid clouds of blue smoke. With full reverse thrust and a lot of power he managed to back the Albatross into the water. He retracted the wheels and eased the throttles into full power. The Albatross was up on the step by the time it reached *Sweet Fanny Adams* and was out of the water by the time it reached the mouth of the bay.

"Goddammit," Longstreet muttered. "That son of a bitch can fly an airplane, damn him to hell."

MacTavish had heard him—again. "Yes, that son of a bitch can fly. And that son of a bitch managed to scoop your girlfriend out from under you. Boo-hoo. Get over it. Get another girlfriend. Like Blind Lemon said: 'Some like 'em black, some like 'em brown. Can't tell the difference, turn 'em upside down.'"

Longstreet snarled, "Up your ass, MacTavish."

MacTavish didn't answer but pantomimed a violin playing "Hearts and Flowers."

Chapter Thirteen

All through the afternoon deluge, Houlihan worked at the chart table in the bridge. Under the awning on the after-sundeck, Ian Spatchcocker lectured Pedro on the adventures of the jolly old RAF.

"I'll never forget the time Wumples had to belly-land his Hurricane. His real name was Featherstone-Haugh, but we called him Wumples ever since that time at Christmas he got his prod caught in a steam radiator in the fourth-floor corridor of the Piccadilly Hotel. He had taken this bint into the corridor for some privacy—"

"Rather! Speaking of radiators, I'll never forget a deeply moving experience I had while in a Theosophical colony in Mozambique. I'd gone there for a chiropractor convention. Boring. Utterly boring, so I—"

"—she was willing and he was in such a hurry he made this mighty thrust at her without lifting her skirt. Kerchuckle-snerk. Boo-haw, boo-haw—"

"—hopped into a rickshaw and told the coolie to take me to the country. I wasn't actually a chiropractor at the time—"

Pedro's solution was to lean back in his canvas deck chair and snore. Occasionally he would wake, roll his eyes, and wistfully finger the butt of his automatic pistol. Neither Spatch-cocker nor Ratcliffe took the time to observe this gesture.

At supper that evening, Longstreet asked Houlihan, "Found anything yet?"

"Maybe. Yes. But I'm not sure about it. I should have something to report tomorrow. What do you say we wait until Van Dusen gets back to fill up his avgas drums? That way I can tell everybody the story at the same time?"

Van Dusen and Delia returned the next morning and spent the first hour transferring fuel from their ferry tanks into the drums on the beach. Delia stayed with the Albatross—and the mosquitos—while Van Dusen rowed *Chicken S.* out to the ship.

Houlihan had set up a large sketch map of Cocos Island on the wall of the main cabin. He had drawn it on the back of a chart. "Okay, here's what we've found. Before we start, you must understand geophysics is still somewhat of a black art. The jury is still out as to how useful it actually is. Let me emphasize that a magnetometer indicates only different levels of magnetic flux. These readings can only register on iron bindings on chests or perhaps the steel in the sword blades—if the swords are there at all. They can also show natural magnetism. There's always natural pockets of magnetic material. We're going to have to do a lot of exploration on foot with the backpack magnetometer and the metal detectors."

"Perhaps we should consult soothsayers? Crystal balls? Voodoo? Witch doctors? Oh, I say! How about an astrologer? Kerchuckle-snerk, sniff-sniff. Boo-haw, boo haw—"

"—don't sneer at magic, Ian," Ratcliffe said. "I'll never forget the time that a Sufi mystic cured me of the bite of a venomous scorpion by reciting a verse from the Koran. We were in a high mountain pass north of Kathmandu—"

"Simply marvelous. Utterly fascinating," Houlihan said, "but let's stay with the magnetometer for now. When we need a Sufi mystic I'm sure Mr. Van Dusen could fly one in for us."

"You may laugh, but you have no conception of the powers of—"

"Please, Kevin! Please save it for later! We found two areas. The first one covers five or six acres in the hills above South Bay. No pirate skipper in his right mind would try to anchor in South Bay. Any ground shallow enough for anchorage is right up on the beach and most of the time South Bay is a lee shore." Houlihan indicated an area on his sketch map crosshatched in red crayon. "I'd say we count that one out. This island is volcanic and I suspect the magnetism in this area is a result of ferrous material.

"The other area is here." Houlihan indicated a small red blotch on the map. "The first time I saw it I thought it was a hiccup on the equipment, but after we went over it a couple times I got the same strong resonance from the same small area. If the magnetometer can tell us anything, it's that this is the only area worth investigating. It's comparatively level and it's about a quarter-mile farther in from Wren's cave—thanks to that piggy. A delicious piggy, I may add."

"Well, let's go dig it up!" Ratcliffe said.

"Oh, rather!" Spatchcocker agreed.

"*Jue puta!*" Pedro fingered the butt of his pistol.

"Whoa!" Houlihan said. "I can narrow it down to about three acres, but that's as close as I can get. We have a lot of bushwhacking and stumbling around with the back-pack magnetometer and the metal detectors before it makes any sense to do any digging. We're going to need the backhoe, too. Any ideas on how we unload it? It won't swim to shore."

"Yeah," Longstreet said. "I've thought about it a lot. It's going to be a real son of a bitch. I think there's an area of smooth sand off the mouth of the creek. I don't think the coral heads can take the fresh water. We'll have to beach *Sweet Fanny Adams* there and wait on the tide. I think she'll careen without too much damage. But it's a risk. A big one."

"To be marooned on a deserted, tropical island! I might've jumped at the chance once," Ratcliffe said. "But it's dreadfully hot, and wet. My clothes are rotting. And the insects! No thanks. I'd much prefer an island I once—"

"We could never take the chance without backup transport from the Albatross," Longstreet said. "One good thing: we haven't seen any snakes yet, poisonous or not. Central America is famous for snakes: fer-de-lances, bushmasters, pit vipers."

"*Jue puta!*" Pedro said. "An' *matabueyes*, dat mean to kill the ox. *Peligrosisimo*—very very dangerous! Very, very dangerous. In Costa Rica we have *matabueyes*, many."

"Not on this island, though," Longstreet said. "I wonder why."

Roger offered, "I don't think pigs are harmed by snake poison and a pig will eat anything it can catch."

"How about when you eat the pig?" MacTavish asked.

"I don't think there's any risk," Roger answered. "We ate one and we're alright, aren't we? I think snake poison has to be injected into you. No harm in eating it—unless maybe you have an open sore in your mouth or something."

"So," Longstreet said, "what do we do first? Wren's cave, the magnetometer area, or unload the backhoe?"

Everybody started talking at once and everybody had a different opinion. Houlihan listened to the uproar for a while. Then he slapped the table sharply. "Let's not waste time. Put it to a vote. I'll put my vote in first. I favor Wren's cave."

"Suits me," MacTavish said.

"Yeah but the Loot of Lima—" Roger said.

"Why don't we send Van Dusen to Persia? Get him to fly us a Sufi mystic—kerchuckle-snerk, sniff-sniff. Boo-haw."

"Sometimes, Spatchcocker, old buddy, you can be a bleeding, reeking pain in the ass," Longstreet said.

"With purple crotch-fungus and a cherry on top," MacTavish sniggered.

"Hey now," Houlihan barked, "easy does it."

"Okay. Sorry, Ian." Longstreet mumbled.

"Hold the cherry; easy on the crotch-fungus," MacTavish said.

"Apology accepted," Spatchcocker reached in his pocket for a Woodbine, then thought better of it on receiving a wintery glance from Houlihan. "Without a Sufi mystic, I say we try for the Loot of Lima."

When the votes were all in, the Loot of Lima had it.

The first order of business was to unload the backhoe. Longstreet, MacTavish, and Houlihan took *Cunning Punt* and a sounding pole and inspected the waters off the beach. The only area of smooth sand, free of coral heads and rocks, seemed to be near the mouth of the creek on the western end of the bay. At high tide in the early morning they lifted the anchors and slowly maneuvered *Sweet Fanny Adams* into that smooth sandy spot until she grounded. They applied power to drive her farther in. Nothing more to do until the tide went out. As the water receded, they decided to shut off the generator set. Roger clucked like a mother hen over his food in the refrigerator and the freezer.

"No help for it," Longstreet explained. "Insulation is good on those boxes. Maybe the food will hold out until we float again."

"In this heat? Are you joking?" Roger said.

"Yeah but that genset is water-cooled," Longstreet said. "When the water intake is exposed it will burn up."

"Couldn't you rig a hose down from the creek? And aren't you going to need the genset running to operate the winch?" Roger asked.

"Dammit. You're right. I should have thought of that. We have enough fire hose to do it."

They had to use the fire pump to prime the hose, but they had water to the genset and the food was saved.

As the water receded, *Sweet Fanny Adams* settled slowly and evenly onto her bottom. They stripped the tarpaulin from the cargo hatch and removed the hatch planks. MacTavish manned the winch. Slowly and very carefully they lifted the hy-hoe up until it was clear of the railings. MacTavish locked the brake and disengaged the clutch on the cable drum. With the gypsy windlass head they swung the boom to port so the hy-hoe was almost over the side. Only a bit farther and they could lower it, but the weight of the hy-hoe made *Sweet Fanny Adams* lean to port. Then gravity took over and rapidly swung the boom perpendicular to the ship. The ship rapidly tilted more and didn't stop until she rested on her bilges and had about a thirty-degree list.

They heard a subdued crunch.

"What the hell was that!" MacTavish shouted.

"Probably bad news, very bad news," Longstreet said, "but lower the hy-hoe onto the sand. Maybe the ship will right itself once we get the weight off of the boom."

When the hy-hoe was on the wet sand they unrigged the lifting tackle. The ship didn't right itself and kept her list to port. They rigged the winch line from the top of the mast to a tree to starboard on the shore. MacTavish carefully put a strain on the winch line. More strain. More strain. The ship slowly righted until she was once again on an even keel.

They climbed down onto the sand and stared under the ship to find the cause of that crunch. A coral head, about the size of a watermelon, had made a watermelon-shaped hole in the planking.

"What are we going to do?" Ratcliffe wailed.

"Turn on the radio and call Van Dusen," Spatchcocker said. "He must bloody well come and evacuate us immediately."

"I wouldn't count on that," Longstreet said. "He's on a freight run and God knows where he is. I think we'd better rig some kind of a patch and do it in a hurry before the tide rises again. Besides, do you want to give up now? What about the Loot of Lima?"

"I suppose I might consent to staying," Spatchcocker said. "But only if you can guarantee we won't sink."

"I don't guarantee a goddamned thing."

Houlihan said, "Easy does it, Spatchcocker. You're not the

only one here. If you want to give up and bail out, we'll see if Van Dusen will give you a ride but you will kiss goodbye to any share of the loot."

"Oh, I say! That's not cricket, you know."

"Cricket, be damned," Houlihan said. "It's not football either, but that's the way it's going to be."

MacTavish said, "Crickets? Schmickets? Cockroaches? You got any other kind of bugs that it's not?"

Longstreet said, "Let's cut the bullshit. The tide will turn soon. We don't have much time to get a collision patch on that hole. Let's get to work."

They worked like madmen. They doubled the tarpaulin hatch-cover to make a serviceable patch, but there was scarcely enough room under the ship to fasten it down. Nobody was particularly eager to slither on their backs into a twenty-inch space under a hundred tons of ship to nail down the patch.

MacTavish started the hy-hoe and scooped an access tunnel under the ship. The water flowing from the creek quickly filled the tunnel but at least they could work safely. Up to their shoulders in water, they covered the hole with the tarpaulin patch. They split some battens from the hatch cover planks and spiked the battens down to the hull around the edges of the patch.

By the time they finished, the tide was rising. "I think that's about as good as we can do," Longstreet said, "The planking is sprung and she's going to leak but I think maybe the pump can keep up with it. We have one bit of luck. The damage is in the cargo hold. It was a fish hold at one time so there is a watertight bulkhead between it and the engine room. Even if she leaks we can maintain power."

"Whatever, but now I've got to get that hy-hoe off the beach," MacTavish said. He drove the hy-hoe up the beach and parked it between the coconut palms.

At full tide, *Sweet Fanny Adams* was floating aft but still aground forward. They fired up the main engine, put it in reverse, and gave it full throttle. Using the rudder, they managed to wiggle the stern. Slowly, and giving grinding sounds, the ship eased back until it was fully floating. They anchored her in her old position, mud-books fore and aft, complete with deadmen.

There was some water in the cargo hold. It had been built to contain ice and fish and was equipped with a four-inch, centrifugal pump. They managed to clear the water in short order.

By the time they finished they had worked through twilight into the night. Roger, that stalwart, had kept doing his job. On the table stood slabs of smoking-hot cornbread and bowls of delicious soup. They were so tired that even Ratcliffe refrained from conversation. They ate and hit the sack.

In the morning Longstreet checked the fishhold. It had leaked some but not alarmingly. They pumped it dry in fifteen minutes.

"I can build us a road with the hy-hoe, but I'll need a lot of help," MacTavish said. "You'll have to break out the axes, machetes, and shovels."

Wren was especially good with a machete. She had filed it to a razor edge and could work her way through the bush almost at a slow walk, no mean trick. She didn't wave her machete around either, only little flicks of the wrist.

"Where did you learn that?" Longstreet asked.

"I was a farm girl—or maybe you should say a stump-ranch girl. When he wasn't creating more daughters and laughing at his own jokes he worked a section that he had to clear. I was cutting my way through brush by the time I was ten."

Spatchcocker selected a short-handled axe and was especially bad with it. Before he had gone ten feet he bounced his blade off of a creeper and gave himself a nasty cut on his shin. "Suffering Christ on the cross! I'm wounded!" he shouted. Houlihan took him to the ship and bandaged him from their first aid kit. They returned to the beach.

Ratcliffe took a safer approach and manned a shovel.

Pedro stood slightly apart with the bill of his fatigue cap pulled down above his eyes and his right hand resting on the butt of his forty-five.

Houlihan spoke to him in Spanish, "¿How do these activities appear to you?"

"They appear foolish. That RAF bobo appears to be a little more foolish than the others."

Houlihan said, "We must watch the wound on that bobo. In this heat and in this jungle he probably becomes infected." Houlihan picked up his machete and joined the rest of the bush-cutting crew.

MacTavish eased off the throttle and shouted, "Look, don't toss the cut brush out of the way. Lay it down in the road so I can walk over it with the hoe. It will help keep the machine out of the mud."

It was slow going, even with the hy-hoe doing the lion's share of the work. By the time the afternoon deluge made work impossible they had gone fifty yards. They returned to the ship for soup and sandwiches.

Spatchcocker was sitting with his bandaged leg up on one of the benches. "I am in serious pain. I need medical attention."

Longstreet said, "Van Dusen should be flying back through in a day or so. We'll see if he can fly you into Panama or San Jose and get you stitched up."

"Contact him on the radio. He must come immediately."

"I'll try. I don't think I'll succeed." Longstreet went to the shortwave radio in the pilothouse, switched to the company frequency, and tried to contact Van Dusen. No response.

Two days later, Spatchcocker's leg had, indeed, gotten badly infected.

The Albatross snarled down through the afternoon scud and made a perfect landing, as always with Van Dusen at the controls. He taxied the plane up on the beach by the gas drums. Delia and Van Dusen got busy transferring gasoline from the drums into the ferry tanks. Houlihan and Longstreet rowed *Cunning Punt* onto the beach with Spatchcocker sitting groggily in the stern sheets, almost unconscious from heat and infection. He had also absorbed a good skinful of the ship's supply of medicinal rum. "Dulls the bloody pain, don't you know."

"Hello, Van," Houlihan said. "In the nick of time. This man needs a hospital."

"That will have to wait until we return," Van Dusen replied. "We can't break our freight run. Our next stop is Canada."

Houlihan said, "No, Van. Listen to me. That won't do. Spatchcocker's leg is seriously infected. I suspect blood poisoning. He needs a hospital with penicillin, a lot of it, and right away."

"Goddammit, I hate to interrupt a freight run."

"Well, your freight run must be interrupted. Without antibiotics he'll be dead in a few more days."

"He doesn't look all that bad to me. His color is good."

"You'll have to take my word for it. He definitely is all that bad. What you take for good color is the rum sloshing around inside him."

"Alright, dammit, I'll take him. But it will have to be Panama, not San Jose. I think I can make a water landing in Panama and drop him off without dealing with Customs or Immigration. But that jog in our route means we'll arrive in Canada running on fumes."

"Why not make a landing on wheels and gas up?" Longstreet asked.

"You're snooping again, Longstreet. Get that goddamned invalid over to the airplane."

Delia studiously stayed out of the conversation and continued to pump gas.

"Are you having a good time, Delia?" Longstreet asked. His abdominal Turk's head was spinning at white heat.

Delia didn't answer him. She nodded.

"How are you enjoying being a copilot?" Longstreet asked.

"Fine," she answered. "Now, leave me alone and let's get that man in the airplane."

"It's Van Dusen now, is it?"

"Yes."

"He's that downtown guy you were talking about, a mover and shaker, with that big Ipana smile?"

"Get off my back, Longstreet, and you can take that 'Ipana smile' thing and stuff it. I've heard it too many times."

With his arms over Houlihan and Longstreet's shoulders, Spatchcocker hopped on one leg over to the Albatross's hatch. Van Dusen boosted him in and eased him onto a thin mattress aft of the ferry tanks. He spread a blanket next to him. "It's hot here, but when we get to cruising altitude you'll need the blanket." Van Dusen climbed out to the beach and closed the hatch behind him.

Houlihan and Longstreet rowed back to the ship.

"Hurting?" Houlihan asked.

"Yeah. Delia and I were real close once."

"So. Hurting's no fun, but you can take it. I worry about Delia, though. She might be in deep trouble."

"How do you mean, 'deep trouble'? She's got what she wanted. A downtown guy with a great big Ipana smile."

"Maybe you're right. I hope so, but my gut instinct says you're wrong."

"Wrong? How?"

"I can't say for sure, but there's a half-empty case of vodka hidden back in the tail section, behind the magnetometer reel. Mickeys. Little bottles. Quick drinks."

"Might be Van Dusen's?"

"Why would he hide it? And why mickeys? That's for sneak-drinks."

Longstreet thought about this. "Huh. She always did like a drink or two—or sometimes more, but I never saw her get drunk or even close to it. She can hold her booze better than anyone I ever saw. I know she could drink me under the table, but I'm not very good at drinking."

Houlihan said, "You're probably right. Let's leave it alone for now. We'll see what happens."

After the ferry tanks were topped off, Van Dusen and Delia climbed on board. They fired up the engines. Van Dusen used full reverse thrust to back the Albatross into the bay.

When the Albatross reached cruising altitude, the cooler air brought Spatchcocker out of his torpor. He limped around inside the fuselage. In back of the ferry tanks was Van Dusen's cargo: cardboard boxes full of sealed plastic bags of a white, granulated material. He took one of the bags forward to the cockpit.

"I say, Van Dusen, what is this bloody stuff? Some variety of foodstuff?"

"You're right on the money, Ian. They have salt pans down along the coast of Ecuador where they collect this fabulous table salt. I tell you, the gourmet stores in Canada can't get enough of it."

"Fascinating. Utterly fascinating. Who would ever have imagined that table salt could be so precious as to warrant importing by air. Could I taste it?"

Delia piped up from the copilot's seat, "I wouldn't do that if I were you. It might cramp your inimitable squid style."

Even with a fever, Spatchcocker still knew how to resent.

"Squid style indeed! Nev-ah, in all my life—"

Van Dusen patted his arm. "Easy does it. She was just kidding. Please don't open the package. Salt is very hydroscopic. The whole bag will spoil if you open it in this damp air. Besides it would alter the quantities on the Customs invoice. That would cause no end of trouble. Now please, put that bag back right where you found it, okay? Then you'd better lie down again. You don't look too good. That infection is no joke."

"Roger, Roger Wilco, as we used to say in the jolly old RAF." Spatchcocker returned the bag to the packing case. Pain, infection, and rum took over. He flopped onto the blanket and drifted away into sleep.

The Albatross landed in the channel in the Canal Zone. Van Dusen taxied up to the yacht club dock. Delia popped out of the forward hatch and flipped the painter around a cleat on the dock. Van Dusen opened the after-hatch and shook Spatch-cocker awake. "This is as far as I go. You'll have to get a taxicab to the hospital."

"I say! That's not cricket!"

"Whatever, but this is it. Get out." Van Dusen hopped out onto the dock and pulled the Albatross in close.

Spatchcocker was too groggy to argue. He climbed out of the hatch and onto the dock. Van Dusen jumped back into the Albatross and shouted to Delia, "Cast off, sweetie-pie."

"Aye-aye, sir. Toodle-oo, Squid."

The Albatross drifted away from the dock and slow-ly downstream. The engine started and the Albatross tax-ied to mid-stream and took off, engines and three-bladed props snarling like the trombone section of the Berlin Philharmonic.

Spatchcocker lit a Woodbine and limped slowly up the dock to the yacht club. He plumped down in a chair. The bar-tender approached him. "That bloody woman! Squid, indeed! Nev-ah! In all my life! Have I—"

The bartender nodded. "Quite so, sir. That bloody woman indeed. Women are like that. Do you require anything, perhaps a cold beer, sir?"

Spatchcocker ordered a beer, but he passed out before he got it. The bartender tried to nudge him awake with no luck. He pulled the butt of the Woodbine from Spatchcocker's fingers before it burned them. He took a closer look, put his hand on Spatchcocker's forehead, and commandeered one of the guests to drive Spatchcocker to the hospital.

Chapter Fourteen

A couple of days in a bed and monstrous doses of penicillin restored Spatchcocker to his usual talkative self. He blathered to anyone and everyone who would listen, about his flight in the Albatross and Van Dusen's wonderful sea salt business.

A gentleman in a seersucker suit came to visit. He sauntered up to Spatchcocker's bed. He was a charming, agreeable fellow with a toothpick vibbling up and down in the corner of his mouth. He pushed his Panama hat back on his head. He pulled the toothpick out of his mouth, holding it with his left thumb and forefinger, and twirled it slowly as he smiled down at Spatchcocker. "Well, my friend, you're looking a lot more chipper than you were a couple of days ago."

"Oh, I say! You have visited before?"

"Why sure. I like to see that all our guests are comfortable. You were sleeping so I didn't wake you. You had a close call, my friend."

"Yes, ra-ther! You are a doctor?"

"No, let's say an interested party. I visit the sick as an act of charity."

"A close call, indeed! I was in a bad way. Simply marvelous stuff that penicillin. When I was with the jolly old RAF—that

159

was back during the war, don't y'know—an infection like that would have been fatal."

The agreeable man nodded. "Quite so. Yes indeed. Wonderful stuff, penicillin. Invented by a Canadian, I believe. Speaking of airplanes—you mentioned the RAF—I understand you were flown here in some kind of an amphibious airplane, is that right?"

"Oh, yes! Our company Albatross. Of course we didn't use amphibians in the jolly old RAF. Our birds landed on wheels. But you might be interested to learn that the famous Spitfire fighter began its life as a seaplane. The Supermarine—"

The man waved his toothpick. "Marvelous, marvelous. Very, very interesting. This company Albatross, now, what was the company name again?"

"We are called International Historical Salvage Limited, a Canadian limited company. We investigate possible, shall-we-say, historical deposits."

The agreeable man made stabbing motions with his toothpick. "Marvelous, simply marvelous. What a wonderful adventure! This Albatross, now, was it carrying any freight?"

"Why, now that you mention it, it was. Our company president, Van Dusen, has a freight business on the side. Nothing to do with International Historical Salvage Limited. He imports a very rare sea salt for the gourmet trade."

"Gourmet table salt, eh? Of course! That's what it is. I should have been able to figure it out. There's been a lot of this table salt circulating in Western Canada. Some of it makes its way into the United States. Interesting to find out that it travels by air. Enterprising people, these Canadians. First penicillin, and now Ecuadorian table salt. This company, International Historical Salvage Limited—what did you say they were do-ing now?" He popped the toothpick in the other corner of his mouth and vibbled it again.

"Digging for treasure on Cocos Island—entirely legal, of course. All tickety-boo. We have cleared the whole matter with the Costa Rican government. We even have a Costa Rican po-liceman with us."

"Wonderful. And you flew into Balboa on this, uh, Albatross?"

"And bloody lucky it was, too. I might have lost my leg otherwise. I must say it was rather abrupt the way Van Dusen landed me. He simply pulled up to the yacht club dock and dumped me out. Then he took off again."

"Yes, that was rather rude, wasn't it? I suppose he didn't clear Customs or Immigration or anything like that?"

"He didn't have time. He was in a dreadful hurry, don't y'know."

The man studied his toothpick and mused on these in-teresting facts. "I guess all your crew do their traveling on this Albatross, eh?"

"Good heavens, no. This was my first trip on the Albatross. We travel on our boat, *Sweet Fanny Adams*. It's on Cocos Island right now. Van Dusen brings us supplies in the Albatross and stops by every so often on his freight trips. Van Dusen also runs the sea salt import business."

"Speaking of businesses, have you found any treasures yet?"

"Sniff-sniff. I won't discuss that. We RAF chaps know all about security."

"Very wise. Mum's the word."

"Marvelous phrase that: 'mum's the word.' Amiddican, is it not? I say, your suit, now. Seersucker isn't it?"

"Seersucker. Yes. It's the thing for tropical weather."

"Seersucker. A word from the days of the Raj, don't y'know. It's from the Hindustani, and originates from the words '*kheer aur shakkar*', literally meaning 'rice pudding and sugar.' In the jolly old RAF, seersucker was very popular in the summertime."

The man flipped the toothpick at the window. It bounced off the screen and back onto the floor. "Oh shit. I forgot about the screens," the man sighed, and bent over to pick it up. The butt of a large handgun gleamed briefly from under his seersucker jacket. He picked up the toothpick, stuck it again in his mouth, and vibbled it furiously. "Marvelous, simply marvelous. It's been wonderful to talk to you and I'm so glad you're getting better. Ta-ta for now, Chum. I'll keep in touch."

Chapter Fifteen

The Albatross landed again and tied up in the Balboa Yacht Club. It was empty this time and had cleared Customs.

"Ready for the island?" Van Dusen asked Spatchcocker.

"More than ready. I don't want those bah-stads making off with my share."

"Made any friends here? Done much talking? Tell anybody about the Loot of Lima?"

"Mum's the word, as you Amiddicans say. We RAF chaps know all about security."

When the Albatross delivered Spatchcocker back to Cocos Island, the gang were all hard at work punching trail. Van Dusen unloaded Spatchcocker and pumped the fuel from his ferry tanks into the drums.

The gang returned to the beach in time to see Van Dusen take off. "In quite a hurry, isn't he," Longstreet said.

"Yes, indeed," Spatchcocker said. "His sea salt business is booming."

"How's your foot?" MacTavish asked.

"Much better. Thenks awfully, but we RAF chaps throw off infection like water off our wings, don't y'know."

"Yes, yes. Tougher than cougar shit and twice as nasty." MacTavish sported his burlesque show grin.

"Oh, I say! Tougher than cougar shit? What did you mean by that?'

"Don't pay him any mind," Longstreet said. "He's kidding. For Christ sake, Mac, lay off. Let's go and eat lunch."

"I don't take kindly to your attempts at humor."

MacTavish's burlesque show grin got broader.

"Mac, pretty please."

MacTavish managed to stay quiet.

After lunch they went back to the area indicated by the airborne magnetometer. They set up some markers for a methodical search with the backpack magnetometer. The afternoon deluge hit before they could begin.

Next day they started early and carefully traversed the area looking for the hotspot. They had to take turns. A backpack magnetometer is heavy and awkward and operating it a killing job in the murderous heat. In the afternoon, before the downpour, the backpack magnetometer needle abruptly jumped into the maximum range. The metal detector responded faintly, too. The cache was evidently buried deep. By the time the rains began, they had defined an area about three yards wide and eight yards long at the base of the hill.

"Son-of-a-gun!" Wren said. "We found it! The Loot of Lima! What are you going to do with your share, Ratcliffe?"

"I believe I'll found a nondenominational transcendental monastery, probably in the Hebrides. Anyway, somewhere the distractions of the world won't be present to interrupt serious meditation."

Houlihan said, "I suggest we continue this discussion back on the boat."

MacTavish said, "And not standing fully dressed in a downpour. Let's go see what Roger has for us. We could break out the beer. We have something to celebrate."

When they had reached the boat and dried themselves off, they sat around the table munching Roger's canned ham sandwiches on his freshly baked bread, garnished with sliced pickles and a bit of sharp mustard. They sipped cold beer, fresh from the hoard in the refrigerator.

Wren said, "What will you do with your share, Mac?"

"I think I'll find out where that fishing skipper who built *Sweet Fanny Adams* went. Somewhere in the Far East. I'll build myself a little house there and populate it with what that fishing skipper found, tits and all."

Longstreet said, "And you'd screw yourself to death in a month."

"Yes! A wonderful way to die!"

Wren scowled. "There you go again, Mac. Tits, tits, tits! That's all you can think about. Besides, those little Oriental girls are tough as nails and practical. With their background you'd be just a perfect target. Before that month was out they'd empty your wallet, roll you up into a spitwad, and flick you into the scrap heap."

"Yeah, yeah. Roger, what would you and Wren do with your share?"

Wren said, "We'd decide that together, but I'd vote for building a modern restaurant on the site of our old diner, with a nice layout: mahogany tables, upholstered chairs, real linen, good silverware, curtains, flowers, and all like that."

Roger said, "I'd go along with that, sweetheart, but I want a first-class kitchen, too, all natural gas fired, a big sala-mander or two, a first-class dishwasher with a scullion to run it, walk-in fridge, walk-in freezer, quarry tile floor with sanitary cove and sloping into drains. Yeah, and maybe my own set of hand-forged, Japanese, carbon steel knives. What about you, Spatchcocker?"

"I believe that I would take flying lessons."

"I thought you were a flyer in the jolly old RAF?"

"Well, I wasn't actually in the RAF proper. I worked in a supporting capacity."

MacTavish said, "A supporting capacity, eh? What the hell was that?"

"Well—NAAFI. We were responsible for the morale of the flyers and mechanics."

"NAAFI, I've heard of them," Roger said. "You ran stores where they could buy cigarettes and booze."

MacTavish pressed, "You weren't actually enlisted in the RAF, then. You were a civilian."

"Well, close to it. If it hadn't been for NAAFI, there's no telling what would have happened to morale."

"Let's get specific," MacTavish bored in. "Exactly what did you do with Nasty, or whatever it was called?"

"NAAFI, and I worked mainly at dispensing alcoholic refreshments."

Longstreet said, "So, in fact, you were a bartender."

"In point of fact, dammit, when those poor devils came in after aerial combat we NAAFI were responsible for—"

"Ain't that something!" MacTavish said. "In the 'Amiddican' army, they have a badge called the Combat Infantry-man's Badge, the CIB. It's worn by those few soldiers who have actually been shot at. I can see your uniform now with its Combat Bartender's Badge, the CBB. A martini glass rampant on a field of beer, emblazoned with crossed swizzle sticks and a stuffed olive crest."

"Snerk! Snerk! I do *not* take kindly to your insolence!"

"A Combat Bartender's Badge! Good stuff," Longstreet said. "Not like a CIB. I got one of those for being there, not that I wanted to. Scared as hell, too. And I got a purple heart when the mess sergeant dropped a pot of beans on my foot. A ghastly wound. Hurt like the devil. War is hell. But you must have had some narrow escapes tending bar on an airstrip. Know any good combat stories?"

Spatchcocker, momentarily speechless, inflated his lungs for a rebuttal. Before the fight could start, Houlihan shouted, "That's enough! Can it! Stick to the point! As for me, I haven't actually decided what I would do with my share, if there is any. Let me tell you again what a magnetometer can't indicate: precious metals. If this deposit actually is the Loot of Lima, it's going to take a lot of work to uncover it. It's at the base of a steep hill. We've been on Cocos Island long enough to see landslides. How many landslides do you think might have rolled over it? So everybody should enjoy their beer and their sandwiches and relax because we have days—perhaps weeks—of work to do before we could say that we'd discovered anything at all."

The next morning they were at work early, MacTavish in the hy-hoe methodically clearing the area, the others dragging brush out of the way. By the time the afternoon deluge arrived, the hy-hoe had dug a hole in the suspect area about a foot deep and five or six feet into the hillside.

They trudged back to the ship in the rain.

When they returned the next day, they discovered the daily deluge had turned their hole into a wading pond about a foot deep, and the hillside had slid and filled a good portion of it. The day was spent digging a ditch to the creek, low enough so the hole would drain.

They trudged back to the ship in the rain.

When they returned the next morning, the hole had drained satisfactorily but had turned into a slimy mud bath. MacTavish managed to dig the hole two feet deeper but had to spend the rest of the morning clearing an area for the spoil. The dirt pile was getting unmanageable.

Pedro had selected a spot in the jungle with good visibility of the hole. He cleared away some of the vegetation and fashioned himself a seat from cut brush. He even made himself a little roof out of interwoven coconut palm fronds. Relaxed, he sat on his seat and watched the others work and sweat in the mud. From time to time he would exclaim, "*Jue puta!*" He'd smile and shake his head.

"You are comfortable?" Houlihan asked him.

"Yes. Very comfortable. My, what energy! What industry!"

"Don't make fun of us. My comrades have little sense of humor," Houlihan said.

Four days later, when the hy-hoe was working in the bottom of the hole, they had a small landslide. The next two mornings were spent excavating the hy-hoe with shovels and by hand.

They carried in the fire pump and used it to blast the mud from the hy-hoe's engine compartment, tracks, and cab. They all held their breath as MacTavish engaged the starter. It started! MacTavish rotated the machine on its tracks. He extended the boom. He worked the bucket. Wonder of wonders, everything worked. When they returned to the ship in the afternoon, they allowed themselves another bottle of beer in celebration.

After two more days of excavation they brought in the backpack magnetometer and the metal detector. The magnetometer showed even stronger indications of a magnetic deposit. The metal detector peeped shrilly and often.

Another day of excavation and they uncovered a deposit of coarse black sand. It covered the whole area and seemed to be bottomless. "I've got bad news for you," Houlihan said. "This is magnetite. Ferrous-ferric oxide, the most magnetic of all natural occurring minerals on earth. The Loot of Lima it is not and never will be."

"That's not fair!" Ratcliffe whined.

"Oh, I say, are you sure?" Spatchcocker asked.

"I'm sure," Houlihan said. "I've seen enough magnetite."

"No treasure?" Pedro asked from his comfortable seat.

"No treasure. Nothing," Houlihan answered.

Pedro laughed. "So, these poor bobos not getting rich today."

Spatchcocker raised his shovel. "You think we are funny, you Dago shit!"

Pedro stopped smiling. The forty-five automatic appeared in his fist and pointed directly at Spatchcocker's stomach.

Houlihan stepped between them. "Put that shovel down, Spatchcocker." "And if you don't mind, sir, I would like you to put that pistol back in its holster. Please don't shoot the bobo. It's not worth the trouble."

Pedro complied.

Spatchcocker lowered his shovel. "Of course I knew I was in no danger. These Spanish fellows are all bluff and no action."

"Shut up," Longstreet snapped.

"I beg your pardon! I'm not accustomed to taking orders from—"

"Shut up," Houlihan barked.

"Never, in all my life, have I—"

"Shut up," the whole group shouted.

Spatchcocker shut up.

MacTavish pulled the idle cut-off to stop the hy-hoe engine. They left it in the bottom of the hole and trudged back to the ship in the rain. Supper that evening was a silent meal.

Chapter Sixteen

They sipped their second cup of coffee. After Wren and Roger had cleared away the breakfast dishes, they came out of the galley and sat down at the table with the others.

"All right. What do we do now?" Ratcliffe asked.

"We throw in the sponge," Spatchcocker replied. "I'm bloody sick of heat, mud, sweat and tears. I'm bloody sick of bloody Amiddican rudeness."

"Most of us are Canadian except for me," MacTavish said. "How about Canadian rudeness? Do any of you Canucks have any Canadian rudeness to offer? I think I could come up with a bit even if I am only a Landed Immigrant."

Longstreet said, "Yeah, now that you mention it, I'm pretty good at Canadian rudeness, too—"

"Longstreet, I'd as soon you didn't," Houlihan interrupted, "and Ian, I'd as soon you put a lid on provocative remarks. That goes for you, too, MacTavish."

"Provocative remarks! Never! In all my life, have I—"

"Spatchcocker! Stop. Right there."

"But—"

"Stop."

Pedro said, "I'm going on deck to enjoy the morning air.

When the fools have reached a conclusion, tell me about it. I would like to go home." Pedro got up from the table and walked out on deck.

"Spanish! Bloody Spanish! What did he say? What did he say?" Spatchcocker said.

Houlihan translated: "He said he hopes we decide something. He would like to go home."

"So would I," Spatchcocker said.

"All right," Houlihan said. "That's two votes for going home. Any others?"

Longstreet said, "There's another thing. We have enough fuel to run the generator and stay here perhaps ten more days. Then we're going to have to leave—or perhaps you guys would like to row back to Panama in or ?"

Ratcliffe asked, "Couldn't Van Dusen fly us back?"

"Nope." Longstreet answered. "He was pretty clear about that. No passengers on his goddamned freight runs, whatever the hell they might be. Besides, he is getting difficult to reach on the radio. Don't count on Van Dusen. We are stuck."

"How badly is this craft leaking?" Houlihan asked.

"As long as we have power to pump twice a day, that big four-inch pump keeps it under control, but don't count on that patch holding up forever," Longstreet told him.

"Well, bloody good," Spatchcocker said. "That settles it. We go home."

"What about Wren's pig cave?" Houlihan said. "We haven't investigated that yet. Cangrejo said that Bonito of the Bloody Sword buried 'twenty tons of silver and some Church treasures.' Isn't that worth a try? I, for one, certainly think so.

I doubt that it is a full 'twenty tons.' Let's call it ten tons, but ten tons is a fair piece of change." He calculated swiftly, "Silver is about two dollars and a half an ounce these days. Ten tons is, let me see, about two hundred forty thousand ounces. At two dollars and a half, that's six hundred thousand dollars. That's not to be sneezed at. It would pay off Costa Rica and our expenses, and give each of us a tidy little grubstake. Besides, Ratcliffe, didn't Cangrejo tell your ancestor about 'other Church treasures?'"

"He did, indeed. But his notes don't say what."

Houlihan said, "Well let's make an assumption. Back in those days the Church was flush. Let's round that number off to a cool million. That's not chicken feed. I would vote for staying and excavating Wren's pig cave."

MacTavish said, "Too bad, all you cute little Oriental girls. Your tits are going to have to wait a bit. Daddy needs money. I'll go for the pig cave."

Wren barked, "Tits! Tits! Jesus H. Christ, MacTavish, there you go again. You don't know shit about women." MacTavish blushed. Wren continued, "I don't want to go until we find out what's in that cave. Don't you agree, Roger?"

"Yes indeed, sweetheart."

Houlihan said, "That settles it. The cave has it."

"Bloody hell!" Spatchcocker sputtered. "I bloody well don't want to sit here any bloody longer in this bloody heat, swatting bloody bugs, and suffering bloody insults."

"No problem, bloody-boy, "MacTavish oozed sweetly. "We need bloody but you could bloody well have bloody *Chicken S.* for your bloody trip back to bloody Panama. Feel bloody free."

Houlihan said. "Mac, skip the wisecracks. You, too, Ian. Shut your face. Let's get to work."

It had been a particularly wet night. The trail was one continuous mudhole. Slipping, sliding, and mud up to the knees they reached the hole they'd dug for the Loot of Lima. There had been a substantial landslide. The hole and the hy-hoe were buried under tons of mud and rocks.

"Jue Puta!" Pedro said and snickered.

"What do you think, Mac?" Houlihan asked. "Do you think it's worth digging it out?"

MacTavish said, "Not only no, but hell no. At the very least, we would need burning tools, a welding machine, and parts, a whole lot of parts—hell, we'd need a whole machine shop. Tell these nice people, Longstreet old buddy, how we are fixed for parts."

"We have no parts."

Spatchcocker said, "Well, that settles it. We go home."

"Wait a minute," Wren said. "We don't need a hy-hoe for the pig cave. Picks and shovels should do the trick."

Ratcliffe said, "Right! Absolutely right! Amazing what can be done by hand. I'll never forget when I was on the excavation team in Luxor, we couldn't use machinery. Too dangerous for the priceless artifacts. We did all our digging with whisk brooms and camel's hair brushes. Some of our native helpers could move two cubic yards of dirt a day with a camel's hair brush."

"Yeah, yeah," MacTavish snorted. "And no doubt they used their assholes for wheelbarrows—"

"Shaddap, Mac," Longstreet snapped.

Ratcliffe's eyes puddled up. "Sarcasm. I simply abide sarcasm."

"Oh, I'm sure MacTavish didn't mean anything sarcastic." Houlihan kicked MacTavish on the shin under the table. "Did you, Mac?"

"Ouch! That hurt! No, no I wouldn't dream of being sarcastic, honest. I was cracking a joke."

Chapter Seventeen

Two days later they had cleared enough dirt, rocks, and rotten vegetation away to discover that there was, indeed, a cave in the side of the hill. They brought flashlights and metal detectors. The cave was twenty-five feet long and hip-deep in pig shit, leaves, sticks, scraps of bone, and flat scraps of wood that could have been the remains of crates. Perhaps the crates for silver ingots, but no ingots were to be found.

They combed the rubbish with the metal detectors. Nothing.

"Ratcliffe, what do your notes say about this cave?"

"If it's the Bonito cache that poor Cangrejo mentioned to my ancestor, it should contain twenty tons of silver bars, church ornaments, and the body of that crewman that Bonito buried alive."

"Well there's not much chance of finding a body," Roger said. "Not with pigs around. Maybe some of those bone scraps are human, but after the pigs have crunched them up it would take an expert anatomist to identify them."

Ratcliffe asked, "Even the skull?"

"Especially the skull," Roger replied. "Did you ever take a close look at the jaw muscles and teeth of a pig? To an adult hog, a human skull would be candy. There would be nothing left but little scraps of bone and perhaps a few teeth. Does anybody want to sieve through this junk for a few human teeth?"

"Not me," Longstreet said. "I guess that's it for this find. No Church treasures. No silver bars—if there ever were any. Shit."

"You can say that again," MacTavish said. "As a matter of fact I will say it again. Shit."

"Shit. Shit. Shit," Ratcliffe said.

Spatchcocker looked as if he was going to cry. "Shit," he sobbed.

Pedro laughed. "Many, many *bobos y pendejos* have waste the money digging *huecos aqui*. Holes, I mean. Not find nothing. All gone. Somebody else get. *Desde hache muchos años.*"

"Many years ago," Houlihan translated. "I wonder if they got everything."

"Do you care?" Spatchcocker said. "The rain is beginning. I'm going back to the bloody ship for a smoke and something to eat. Shit."

"You go ahead," Houlihan said. "I'm going to sort through this junk and search the cave again."

"What for?" Spatchcocker whined. "If there had been anything the bloody metal detector would have found it. Go ahead. Search if you choose. I'm going back to the bloody ship."

Spatchcocker, Ratcliffe, MacTavish, and Pedro left for the beach.

"I guess we should go, too," Roger said. "I don't fancy that bunch ransacking our provisions to make lunch. Are you coming, sweetheart?"

"I don't know. Houlihan, are you going to need my help?"

"No. You go on back with Roger." Houlihan started methodically searching through the trash, taking his time, examining every piece.

Longstreet said, "Well, what the hell. I don't know what there is to find, but I'll start searching the cave." It was their good luck that the afternoon rains held to a few scattered showers.

"A lot of these wood scraps are sawn timber, manmade stuff," Houlihan said. "I suspect they were once boxes for silver ingots. But somebody's got them already."

"What exactly are we looking for, Joe?"

"A small container like a jar or a bottle."

"You mean like this one?" Longstreet asked, waving a dirty cylinder. "This was up in the corner of the cave in a little crevice in the rock. I guess whoever looted this place missed it."

"Yes, by golly, yes!" Houlihan said. "That might be it!" He scraped the accumulated dirt and mold to reveal that the object was, indeed, a glass container that had been fused shut to protect its contents. "We'll take it back to the ship where I can clean it carefully."

In the galley, Houlihan worked patiently with a scouring pad to clean it. After an hour or so he brought it out and put it down on the table. Everyone crowded around to have a look.

"I'll tell you what I see," Ratcliffe said. "A mummified piece of gristle and dried skin with a nail on it, probably a finger or toe of a person or maybe a big monkey, but treasure it most definitely is not. Like that time in Luxor. Using only whisk brooms and camel's hair brushes, we were excavating—"

"If it turns out that I've spent bloody years of my bloody

life to be rewarded with the bloody mummy of a bloody monkey's finger, I will be most bloody annoyed."

Longstreet chuckled, "We could say that history has 'given us the finger,' couldn't we."

MacTavish agreed. "Not only the finger—I think history has given us the whole arm, right up to the elbow."

"Oh, I say, I get the joke. Jolly good," Ratcliffe said. "To 'give the finger,' that refers to the obscene gesture, common to most of the world, with the middle finger of the hand. Sign language can be so expressive. It signifies copulation, aggressive copulation, as an act of violence. Come to think of it, I will never forget the time that I got the finger in Algiers. In the Casbah, as a matter of fact. We had gone there on a fact-finding expedition to ascertain whether Pépé le Moko had actually existed or was only a legend, as was so vividly portrayed by Charles Boyer and Hedy Lamarr, in the film, *Algiers*. Did any of you know that Hedy Lamarr, besides being a ravishing dish, was also an electronic genius? She and her friend, George Antheil—"

"Bloody hell!" Spatchcocker snarled. "Give me that bloody bottle!"

He snatched the bottle from the table, raised it over his head, and would have smashed it to the floor if Houlihan hadn't grabbed his wrist. "Don't. I want it for a souvenir."

"Souvenir? Souvenir! That bloody piece of garbage? Give it to me. I'll get rid of it. I'm going to throw it over the side. It has no value. It makes me angry."

Houlihan said, "No. I want it. I financed a lot of this expedition. You'll have to allow me this."

"Well, take the bloody thing. Get it out of my sight."

"I will." Houlihan took the bottle, wrapped it carefully in a towel, and tied it with string. He took it down to the storeroom.

Longstreet said, "We have another problem. I have to pump the hold three times a day now. The patch is leaking. How are we fixed for fuel, Mac?"

"Probably only enough to run the genset for a week or two and take us back to Panama, but that would be cutting it close."

"How's the grub situation, Roger?" Longstreet said.

"Pretty slim. We have some canned goods left and as long as Wren catches fish we can make do on fish and rice, but that's about it, unless Van Dusen brings us something."

"Where is Van Dusen?" Wren asked. "Has he called?"

"No. I haven't heard a peep out of him. I called him on the blower a few times but he's not answering. The last time we heard from him was when he stopped by and filled his beach drums from his ferry tanks. He must be down south loading sea salt or whatever it is."

Longstreet said, "Well, that does it. We got two choices. Leave, or go native. Move on shore and eat pigs, coconuts, and fish. Look for treasure and swat bugs."

Ratcliffe said, "Oh, yes. Go native. But I did that and the mosquitos ate me alive. I'd rather not live on shore. Not again. Why, did you know that mosquitos in Alaska—"

"I'm bloody sick of this," Spatchcocker said. "There is no treasure. I say we go back to Panama."

"What about you, Wren?" Longstreet asked. "What do you and Roger think?"

"But Roger has his heart set on finding—"

"Roger's heart is no longer set on finding," Roger interrupted. "Let's go back to Medicine Hat and do something we know something about. I'm ready to go home."

"We go back," Pedro declared. "You can talkee-talkee all you like. I myself am the law here. This nation is Costa Rica. I not asking nobody nothing. I am saying. We go back." He wasn't smiling. His hand rested on the butt of his forty-five.

MacTavish said, "That's it, gang. The law has spoken. The rag is damned well torn off the bush."

Pedro said, "Yes. The rag is off the bush. We go back."

Longstreet said, "Before we leave, let's see if we can rig something to slow down that leak."

Roger said, "Before you start monkeying around in the hold, I'll make some sandwiches. I made fresh bread. We have some canned corned beef and sauerkraut. Pickles, too. Maybe some hot mustard? And Wren and I have a secret, haven't we, Wren?"

"Yes. We squirreled away some beer. It's good and cold. We could each have two bottles. We were saving it for a situation like this."

MacTavish said, "Goddammit, Wren, Roger. Sandwiches. Cold beer. You two are my fairy godparents."

"We're going to hold you to that," Roger said. "I could use a godson, even a fairy one."

Wren added, "And we have some plans for you. You need a change of attitude and lifestyle. If I can do it, your life as a tit-happy deck ape is about to change."

After lunch, Wren busied herself with the cleanup. Roger, Longstreet, and Houlihan descended into the hold to study the leak.

In the main cabin, Spatchcocker, squinting around clouds of Woodbine smoke, backed Pedro into a corner. "Pedro, or whatever your name is, I've seen the way you Spanish people park your aircraft."

"*Pendejo*, I am not Spanish, I am *Costaricense*. I tell you this many times."

"Whatever—Spanish, Costa Rica, the same bloody language, the same people, and my name is not Pendejo. Why do you insist on calling me Pendejo. You park your aircraft any which way. For instance, in the Jolly old RAF we would never allow—"

"*Jue puta! Mierda!*" Pedro muttered and shouldered his way past Spatchcocker. "*Con permisso, Pendejo,* I tink I get the air." He scrambled out on deck only to run into Ratcliffe, gazing into the distance and leaning over the rail.

"Oh, Pedro, this is so reminiscent of the South China Seas. I will never forget that morning in Mandalay when I was standing by the old Moolmein pagoda. It was at dawn. Dawn is magnificent there. It comes up like thunder out of China, across the bay. The temple bells were ringing softly and the morning breeze whispered through the palm trees. I caught sight of one of the last of the great Foochow pole junks gliding by. Under the right Chinese skipper, called a 'lodah,' those junks can make the most remarkable progress on even the slightest breeze. Of course, 'Foochow' is an anglicized version of its real name: Fuzhou. The food in Burma is wonderful but ten times spicier than it is farther north. Words are not adequate for me to describe the magnificence of—"

"*Jue puta! Mas mierda! Con permisso, Pajero,* I tink I help de oder mens." Pedro scuttled down a ladder to the hold where Longstreet and MacTavish, up to their knees in bilge-water, worked to uncover the leak.

Roger and Houlihan passed lumber and tools. They uncovered the hole. Scraps of shattered planks were still in place. They could see portions of the tarpaulin patch. Water ran in briskly, faster than filling a bathtub.

MacTavish asked, "Do we have anything we could use as a collision mat? Something flexible but waterproof we could push up against the inside of this hole?"

Longstreet said, "Nothing that I can think of. Mattresses or cushions would leak."

"How about bacon?" Roger suggested. "We have three sides of bacon left. That might do the trick."

"Hell yes!" MacTavish said. "That would work like stink. We could back it up with pieces of the planks from the hatch cover."

"Would you get that bacon, Roger?" Longstreet asked.

"But there would be no bacon left for breakfast."

"Have we got any canned ham left?"

"Yeah, a little."

"We'll eat ham. Better than drowning."

Roger brought the bacon. They covered the hole with it, clamped it down with pieces sawn from hatch cover planks, and braced the whole mess with pitprops against the upper deck, also made from hatch cover planks. The leak slowed to a mere trickle.

"Home free," MacTavish said.

"So long as we don't have any heavy weather on the way back," Longstreet pointed out. "We've got absolutely nothing to cover the cargo hatch. We've used our only big tarp and all the hatch planks."

"Jesus! I didn't think of that," MacTavish said. "If we got swept with some big seas—"

"We should pray that we don't meet heavy weather or big seas," Houlihan said.

"I'm not very good at praying," MacTavish admitted.

"Me neither," Longstreet said.

"I can pray," Pedro said. "But, *jue puta!* I not been to Santa Misa or *confesarme* since many weeks."

Houlihan said, <We will fix that.>

<I would be very grateful. Holy week will come soon. ¿But how will we fix that?>

<We will talk about that later.>

"I could try praying," Roger said. "I learned some prayers in parochial school. I even had to memorize a lot of stuff for my confirmation, but I don't think I can remember much of it. I haven't been to church in years."

"You could fix that easily," Houlihan pointed out. "Like the man said: 'There are no atheists at sea.' Give it a try. I might even give it a try myself. Like the man said, 'For everything, there is a season.'"

"I'd give it a try too, but I don't understand the technique," Longstreet said.

"Don't worry about that," Houlihan replied. "Like the man said, 'fake it until you learn how.'"

MacTavish said, "Well, that goes for me, too. I'll fake it. I'll take praying over drowning any damn day. But now that we're on the subject, let me get this straight. Who was that damned man anyway? The one who said all that stuff."

"Are you kidding? He was the man who said stuff," Houlihan explained. "That's all he did."

MacTavish said, "He only said stuff? That's all he did? He didn't eat? He didn't sleep? He didn't drink beer? He didn't chase pussy?"

"That's him."

"He must have been a real pain in the ass."

"He was. No doubt about it."

Longstreet said, "Like the man said, 'stick to the point.' It's my turn with that 'like the man said' bullshit."

"Longstreet, old friend, I don't own it. Use it any time you choose."

They climbed out of the hold.

Getting the anchors up was difficult. The afternoon deluge didn't make things any easier. The bow anchor slid in like a trained pig but the stern anchor had snagged around a couple of coral heads. After several hours of twisting and jerking, the anchor line parted.

The rain coursed down Longstreet's face and into his mouth. "Goddammit! I hate losing an anchor. No telling when we might need it. The water's shallow here. Maybe I could dive for it."

"Sure. Why not." MacTavish grinned. "But before you do, take a look over there." He pointed to where a couple of mako sharks and one hammerhead lazed in the water. "They're waiting for our garbage but I'll bet they'd really like a tender young diver. Yum yum!"

"Thanks but no thanks. I guess we leave the anchor."

Houlihan was at the wheel and steered slowly and carefully out of Wafer Bay. It still rained heavily. Several horsetail waterfalls splattered down the rocks. The island was misty green, mysterious, and beautiful.

"Goodbye, Cocos Island," Longstreet muttered.

"Goodbye, Cocos Island," MacTavish echoed. "And goodbye sharks, mud, mosquitos, dead pig, busted hy-hoe and all."

"Not a romantic bone in your body, is there, MacTavish."

Chapter Eighteen

Next morning at about eleven, Longstreet stood on the wing of the bridge looking at the misty horizon over the foredeck. Houlihan had the con. Longstreet would relieve him at noon. They heard a continuous, grinding mumble from the cabin below.

"What you Spanish chaps never seem to understand—"

"*Pendejo*, I tell you I am *Costaricense*, not Spanish."

"Bloody Spanish, bloody Costa Rican, it's all the same. Same language makes the same thought patterns. Now, what you bloody Spanish chaps never—"

"Shut up! Shut up! Shut up! Shut up—"

Spatchcocker backed out of the cabin and across the foredeck until he was against the bulwarks at the bow. His face was pale; his moustache quivered; he stared down, cross-eyed, at his nose, under which the muzzle of a forty-five automatic pistol was jammed, its butt firmly in the right hand of Pedro, livid with rage, shouting: "Shut up! Shut up! Shut up! Shut up! Shut up! Shut up! Shut up! Shut up—"

"Longstreet! Take the con!" Houlihan shouted and dashed down the companionway. When he was on the deck, he shouted, <Pedro, Pedro, my dear boy. Please! Don't shoot, don't shoot.>

<¿And why not?>

<It is a sin to kill. Even utterly useless fools.>

<No one would miss this one.>

<Quite right, but it's still a sin. I know you would be within your legal rights as a Costa Rican Guardia Civil, but think of the paperwork!>

<True. That is the truth.>

<Pages and pages of paperwork. Days of questioning and conversation. And more paperwork. Interviews with the foreign press. More paperwork.>

Pedro lowered his forty-five and burst into tears. Houlihan put his arm around Pedro's shoulders. Wren hurried forward and put her arms around Pedro's other side and hugged him. Spatchcocker scuttled back into the cabin where Ratcliffe and Roger stared through the portholes. Spatchcocker said, "Of course, I was perfectly safe. I knew he wouldn't pull the trigger because—"

Ratcliffe and Roger shouted in unison, "Shut up! Shut up! Shut up! Shut up! Shut up! Shut up! Shut up!"

"These Spanish fellows, all bluster and no action. Typical—"

"Shut up! Shut up! Shut up! Shut up! Shut up! Shut up! Shut up!"

Ratcliffe said, "This is quite reminiscent of that time I witnessed a gunfight in a Malemute saloon. Fifty shots were fired but only one man had a hurt finger—"

Roger shouted, "Shut up! Shut up! Shut up! Shut up Shut up! Shut up!—"

At about three in the next afternoon they motored through a flat, glassy calm. The horizon was misted and indistinct. Altostratus clouds streaked the sky.

"Not good news," MacTavish said. "There's a norther moving down."

"And that leak is getting a lot worse," Longstreet added. "That patch must be coming loose."

The next morning they lost the outer patch completely. Water squirted through the timber and bacon patch and into the hold. They engaged the four-inch centrifugal pump. It roared and sucked, lugging down the generator set. They peered down into the open hatch. The pump didn't appear to be gaining on the leak. They reduced speed to six knots and that seemed to help. The water level subsided in the hold.

Longstreet called the gang together. "We got problems, big ones."

"I insist that we summon Van Dusen," Spatchcocker said. "He must bring the bloody airplane and take us off immediately."

"Don't think I haven't tried," Longstreet said. "He doesn't answer the radio. God alone knows where he is. He could be anywhere between here and Vancouver, or Ecuador, or wherever he picks up that damned sea salt. We're going to have to save ourselves."

"There's heavy weather brewing," MacTavish said. "With that hatch uncovered, what do you think our chances are at reaching Panama? I think damn near zero."

Spatchcocker snarled, "Dammit! You are bloody well not listening to me! I demand to be taken off this bloody wreck."

"Go ahead. Demand your head off." MacTavish explained, "Any seaman worth a fiddler's fuck knows the only one who can save you at sea is yourself. We're about sixty sea miles south of Puerto Armuelles. I'm pretty sure we could make it."

Houlihan said, "Well, as the man said, 'any port in a storm.' I'd vote for Puerto Armuelles—if we can make it."

He got no argument. They altered their course to the north.

Toward noon, an American military observation plane began to circle them. Longstreet got on the emergency channel on the radio. "Observation plane, this is *Sweet Fanny Adams*. Observation plane, this is *Sweet Fanny Adams*. Come in, please. Over."

"Well hello there, *Sweet Fanny Adams*. We have been looking for you. What are those clowns doing on your foredeck? Over."

Longstreet took a look. Spatchcocker and Ratcliffe were flapping a bedsheet and screaming: "Help! Help! SOS! Mayday! Save us! Mayday! Mayday!"

"Observation plane, this is *Sweet Fanny Adams*. A couple of our gang are a trifle overwrought. They think we're sinking. Over."

"Well, that's a good question. Are you? Over."

"No. Not presently. We have a leak but we seem to be holding our own. We are making for Puerto Armuelles. Over."

"That's a good idea. There's a major storm headed south but you might get to Puerto Armuelles before it hits. Over."

"Good to know. Over."

"Yes, *Sweet Fanny Adams*. We'll be checking on you all the way. And we'll have a real nice welcoming committee waiting for you in Puerto Armuelles. Over."

"Real nice welcoming committee? What's that? Over."

"It will be a wonderful surprise. Over and out." The channel went dead and crackled with static.

Chapter Nineteen

The banana is a vegetable made for commerce, particularly the Cavendish cultivar. This variety was named for William Cavendish, sixth Duke of Devonshire, from whose hothouses the cultivars were first developed. Cavendish Bananas ripen naturally until they are picked. Once picked, they no longer turn yellow on their own. They need to be gassed with ethylene to start ripening again.

"Bingo!" shouted a gaggle of enterprising businessman. "Grows like a weed in the tropics! Easy to ship! Cheap food for our workers. We can control it completely. We can make lots of money!"

Imagine throwing a chunk of meat into a cage of hungry wolves. Now substitute the bananas for the meat and enterprising businessman for the wolves. The fight was on! In Central America, through most of the twentieth century, the winning wolf was the United Fruit Company. They owned the ships. Through bribery, political chicanery, and sometimes armed force, they controlled extensive plantations. United Fruit planted the bananas and built the ports and the railways to connect the two. When a shipload of green bananas had grown to proper size, the stems were picked and sent by rail to the port where a ship waited, and what a ship! Towering, white like a wedding cake, spotless, refrigerated and well stocked with ethylene, this ship was one of 'The Great White Fleet.' The crews said:

"Here's a toast to the Great White Fleet,

Lots of work and nothing to eat."

The United Fruit Company ran their plantations on the same principle. They paid little, and when they did it was not in real money, but script for the company store. Whisper the word "union" and you were up to your neck in goons. When it appeared a union might prevail in spite of bribery, armed force, and political manipulation, the Company moved on and raised their bananas in a more tractable location. In those days, there were plenty of tractable locations where crooked politics and poverty ruled.

Puerto Armuelles was one of these banana towns. It was only a sleepy little hamlet, until a shipload of the fruit was at the right stage. A great, white, refrigerated ship would arrive and tie up to the pier. In the late afternoon the plantation workers picked the fruit and loaded the trains. In the evening the trains started to arrive on the pier. The pier workers unloaded the stems of bananas and trotted them into the holds of the ship. All night long the trains rumbled and only stopped at daybreak. Harvested bananas must never see the light until shipped to a major northern city and, gassed with ethylene, they arrive at your neighborhood fruit stand. During the day, the town swarmed with workers and their families, eating, drinking, shopping, and blowing their pitiful paychecks. Puerto Armuelles didn't sleep when a ship was in.

At about eight in the morning, *Sweet Fanny Adams* sighted Puerto Armuelles. No ship waited at the long pier. No trains ran. The town simmered and sweated quietly in the blazing sunshine.

Sweet Fanny Adams had reduced speed to four knots. The leak had gotten worse. Longstreet had the con. He heard a muffled crash and the sound of gushing water. "Shit! What the hell was that?"

MacTavish ran and looked down into the open hold. He shouted, "The patch is gone, bacon and all! Give her full throttle. Beach her. Make for the beach to the east of that pier.

Longstreet pushed the throttle lever full forward. The 12-V71 Detroit diesel bellowed like a wounded dragon. *Sweet Fanny Adams* twanged like a fortissimo banjo and was doing sixteen knots when she plowed a furrow through mud, sand, and oyster shells up onto the beach. Crockery and pans shattered and clanged in the galley. *Cunning Punt* and *Chicken S.* burst from their chalks and shattered to kindling against the main cabin. The stays snapped. The mast toppled forward and dented the back of the pilothouse. Longstreet was slammed against the windows of the bridge. The engine still roared and the prop thrashed, half out of water. Longstreet managed to stagger to his feet and kill the engine.

Silence.

Spatchcocker and Ratcliffe, encased in life jackets, burst onto the deck, dragging their huge duffel bags. They ran to the bow, too high for a jump. They ran aft to the fishing platforms at the stern, still in deep water. "Help! Help! Help! SOS! Mayday! Mayday!" they screamed.

Wren and Roger came out on deck from the galley. Wren was unscathed. Roger had a nasty cut on his forehead. His shirt and apron were spotted with blood but otherwise he looked okay. He called up to Longstreet and MacTavish on the bridge. "Land ho, by George!"

Houlihan picked himself up from the scuppers at the bow. "Like the man said, Land ho!"

That got a good laugh, except for Spatchcocker and Ratcliffe in the stern sheets shouting, "Help! Help! Help! SOS! Mayday! Mayday!"

Longstreet said, "Joe, do you think you could cool those assholes out? The noise is driving me nuts."

Houlihan said, "I don't think I told you, but I cool assholes professionally. Part of my job." He strolled aft.

MacTavish took Roger into the cabin to the first-aid kit. He put pressure on the cut with a dishtowel to stop the bleeding. He cleaned Roger up with another dishtowel that he had wetted at the sink. He cut two butterfly bandages from a roll of adhesive tape. He closed the wound and finished the job with a neat dressing.

Wren produced a clean shirt and apron for Roger. She inspected MacTavish's work. "Not bad. Not a bad job at all. Where'd you learn first aid?"

"In the Navy. I was a medic for a year or so until they found out I was a good mechanic."

"You know, you might be a decent guy if you weren't so cunt-struck."

"Cunt-struck? Cunt-struck! Me?"

"Yes, you. It's a terrible disease. Makes assholes out of

otherwise decent men. All they can think about is 'tits, tits, tits.' But maybe there's hope. If the right woman took you in hand, she might be able to cure you."

"I'm ready for the 'right woman.' Will she have big tits?"

"There you go again. Maybe you're incurable. But I'll see what I can find. Maybe in Medicine Hat. Come to think of it, I might introduce you to my little sister, Teebie. See what she thought of you."

"Has she got big tits or has she had a mastectomy like you?"

"Oh for God's sake, MacTavish! Stop it with the tits! She's intact, for now, but our whole family is inclined to breast cancer. Only reason I mention her, she was married to a used car salesman who would make you look like a cross between Dagwood Bumstead and Prince Albert. He drank. He lied. He cheated. He used stinky hair oil. He stole from her. He beat her. She loved him and took it for years until he ran off with a schoolgirl he met in a bar. She was sexy as all hell, but under sixteen. Her dad ran the slaughterhouse in town, had razor sharp knives, and was cozy with the police. Teebie's husband skipped and right in the nick of time. He's hiding out down in the States or maybe Mexico. Teebie finally divorced him. She went back to school and studied law. Now she's got a job with the Crown Prosecutor. She's happy again, but if the family curse should strike her, she could use a decent man who could take care of her. I've seen you operate a hy-hoe. You're good. You like to work and it's a good trade. You're a good mechanic, too, and you're not a drunk."

"That's kind of cold-blooded, isn't it?"

"Come off it, Mac. You know good and well that's the way things should work. We look out for each other."

"Yeah. You're right, I guess. But your sister. She's named after a disease—tuberculosis. I thought all your sisters were named for vegetables."

"She was too. How'd you like to go to school with a name like Tuberous Begonia Beaverbrook?"

"Beaverbrook? Your dad was named Beaverbrook?"

"Yes, he was. His dad, my granddad, was an honest Ukrainian farmer with an honest Ukrainian name that sounded a lot like 'Cut ya fukin corset off.' He changed it to Beaverbrook when he immigrated, not after some fool Englishman but because there was a beaver colony in the brook on the quarter section he got from the government."

Longstreet shouted from the bridge. "Here comes that welcoming committee that flyboy was talking about on the radio. They don't look all that friendly."

The tide was receding. On the road at the edge of the beach, several olive-drab military trucks arrived and disgorged a platoon of troops. Police? Panamanian Army? Anyway, they looked businesslike. They set up a thirty-caliber Browning light machine gun at the edge of the road and spread out and advanced, carrying M-I rifles and 'grease-gun' submachine guns. One carried a three-point-five-inch bazooka and was followed by an ammunition carrier. They took up positions around the ship.

The troop's Commandant had a bullhorn. He drew his pistol, aimed it in the air, and fired a few shots to get their attention. The Commandant said through the bullhorn: "Listen me. I am wanting all everybody on the deck with the hands up in the air."

"What the hell," MacTavish said. "This doesn't look good."

Everyone lined up on deck beside the pilot house with their hands raised except for Ratcliffe and Spatchcocker, who stood on their huge duffel bags in the stern waving their arms and shouting, "Help! Help! Help! SOS! Mayday! Mayday!"

The Commandant motioned two of his men forward. They splashed, hip-deep, through the receding tide and boarded the ship via the stern fishing platforms. Spatchcocker and Ratcliffe advanced to greet them but were rebuffed and forced up on deck to join the others. More troops boarded the ship. Pedro was relieved of his pistol.

Spatchcocker waved his long finger under the nose of the nearest trooper. "This is bloody outrageous. I am a British subject! I demand to be taken to the nearest British consul!"

He was answered with a rifle butt placed neatly on the side of his head. Not too hard, but enough to leave him gasping on the deck. For once, Ratcliffe said nothing.

The soldiers made a quick search of the ship. <Everybody is here, Commandant,> they shouted. The Commandant came on board. He stood in front of the gang and looked them over.

Houlihan said, <Forgive me, sir. ¿May I ask why we are being treated in this manner?>

<You may ask. Perhaps we will answer later.>

Pedro said, <I am Costa Rican. A member of the Guardia Civil. ¿Would you be so kind as to contact my commander in San Jose? He will verify my status.>

<Interesting if true. This too we will discuss later.>

The gang was herded into the storeroom under the main cabin. The door was closed and locked. A guard with a submachine gun stood outside. The heat was stifling. They opened the portholes and it helped a little. Rivers of sweat poured down them. An hour passed.

Spatchcocker got some of his sand back. "Never, in all my bloody life have I been subjected to such—"

"Shut up! Shut up! Shut up! Shut up! Shut up! Shut up! Shut up!"

Houlihan said, "I think it's appropriate for me to 'come out of the closet,' as the man said."

"There's that damned man, again," MacTavish complained. "And 'out of the closet'? What closet? Where?"

"Watch," Houlihan said. He pulled some garments out of his duffel bag and donned a black cassock with a white clerical collar. "That closet."

Longstreet said, "A priest suit? What in God's name are you doing with a priest costume?"

"Well, 'in God's name,' it's not a costume. It's my working clothes. I am, in fact, a priest."

"Jesus, Joe! You are a priest?"

"Yes. 'Jesus, Joe.' You're pretty close to right. I am Father Joseph, of the Society of Jesus."

Spatchcocker got to his feet and opened his bruised mouth. "This is bloody outrageous. You lied to us. You never told us you were a bloody Popish priest."

Houlihan snapped, "I don't lie. Not ever. You never asked."

Longstreet said, "But I thought you were a prospector and a geologist."

"That too."

"How did it happen?"

"It's a good yarn. I'll spin it if you like. It'll help pass the time."

"Yes."

"Tell us."

"Okay. Picture a tough Mick in Winnipeg with a tough Mick father. He was an engineer on the CPR. Along with being tough, my dad was a straight arrow. Right was right. Wrong was wrong, and that's all there was to it. Me? I didn't want to work for the railroad. I wanted to get rich, and I didn't want to get crooked. I scraped through a geology course at the University and then hit the bush. The way a geologist gets rich is to find something. I tried that for quite a few years, but I finally wised up. Only one geologist in a thousand finds anything. There's another way a guy who knows his way around the bush can get rich. It's risky and the guy doesn't make very many friends, but it's not crooked. He files splinter-claims."

"Splinter-claims? What are they?"

"When a big mining company wants to develop a property, they make a whole series of deals with a bunch of prospectors and smaller exploration companies. They get control of all the claims in an area. They keep very quiet about this. Now picture a sharp young fellow who finds out about this process early in the game. He goes to the registry office and studies these claims. He identifies holes in the patchwork, little slices, little splinters. He goes out in the bush and stakes a whole bunch of these little slices. By the time the big company catches on, they find that all these properties they bought are useless because all these little slices make their property impossible to develop. They have to buy the splinter-claims, for a lot of money. You get it?"

"Yeah, so far, but what's that got to do with being a priest?"

"I'll get there. I was out in the bush, busy staking splinters, when I broke both my legs."

"How in hell did you do that?"

"I'd rather stick to the point. As I told you, splinter-claim specialists are not very popular. Anyway, there I was at the bottom of a gulch with two broken legs. I should have died, but as the man says, 'There are no atheists in foxholes.' And there are no atheists out in the bush, in a gulch, with two broken legs, either. In the process of crawling out—it took me two weeks—I made some vows. I kept them. I'm Father Joseph, SJ."

"So what's with 'Houlihan'? Is that a fiction?"

"No. Not really. That was my name before I took orders. It's still my name on my passport."

"Yeah, but what're you doing on a treasure hunt?"

"Our order is noted for historians. Remember that pirate, Bonito? That mule train of silver Bonito snatched had one mule that belonged to the Church. It was carrying something infinitely more valuable than silver: the index finger of St. Isaac Jogues."

"You're putting us on."

"No. In 1642 that finger was chewed off by a Mohawk Iroquois while St. Isaac was being tortured. Afterwards, this Mohawk was struck with profound regret. He spit the finger out and kept it in a small deerskin bag hung around his neck. Soon after, he converted to the Church and gave the bag with the finger to his confessor, also a Jesuit."

"Honest to God, Joe, this is pretty farfetched."

"Farfetched or not, it's the truth."

"So how did this guy, Isaac Jogues, become a saint? After the Mohawks were through torturing him, did they kill him?"

"No. They kept him as a slave for a few years until he escaped through New York and returned to France. He got a Papal dispensation so that he would be able to say Mass without using the prescribed fingers. In those days, the host could only be touched with the priest's thumb and forefinger."

"You're kidding."

"I wouldn't kid about something like that. Isaac Jogues was comfortable, but the easy life wouldn't do for him. He went back to the Iroquois. He was successful at first. He converted a whole tribe, but a few years later, sickness and crop failure hit. They decided that Isaac Jogues's God had led them astray. They whacked his head off with a tomahawk."

"Ouch!"

"Yes. Ouch."

"So that little chunk of bone and gristle you have in that glass container—"

"You got it. That finger is a relic. It belongs in the care of the Church. Because of my background my order figured I was the man for the job. I was instructed to keep quiet about being a priest and join any group that might produce results."

MacTavish said, "Well, if that don't beat hell!"

"You can say that again," Houlihan agreed.

"Okay. I will say that again. If that don't beat hell!"

Chapter Twenty

An hour later, the door of the storage was opened and a soldier glanced in to inspect the prisoners. He saw Houlihan in his new clothes and his eyebrows went up all the way under his helmet. Houlihan said, <¿Are you surprised, Señor? I am, in fact, a priest. ¿Would you do the favor to tell the Commandant?> The soldier nodded and left quickly.

Houlihan was brought up from the storage room to the bridge, where the Commandant had established an office. He said: "Commandant, I'm not for a minute questioning your authority, but I would like to ask you why we are being subjected to such rough treatment."

The Commandant said, "The English of me, it is not so good. To converse with me, please we speak the Spanish?"

Houlihan said: <I apologize, Commandant. Let us speak Spanish. I would like to ask you why we are being subjected to such rough treatment.>

<As far as your treatment is concerned, my men suspected your group is in the drug smuggling business. I will speak frankly. Some of my men hate el bisneo, but most of them, unfortunately, turn a blind eye if they receive the customary princely bribe, sometimes more than a full year's salary. They

were convinced you were drug smugglers and too tight to give the appropriate recompense.>

<Your troops' reaction is pretty severe,> Houlihan said.

<Yes it is. As you well know, this is Holy Week. They have been assigned to guard you, so they are unable to confess or attend Mass. Many of them feel their faith and perhaps their immortal souls are in danger. Currently, there are no priests in Puerto Armuelles. Again, I will speak frankly. It will be difficult for me to prevent your friends from, shall we say, being shot while trying to escape.>

Houlihan said: <I could resolve this unfortunate situation. ¿Could you give me freedom of the ship? I could hear confessions in the main cabin, and I will celebrate Masses as soon as I have proper communicants.>

<Splendid! I will allow you and your comrades freedom of the ship. Inform them, however, that if they try to leave, they will be shot.> The Commandant gave some orders, which were passed down through the ship and greeted with loud cheers.

Houlihan said, <I have one other request, if you would be so kind. Our generator set was water-cooled. It has burned itself up. Our cooling fans, refrigeration, and other kitchen utensils are electric. ¿Would it be possible to provide us with a temporary power line? It would be most convenient for our Mass.>

The Commandant shouted for his sergeant and gave a few more orders. The sergeant saluted and left the ship, accompanied with two of the soldiers. Power was restored to the ship in an hour.

The gang was released from the stifling storeroom.

Spatchcocker, plastered with sweat and with his sparse whiskers sticking out in all directions, shuffled up to the Commandant and waved his forefinger under the Commandant's nose. "I am a British subject. Never, in all my life—"

Pedro shouted, "Shut up! Shut up! Shut up!"

Spatchcocker said, "This is absolutely outrageous! The British consul will—"

The whole gang shouted, "Shut up! Shut up! Shut up!"

But Spatchcocker did not get the message until Houlihan said, "Shut up, Ian. Don't say anything."

The Commandant, and the few of his men that were present, snickered. Spatchcocker opened his mouth again.

The gang shouted, "Shut up! Shut up! Shut up!"

The Commandant said, <There have been interesting developments. I consulted the Archbishop of Panama, Señor Marcos Gregorio McGrath, who, in turn, discussed the matter with the archdiocese of San Jose. He confirmed your story. I apologize, Father Joseph.> He took Pedro's arm. <I have received confirmation from San Jose, lieutenant. I apologize for your inconvenience.> He handed Pedro's forty-five automatic back to him. <Of course, you yourself are free to leave any time you choose.>

Houlihan said, <Pedro, were you ever an altar boy?>

<But of course!>

<Would you be so kind as to delay your departure? I would like you to serve Mass.>

<I am honored, Father Joe.>

On the next day, which was Tuesday, Father Joseph heard confessions on the afterdeck. MacTavish and Roger had helped rig a blanket as a curtain to give the confessants privacy. At first, he heard the guards. Their confessions were remarkably similar:

<Father, forgive me. I have sinned. I have taken bribes.>

<Father, forgive me. I have sinned. I have arrested innocent men/women because they did not offer bribes.>

<Father, forgive me. I have sinned. I have accepted sexual relations with female suspects as bribes.>

<Father, forgive me. I have sinned. I have accepted sexual relations with male suspects as bribes.>

<Father, forgive me. I have sinned. I have arrested impoverished, ugly, innocent men and women because they did not have anything with which to bribe.>

Quite the ordinary admissions from any law enforcement agent of any nationality.

But the word had gotten out. The Commandant had orders to restrain the ship's crew but nobody had ordered him to refuse visitors, so he allowed them. A small gift to the Commandant was considered appropriate to be allowed admission to the ship. The aged and infirm could skip this formality. The Commandant was nothing if not a compassionate man.

On Tuesday evening, a trickle of townsfolk appeared at the confessional.

On Wednesday morning, the trickle became a flood. Farmers, banana carriers, locomotive engineers and firemen, truck drivers, barkeepers, taxi drivers, cooks, hookers, waiters, waitresses, even the town drunk came to confess: <Father, forgive me. I have sinned. I beat my wife to get money to buy guarro.>

Father Joseph had to shut up shop at two a.m. to catch some sleep. At eight a.m. on Thursday morning, he celebrated

Mass on the afterdeck to offer communion to those who had confessed. Pedro served Mass. Then, it was back to the confessional for him. A multitude was waiting.

At about noon, a refrigerated, United Fruit banana ship arrived at the dock. Houlihan heard those of the ship's crew who were Roman Catholics. Their confessions were also remarkably similar:

"Father, forgive me. I have sinned. I have smuggled drugs."

"Father, forgive me. I have sinned. I have bribed law officers to allow me to smuggle drugs."

"Father, forgive me. I have sinned. I have accepted bribes from crewmen to allow them to smuggle drugs."

"Father, forgive me. I have sinned. I have accepted sexual relations with crewmen/women to turn a blind eye to drug smuggling."

"Father, forgive me. I have sinned. I have given sex to officers and government agents as bribes to allow my drug smuggling."

The ship's captain, an old Portuguese sea dog, came last. After his confession, he said, "I'm lucky you were able to hear me today, Father. You can't hear confessions again until Sunday."

Father Joseph said, "Priests can and *should* hear confessions on Good Friday and on Holy Saturday."

Old Portuguese sea dogs don't take correction easily— even from priests. "I doubt that."

It was a mistake. Jesuits, in their priestly role, don't take correction at all—even from old Portuguese sea-dogs. Father Joseph thundered, "*Hac et sequenti die, Ecclesia, ex antiquissima traditione, sacramenta, praeter Paenitentiae et Infirmorum Unctionis, penitus non celebrat.* On this and the following day, the Church, from a most ancient tradition, does not celebrate the sacraments, except for the sacraments of Penance and Anointing of the Sick. Got that, Captain?"

The Captain shriveled. "Forgive me, Father."

"There is nothing to forgive, Captain—my son. Go with God and good luck with the bananas."

On Friday morning came the hoi polloi, the banana carriers and banana farm employees from hovels in outlying hamlets. Because their isolation and poverty didn't allow them admission to the drug trade, their confessions were more interesting:

<Father, forgive me. I have sinned. I have given bribes to company officials to allow me to: carry bananas, cultivate bananas, pick bananas, drive banana tractors—>

<Father, forgive me. I have sinned. I have: lied to, stolen from, murdered, brutalized, fornicated with, sodomized my: wife, children, relatives, neighbors—>

<Father, forgive me. I have sinned. I have committed: murder, robbery, rape, adultery, sodomy, bestiality, forgery, sacrilege—> and even a few crimes unusual for such impoverished folk: <— treason, breach of contract, perjury, barratry, lèse-majesté—>

Father Joseph's day was fortunately cut short at sundown when the banana trains began to arrive from the surrounding farms. Good Friday or not, the entire population was occupied with loading the huge refrigerator ship. Time, tide, diarrhea, bananas, and the United Fruit Company wait for no man, and they don't respect Church celebrations, either.

On Saturday, Father Joseph heard confessions all day but was relieved at sundown when the banana trains arrived and loading the ship commenced. He was able to catch a good night's sleep. He needed it for Easter Sunday, when he and Pedro were occupied with Masses all day long. *Sweet Fanny Adams's* afterdeck was much too small for the multitudes. They had to stand or sit on the beach.

On Monday, the atmosphere was different. The machine gun nest was still up by the road but the gun crew sat around a low table on upended beer-cases. They drank beer out of bottles and a white liquid out of a mason jar. They played a card game requiring cards to be slammed down on the board with a curse or a nasty sneer of triumph.

Spatchcocker's face sported a ratty stubble and a glorious shiner where he had received the kiss of the rifle butt. He was silent and, for the moment, subdued. He sat in a deck chair under the awning at the stern.

Ratcliffe had cornered a soldier in the narrow confines of the bulwarks at the bow. He was regaling him: "Imagine my surprise when, at sundown—you can't imagine the unbelievable beauty of a desert sunset in the Australian bush—I discovered that this aboriginal medicine man had, in fact, studied at Oxford and had with him—in addition to effective incantations and a poultice of kangaroo hair and dog shit—a case of modern drugs, one being an antibiotic, the other, aspirin. If it hadn't been for this, I would almost certainly have died from the poison injected into my shoulder by the spurs of the goombowali bird—a most unusual avian very similar to a crow but distinguishable by its unique cry, 'gitcherkokout-gitcherkokout-eedme-eedme.' I expressed my gratitude with a gift of my broken pedometer and a pack of chewing gum."

The soldier, like many Central American private soldiers, was a man of complex ancestry, sparse education, and no English. He smiled faintly as he looked around Ratcliffe for an escape route.

Roger, Wren, Longstreet, MacTavish, and Houlihan—or rather Father Joseph—sat around the mess table guzzling more coffee and munching on some of Roger's sweet buns. They were swapping jokes and stories punctuated with guffaws.

The Commandant was in his jeep, up by the road, talking into his radio. Calm was dissipated by the whapping approach of a large, American helicopter. It landed on the beach beside the ship and disgorged several nattily dressed men leading dogs and, under his Panama hat, the man in the seersucker suit, his toothpick vibbling jauntily in the corner of his mouth. He climbed onto the afterdeck via a fishing platform.

"I say!" Spatchcocker said. "Jolly good! We meet again. Is that your machine? And those fellows are taking their dogs out for a morning walk?"

"No. The helicopter belongs to Uncle Sam and the dogs are here on government business."

"Oh, I say! The Amiddican government. Jolly good. So pleasant to deal in proper English instead of this Spanish mumbo-jumbo. I would like to register a formal complaint. Never in all my life have I been subjected to such outrageous affronts as I have suffered from these Spanish bullies, and even my own companions have not—"

"Marvelous. Simply marvelous. Now if you would be so kind, move your mangy ass into the main cabin and shut the fuck up."

"Never! In all my life have I—"

"Shut up. Move." The toothpick rumbled across to the other side of his mouth, stopped vibbling, and pointed aggressively at Spatchcocker.

"I beg your pardon! Her Majesty's government will—"

"Shove it up her ass."

It finally dawned on Spatchcocker that this seersucker-suited man was not in the same charming mood as he had been in the Canal Zone hospital. The man fanned himself with his Panama hat.

"Now, on your feet and move. I'm in a hurry. I would like to finish searching this turd-raft and get my hot, sticky ass back into my nice, air-conditioned office. I would have been here sooner but the helicopter pilots refused to fly during Holy Week."

The gang was herded into the main cabin. Panamanian troops stood at the doors. The seersucker man sat in a corner of the cabin and tipped his chair back against the wall. He put his Panama hat over his face (and toothpick) and appeared to sleep. The dog handlers went to rummage through the ship. The dogs were tail-wagging mutts who loved the world. Their noses worked continually. They had to sniff everywhere, everything, and everybody.

After an hour of this, one of the dog handlers came into the cabin accompanied by the Commandant. "Not a thing, chief. The ship is clean as a whistle."

"Okay. We can stand down. Let's get the hell out of here. Commandant, that goes for you and your men. We're all done." The man got to his feet, straightened the creases in his seersucker pants, shifted his toothpick to the side of his mouth, and made for the door.

"Hey, wait a minute, please," Houlihan said. "Would you mind telling us what all this is about?"

"Well, Father, I suppose you deserve an explanation." He sat down again at the table. He took the toothpick out, examined it critically, pitched it on the deck. "Roger, you're the cook, right?"

Roger nodded.

"This toothpick has had the bun. I would really appreciate some fresh toothpicks."

"Yes. Sure. You bet. Coming right up." Roger went into the galley and returned with a bunch of toothpicks. The man spread them out in his palm, selected one, and stuck it in his mouth. He put the rest in the chest pocket of his seersucker jacket, along with pens and a pair of sunglasses.

"You guys may be the world's biggest suckers, but at least you stock good toothpicks. To begin with, have you any idea what this whole mess was about? Probably not. Did you honestly think that Van Dusen had any interest in treasure hunting? Gah! What a pitiful gaggle of patsies! Van Dusen cooked up this whole scheme to give himself his own private refueling station between Ecuador and Canada. His airplane could make the whole trip far enough out at sea to avoid any questions. It was an Albatross, an amphibian, see? He could land on any body of water, take on or discharge any cargo without bothering with Customs or Immigration officers.

"We were beginning to smell a rat because there was a lot of new, high-grade cocaine coming in through Canada. Trouble was, we had absolutely no idea how. But then I ran into this talkative fellow, the one with the shiner"—he indicated Spatchcocker with his chin—"in the hospital in Panama. My God, how that asshole can talk! He made everything clear as a bell."

Spatchcocker began to huff. Father Joseph laid a hand on his arm to shut him up.

"So, we kept that airplane on our radar. We tracked him home to his rendezvous on Sproat Lake in British Columbia. The Royal Canadian Mounted Police watched until he made the swap with his pickup boat. Then they nabbed the boat and the drugs, neat as a pin, and would have nabbed Van Dusen, too, but he managed to power up and take off—one hell of a flyer, he was. He flew very low and off our radar. It was an hour or two later that a Canadian observation plane's radar picked him up. They followed him as far as they could but he kept flying straight out into the Pacific and into the teeth of one hell of a storm. He must have been running on fumes." He waved the toothpick like a symphony conductor's baton. "It's a long haul from Cocos Island."

"Anyway, that was that. Van Dusen must have kept flying until he ran out of gas or his Albatross was torn to pieces in the storm. He might have landed, but an amphibious airplane is not a ship. It can't withstand a full storm at sea. When the storm cleared we searched but found nothing. One way or another, crashed, burned, or wrecked, Van Dusen and his Albatross are gone. End of the road for Van Dusen. Case closed." The toothpick went back into his mouth.

Longstreet said, "Was there a woman with him?"

"I heard rumors. A redhead. Supposed to be quite the looker, but nothing for sure. If there was a broad flying with him, she drowned with him, too."

Longstreet's spinning Turk's head transformed itself into a silent, frozen void in his stomach.

The man clapped his Panama onto his head. "I guess that does it. I'll be off—oh, thanks for the toothpicks. I was running low."

He and his dog handlers climbed off the ship and walked down the beach to the helicopter, the dogs wagging their tails merrily and sniffing everything in their path. They got in. The turbine whined. The helicopter lifted in clouds of dust, noise, and sand and flew away.

The Commandant and his men had already climbed into the trucks with all their armament. The trucks left.

"Well, fellow patsies," MacTavish said, "like the man said, I guess that does it."

"Yeah, I guess that really does tear the rag off the bush—Jesus, Delia too."

"Still packing that torch, eh, pal?" MacTavish said. "I'm sorry about that. But let's get real. As for me, my rice-bowl has croaked. Too bad, but he's not that much of a loss. Like you said, Longstreet, him and his great big Ipana smile. If I was going to insult the dead—which, of course, I would never, never, never do—I'd call him a four-flushing, treacherous, crooked, lying, miserable son of a bitch. But he sure could fly an airplane, couldn't he?"

"Yeah. He sure could fly an airplane, the bastard. He was quite the man for the ladies, too."

MacTavish said, "Okay. But what am I going to do now?"

Wren gave him the news. "You're going to come back with us to Medicine Hat. Roger is going to need a lot of help getting our diner back in shape. There's always jobs for good hy-hoe operators in our town, and who knows? Maybe Teebie might consider giving you the time of day."

"That's a deal. I'll take it. What're you going to do, Longstreet?"

"I'm going back to BC to lick my wounds. I've probably picked up some clients, too. I hope so. I have to make some money."

"And you, Father Joe? Going back to Canada with St. Isaac's finger?"

"Probably, but only after the Church sends out a priest for Puerto Armuelles. That might take some time. Also, United Fruit doesn't treat these people all that well. Maybe I could do something about that."

<Do you still need my help at Mass?> Pedro asked.

<No. Not anymore. There are plenty of potential altar-boys here in town. But you have been invaluable, both at Mass and as a good friend. I will miss you.>

<Perhaps not forever. I shall speak to the archbishop. You are one priest in a million. Costa Rica—indeed Central America—needs priests of your caliber.>

"*Bueno. Hasta la vista, ijito.*"

"*Egualmente. Hasta la vista, padrito.*" Pedro left to pack up his gear.

"What about you, Spatchcocker?"

"I've had all the bloody, insufferable, Amiddican rudeness I can stomach. I'm going back to England."

MacTavish said, "Excellent choice, as the French waiter said to the 'Amiddican' customer who ordered a deep-fried telephone book. That way you'll avoid any more bloody, insufferable, Canadian rudeness, too."

"Nev-ah! In all my bloody days, have I ev-ah—"

"Stop! Can it! Put a sock in it!" It was not friendly Joe speaking but Father Joseph, SJ, in a voice remarkably similar to a rawhide Inuit dog-whip. "I've listened to you two mugs squabble all I care to. I'll tolerate it no longer."

"Goodbyes are such a sweet sorrow," Ratcliffe mused aloud. "I can still shed a tear when I recollect the profound sadness I felt when my boyhood sweetheart told me she was moving back to her natal land, Kazakhstan. She hurt my feelings cruelly. She told me her increasing fluency in English had rendered my enlightening conversation to be 'yikkity-pikkity-yakkity-krakkity,' and thus revealed herself as having no appreciation for the finer things in life. She did not appreciate good English bangers and mash, either. And here I had been so considerate and careful to—"

Father Joseph, SJ, barked, "That goes for you, too, Ratcliffe. Put a sock in it. I'm sick and tired of your rambling fictions."

Spatchcocker and Ratcliffe stamped off to stuff dirty clothes and other belongings into their bulging duffel bags.

Roger questioned, "That's all very well and good, but what are we going to eat for dinner? The fridge and deepfreeze didn't like losing power and we have no food."

"What the hell," Longstreet said. "We aren't confined to the ship anymore. Why don't we find out what Puerto

Armuelles has to eat? And Roger, you must be sick of cooking for us."

"No. I'm never sick of cooking, but it would be wonderful to taste the local cooking style."

Wren agreed. "Well, I'm sick of washing dishes. Let's go downtown."

MacTavish said, "I think *Sweet Fanny Adams*'s seagoing days are over. What are we going to do about her?"

Longstreet shrugged. "She's certainly not my worry. Right now, she's a wreck and subject to salvage, perfectly legally. She used to belong to the stockholders, a bunch of Vancouver punters who hoped to get rich from buried treasure. I'm going to walk away from her. Let the punters worry."

"Poor old girl," MacTavish said. "She was our home for a month or two and she got us back to the mainland, even if she did try to drown us. Seems kind of mean to leave her to rot."

"I was right about you," Wren said. "You are, indeed, a soft-hearted slob. But look at it this way. The people around here may be dirt poor, and slaves to the United Fruit Company, but they're not stupid. How long do you think all this lumber, hardware, machinery, and stuff will remain here if we leave it on the beach?"

MacTavish rubbed his head. "You're right, as usual. *Sweet Fanny Adams* is not going to go to waste. Good use for her. Let the Vancouver punters sweat for it. What about that, Father Joe?"

Houlihan thought for a moment. "That might be a dilemma for the stockholders, but she's legal salvage now and up for grabs. It's not the Church's problem, nor is it mine. I'd say we could walk away from the ship with clear consciences."

The tide was in and the stern fishing platforms were awash, but that didn't stop MacTavish. He unlimbered a chain saw and carved a door through the bow. The whole gang walked into town to look for a place to eat.

The sun was down and the United Fruit ship was taking on the balance of her cargo. Town was bustling. Everyone who was not carrying bananas had come to town to spend their pittance wages and pay their debts at the company store. Rattle-trap autos and trucks mingled with donkey carts on the dusty dirt roads. Cantinas blared with tamboura music and dished out beer, rum, and guarro. A scrawny bitch spotted with mange trotted down the dirt street, her dugs swinging beneath her. She looked worried, and with good reason. Her litter had been recently weaned or perhaps died. Latin American canines are not cherished as they are in the North. To make it worse, she was coming into heat again. She was followed by at least fifty hopeful, panting dogs, eyes gleaming, tails wagging, tongues hanging out a foot and pissing on everything vertical that happened to be in their path.

Up one of the busy side streets, the gang found an open storefront with a sign: 'Restaurante Chino.' Cluttered tables filled the room and spread out into the dusty street. Stoves roared. Dishes clattered. Longstreet sniffed carefully at the cacophony of savory smells. "This is the place," he said. "It may look like a rathole, but these guys know how to cook and the food is fresh."

They sat down on rickety folding chairs at a table made from a door. The proprietor himself waddled up to them. He was a toad-like fellow, squatty, thick, no neck, perhaps Chinese or more probably the son or grandson of a Chinese. "Good evening, folks. What can I bring you?" He had a deep tubular voice, similar to that of a bullfrog.

"Hey," MacTavish said. "You speak English!"

"And the cat shits in the woods. And the Pope is Catholic." He caught a glimpse of Joe's clerical collar. "Sorry, Father. No offense intended."

"None taken," Houlihan said. "We'd like some cold beer and something to eat."

"Beers coming right up," replied the bullfrog. "How about some ceviche? We made it this morning. And we got good soup. The fish is fresh, and the *carnicero* killed some succulent goats today. We cook goat with some *fou-qua* and a black bean sauce. Pork fried rice?"

"Yes to everything, and keep that food coming."

First came the ice-cold beer, then the ceviche. Then, the soup, formidable in appearance. Bits of honeycomb tripe and small morsels of hog kidney floated among plantain chunks, spinach, and wontons. It smelled so good that they ignored its appearance and spooned it down. It tasted delicious but unlike anything they had ever eaten before.

"What a treat!" Roger said. "Damn, I love learning something new."

"Sweetheart," Wren said, "some of these ingredients are going to be hard to get in Medicine Hat."

"Whatever. I'll bet I could find them or maybe substitutes, and soup like this would be a real hit in our diner."

"Diner? But sweetheart, I thought all that was behind you. You are going to be a big-time treasure hunter, remember?"

"Don't rub it in, Wren. Because I've been stupid doesn't mean I have to stay stupid. I'm a cook, born and bred. And you and I are going to run the best diner in Canada, maybe the world."

Then Froggy brought out more dishes: tender young goat filets with *fou-qua* and black bean sauce, fried rice with pork fragments and onions, *gai lan* steamed with a pungent garlic sauce, deep-fried tentacles of a small local octopus—

Conversation became possible when they had eaten. They were sipping their third bottle of beer when they were interrupted by the bellow of two Pratt & Whitney R-1830 Twin Wasp aircraft engines from a few hundred yards away. A DC-3 was taking off.

"Hey, Froggy," MacTavish shouted. "What's that airplane?"

"That's the evening flight. Panama to Puerto Armuelles to San Jose—and how did you know they call me 'Froggy' here? Ranito, in Spanish?"

"I'll never tell. It will be a mystery."

When the gang returned to *Sweet Fanny Adams*, they discovered that the local populace had not been idle. The radio set, the ship's wheel, the binnacle, the sextant, and the pilot house doors had vanished. The galley stove was missing its burners.

Pedro, Spatchcocker, and Ratcliffe were missing, too. They had taken that evening plane to San Jose.

Chapter Twenty-One

Longstreet took the ferry to Victoria and the Nordic Air hangar.

"Well hidie-ho! If it ain't the ancient mariner, back from tropical bludy fookin seas," said the Oatmeal Sasquatch.

"Yeesus Christ!" said Einar, "yü're burned black like an African. Did yü catch any interesting social diseases while yü were cavorting wit dem dusky beauties?"

"I don't need this crap," Longstreet snarled. "Gimme my goddamn bill. Gimme my goddamn airplane."

Einer and the Oatmeal Sasquatch detected Longstreet's mood and kept further razzing to a minimum. They had removed the floats and the Super Cub was on wheels. The wear and tear of the previous summer was neatly erased. Einer was so sympathetic that he managed to blush when he presented the bill—but he did present the bill, which Longstreet paid.

They rolled the Super Cub out of the hangar. Longstreet checked the oil and did a walk-around inspection. Damn! She was all fixed up and clean. What a beautiful little airplane! He climbed in and shouted, "Clear prop!"

"Clear!" shouted Einar and the Sasquatch.

The Lycoming started without a hitch. Its chuckling roar

began to lift Longstreet's heart out of Arctic seas. A four-cylinder, two-hundred-horsepower Lycoming might be only a racket to some, but to a flyer it's a siren song of pure joy.

On his flight, Longstreet tried a couple of wingovers and even did a nice spin. Goddammit! It felt good to fly a neat little airplane again. Yes, there was a freezing void in his soul where Delia gasped for air and drowned miserably in the sinking Albatross. But it was only a pocket, not his entire soul. He flew back to Vancouver, doing spins, wing-overs, even a loop whenever he felt like it. He even tried a snap roll. It was not a success and evolved into the beginnings of a flat spin. Not good. Not good news at all. He straightened up, flew right, and didn't try any more snap rolls. "I'll leave that to the ravens."

He called his answering service and found that he had picked up a couple of contracts. None too soon. He needed money. He called Einer. "Floats again."

"Yaw. Ven?"

"How about tomorrow? Too soon?"

"Tings is slow right now. Ve dü it tomorrow. First ting."

"I'll bring her over right now."

Longstreet spent the rest of the day flying the Super Cub to Victoria and catching a flight back to Vancouver with one of Einer's other customers.

His first job was that section of "really nice" poles. A Suit had blundered and closed the deal without a cruise. Now the other Suits were doing shrieking Nervous Nellies in the office remarkably similar to booby courts-martials on Cocos Island.

"What do you mean you bought it? Without a cruise?"

"Where's that cruiser—Longstreet, or something like that. Get the Push on the blower."

When the radiophone blatted, the Push sighed and mumbled something about Suits and very intimate social relations. He picked up the mike and listened to the whines. "Well, sir, if you remember, I told you all about it last fall. He turned the job down flat and went down south somewhere."

"You shouldn't have let him get away. It's all your fault."

"What would you propose? Hit him over the head and chain him to his bunk? That's illegal and you wouldn't get your cruise anyway."

"What are you going to do?"

"Me? I'm not going to 'do' anything. I didn't buy that timber. I suggest you look around for another cruiser, but that's not my problem." The Push was no amateur. He knew the best way to change the subject with a Suit is to ask for something that costs money. "By the way, my best hook tender somehow got ahold of fifty cases of beer. I'll need some new beds and three toilets to replace the ones they threw out the windows. Unless you would like a big drop in production, you'd better send me another hook tender—a hook-and-rig, if you can find one. We have a couple of long corners that are going to need a back-spar. And I'll need a rigging slinger, a chaser, an engineer, and two chokermen. They flew out with the hooker. I guess they charged the flight to the company."

"Why did you allow them to charge—"

"Allow? Are you kidding, sir?"

"And toilets? New toilets? What's wrong with the old ones?"

"Excuse me, sir, but you must know very well that the first thing any good logger does when he gets drunk is break a toilet. Oh yeah, and I'll need two windows for the bunkhouse and a new washing machine."

"Why did you allow such a rampage? We'll have to dock your—"

"Wonderful working for you, sir. You'd better send in a new man to push camp while you're at it. No telling what these goofs might do after I leave today."

"Leave today! Wait! No offense intended."

"No offense? But sir, I heard you say something about 'dock your'—"

"Only kidding, only kidding. Can't you take a joke?"

"No, sir. I don't take jokes. If you want Longstreet, you'd better give him a call."

Longstreet answered his phone, "Yeah? What's on your mind?"

The Suit whined.

"No sir, I don't give a fiddler's fuck about 'all the other jobs you're going to throw my way.' It will have to be cost plus like all the others."

More whining.

"Okay. I'll stay in your camp again. That way you don't have to pay me for rations and quarters."

When he arrived at the camp, Longstreet moored the Super Cub on the inner side of the float. Several ravens were perched on a nearby snag and flew down to give him a once-over, first with one eye, then flirting their heads to bring the other to bear. "Snurr-snick-snick grackle." (Damn my eyes! If it ain't that kid back.)

"Gore. Dick-dak." (Yeah. And his little airplane, too.)

"Kickie-frack." (Hiya, kid. How's tricks?)

Longstreet's freezing void did the talking. "Piss off. I *ain't* in the mood for conversation." He toted his bag up to the bunkhouse. "Same room?"

"Same room," the Push said. "Have you eaten yet?"

"Yeah. Had a good breakfast. I'll change my duds. Do I use the same skiff as last time?"

"Yeah. Use the same skiff. Check the gas. The outboard should be fine. I had the mechanic clean it up after that hooker pissed in the gas tank right after he got back with all that beer. We still can't figure out how he managed that much weight in that little aluminum skiff."

"The same hooker that cornholed the toilets and the windows? That bunkhouse looks like it's been through a war."

"Yes, indeed. The very same."

"Ain't logging fun! Is he gone?"

"Gone."

Ten days later, Longstreet had finished his fieldwork. He tossed his bag in the back seat of the cub and checked his gas tanks for water. The raven flew out of the bush to land on the top of his rudder. "Cackle-cackle-snur?" (Feeling any better?)

"A little."

"Snickie-gaw chuck?" (Where did you go this winter? We missed you.)

"I've been down south. Took a vacation."

"Choor! Gaw-gok?" (Is that what put you in such a rotten mood?)

"Well, it wasn't all that bad. Met some interesting folks, some good times, some bad times, but my girl got killed."

"Snoor, gackle—snoor." (That's tough. We're sorry.)

"Well, thanks for that. I'm sorry too, but what the hell, life goes on." The freezing void tweaked at Longstreet's soul. He wondered if he'd ever get rid of it.

"Gok-gok-gok,"(Sorry kid. I got to run.) He flew away across the Sound. Yes, he did a snap roll.

"Yeah, yeah. So you can do snap rolls and I can't. So what. See you later, Raven." Longstreet finished his run-up and flew back to Vancouver. The freezing void stayed in his gut all the way.

When he got back to his apartment, he didn't even get a chance for Chinese food at Hong-Fat's. The bookkeeper called. A sawmill company had been offered a bankrupt logger's timber lease, two sections of old-growth fir and hemlock—they thought. Was it rotten? How much? Did it exist? They had to know right away. Longstreet called them.

"How much of a cruise do you want?"

"Twenty percent."

"That'll cost you dough and time."

"How much time? We're in one hell of a hurry about this. The bank won't wait."

"Two weeks. Maybe more. And I just got in from a job. I need a bit of a rest. Maybe a week?"

"Jesus Christ no! We need to know like tomorrow."

"Not this child. Call somebody else."

"They're all busy. Besides, you're pretty accurate. We want you."

"Alright. For a rush job I need twice my usual fee."

"Have a heart."

"Can't do it. I lost mine a while back. I've got no heart left."

"Alright, goddammit, alright."

"Set it up with my bookkeeper. Send me the legal description and some maps."

"We'll get them ready. Drop around this afternoon."

"Nope. Courier them to me."

"That'll cost you."

"No. Fuck it. Call someone else."

"Alright, alright, alright! We'll pay the courier."

Longstreet spent the rest of the morning loading up his grub box and getting the rest of his gear together. The courier brought the papers. Longstreet did the job. It took two weeks. And then another rush job. And another.

It was the end of August before he got a short break. He walked into his apartment, tossed his dirty clothes into the washer-dryer and his notes onto his drafting table. The phone rang. "Yeah?"

A weak, tremulous, female voice said, "Longstreet?"

"Yeah."

"It's Delia."

"Bullshit. Bad joke. Delia is dead."

"No, I'm not. I'm alive. Not very much, but I am alive."

"Delia?"

"Yes." The voice quavered. It sounded close to tears. "Would you come see me?"

"Jesus, whoever you are, you sound like hell. What happened to your voice?"

"Lots happened. If you'll come see me, I'll tell you all about it."

"Where are you?"

"I'm in Vancouver General. The psych ward."

After a shower and a lightning-fast shave, Longstreet drove his Beetle to the hospital and took the elevator to the psych ward. He said to himself: "This isn't true. It can't be. Some nutcase is pulling a stunt. They won't let me in. It's all a bad joke." His heart was pounding. He identified himself at the desk, expecting a horse-laugh.

He didn't get it. "Go right in. Fourth door on your left, but be careful. Be gentle with her. She's not strong yet."

It was, in fact, Delia, but a very different Delia. She was emaciated and her hair was cut short. Yes, it was still red, but a much more subdued shade of red, and it showed several streaks of gray. Her lower arms were bandaged from her palms to her elbows. She began to cry. Longstreet began to cry, too. He went to the bed and hugged her gently. She cried harder.

When he could recover his voice, Longstreet said, "Last I heard, you flew off to a watery grave with Van Dusen!"

"That son of a bitch! He was the love of my life. I was scared shitless, but yes. I was all ready to go with him to that watery grave. What a saphead! A misty-eyed, love-struck, high-school girl. The RCMP grabbed the boat with the dope and two other speedboats were closing in on us. Van poured on the gas and managed to take off. He had made the swap downwind and with the engines idling. We flew down the Somas River at about ten feet. We passed Port Alberni, then cruised down the Alberni Canal, still flying right down over the water. He landed

230

at the seaplane dock in Ucluelet. I guess they hadn't heard the news and he gassed up. While he was filling his tanks I visited the toilet in the office. We had a porta-potty on the Albatross but I never did like to shit in a suitcase. I heard the engines start and ran down to the dock. Too late. He took off. The pump jockey gave me a scrap of a map. The son of a bitch had scrawled a note on it: 'You were a great ride, sweetie, but I got places to go and things to do. You're a bit heavy on the sauce, too. Toodle-oo. Love and kisses, Van.'

"Toodle-oo? Great ride? Toodle-oo! That lousy four-flusher! I felt like homemade shit. I couldn't stop crying. So dumb! I'd fallen head-over-heels in love with a slimy crook with a 'great big Ipana smile.' Of course, the RCMP arrived and scooped me up like a poached egg out of boiling water. And I was boiling, for sure. They questioned me for days. I told them the works, sang like a canary, and why not? 'Toodle-oo!' 'Great ride!' 'Heavy on the sauce!' 'Toodle-oo.' I was so goddamned mad! And those cops! But I didn't have any dope and I never took any money. After days of questioning, they had the unmitigated gall to laugh at me and dump me out on the street. No charges."

Longstreet said, "What happened to the money? There must have been a lot of it."

"I was so damned sappy and love-struck that the son of a bitch never had to discuss it, but there were about six heavy suitcases back in the tail section."

"So, the son of a bitch flew off to his watery grave rich, very rich."

"Rich, yes, but watery grave, I don't think so. He had full tanks and a lot of money in an airplane that can land anywhere, an airplane he could do tricks with. I mean, back in Sproat Lake he had put the props in full fine pitch while we unloaded and he never cut the engines. The second he saw cops, he applied full power and used the flaps to horse over two speedboats. Those cops were too scared to shoot. I could see their pasty faces right under the copilot's seat." Delia snickered. "Don't count on that watery grave."

"That's too bad. No watery grave, huh?"

"Yes. Too bad. Boy was I crushed. I felt like a June-bug after she hit the windshield. I got very drunk and stayed very drunk. The gutter and I were real pals. Why I wasn't robbed, raped, and murdered I'll never know, but there must be more decent people out there than we know about. I got bored with the gutters out there in the country and came back to the gutters here in town. I still have my apartment. I was going to sell it to support my booze habit and move into the Vancouver gutter as a permanent residence, but I never got around to it.

"I sent the security guard out for a mickey of vodka. Then I started crying again. 'Fuck it,' I thought, and climbed into the hot bath with the razor blade. I did okay on the slashing part but—wouldn't you know it?—the security guard came in with my vodka, found me, and called the meat wagon before I could do a decent job of dying. It goes to show. I couldn't do a decent job of anything."

Long pause. Delia began to sob again.

"Longstreet—"

"Okay. Yeah. I'm still here."

"Longstreet, I'm not the iron lady I thought I was. I fucked up. No way around it. I fucked up. I'm in a God-awful mess.

I've been on the sauce. It got so bad I'd take my first drink in the morning, puke my guts out, and enjoy it. I wanted to be a big-time operator but succeeded in becoming a cruel bitch, an ass, and finally a drunk. Could we leave it at that? When they let me out of here, let's go have a good dinner at Hong-Fat's. Then maybe, if you feel like it, we could go back to my place?" Delia began to sob again, then she cried openly, noisily, uncontrollably. Longstreet held her until she stopped. "Could you maybe take care of me?"

He looked in his gut for his constant companion, the freezing void. He couldn't find it. He couldn't even find the hole it used to occupy. Longstreet lectured himself sternly. "Are you going to take this crap? What kind of bullshit is this! This snotty broad gives you the gate, takes up with another guy. Now she wants to get together again. Big deal. What a crock of shit! What are you, a man or a mouse?"

He thought some more. He hugged her closer. His heart did a snap roll. "I guess I'm a mouse. Squeak."

"Okay. You got a deal."

The end.